Love
from
London

the PRINCIPLES of L♥VE

Love from London

Emily Franklin

nal
jam
books

NAL Jam
Published by New American Library, a division of
Penguin Group (USA) Inc., 375 Hudson Street,
New York, New York 10014, USA
Penguin Group (Canada), 90 Eglinton Avenue East, Suite 700, Toronto,
Ontario M4P 2Y3, Canada (a division of Pearson Penguin Canada Inc.)
Penguin Books Ltd., 80 Strand, London WC2R 0RL, England
Penguin Ireland, 25 St. Stephen's Green, Dublin 2,
Ireland (a division of Penguin Books Ltd.)
Penguin Group (Australia), 250 Camberwell Road, Camberwell, Victoria 3124,
Australia (a division of Pearson Australia Group Pty. Ltd.)
Penguin Books India Pvt. Ltd., 11 Community Centre, Panchsheel Park,
New Delhi - 110 017, India
Penguin Group (NZ), cnr Airborne and Rosedale Roads, Albany,
Auckland 1310, New Zealand (a division of Pearson New Zealand Ltd.)
Penguin Books (South Africa) (Pty.) Ltd., 24 Sturdee Avenue,
Rosebank, Johannesburg 2196, South Africa

Penguin Books Ltd., Registered Offices:
80 Strand, London WC2R 0RL, England

First published by NAL Jam, an imprint of New American Library,
a division of Penguin Group (USA) Inc.

First Printing, March 2006
10 9 8 7 6 5 4 3 2 1

NAL JAM and logo are trademarks of Penguin Group (USA) Inc.

LIBRARY OF CONGRESS CATALOGING-IN-PUBLICATION DATA

Franklin, Emily.
  Love from London : the principles of love / Emily Franklin.
     p. cm.
  ISBN 0-451-21773-X
  1. Americans—England—Fiction. 2. Female friendship—Fiction.
3. London (England)—Fiction. 4. Women singers—Fiction.   I. Title.
PS3606.R396L68 2006
813'.6—dc22   2005027004

Set in Bembo
Designed by Ginger Legato

Printed in the United States of America

For Mum—for London and everything else

Acknowledgments

Thank you to:
Faye Bender, Anne Bohner, Michele Langley,
and the whole team at NAL.

Adam and the kids—thanks and love.

CHAPTER ONE

My tray table is in its upright and locked position, carry-on luggage safely tucked under the seat in front of me, and my seat belt is securely fastened, but my emotions (and my hair for that matter) are not.

I'm sitting here in my seat feeling like a total mess—and, judging from the looks I've gotten from the woman sitting next to me— looking like a total slob, too. Crumbs from the long-ago digested cheese crackers have amassed on my chest, wrinkles abound from top to pants from sitting in the same position. Granted, seven hours of flying does not make for beauty queens.

"It's okay, dear," the granny-type lady to my left says and pats my hand. She's pruny, tiny, and so sweet I could cry.

"Do you think I made the right choice?" I ask her even though she knows nothing about my life, my upcoming months in the UK, my aunt sick back home, my father pacing until I call to say I've landed, my near-miss boys left Stateside, my transcript waiting for good London grades.

Pruny Lady looks at me and tilts her head, seriously considering. A total "What If God Were One of Us?" moment. I suddenly think— maybe She would come in the form of an elderly plane passenger!

"You know, I do think you made the right decision," Pruny says. "Just keep your eyes open and you heart will fill up."

Prophecy or purely pointless drivel, who can tell. We land with a bounce and bump, and I keep my fingers poised on the belt buckle until we've taxied to the gate. So far, out the tiny window, nothing looks that different.

Inside, however, it's another story.

I've been to Europe (albeit not in the jet-set way of most of the Hadley Hall crew)—a two-week vacation in France before sophomore year at Hadley and an entire summer in Berlin with my dad when I was eight years old—so it's not like I've been completely holed up in the land of Americana, but Heathrow is itself a blend of races, languages, and emotions. Accents, smells, green fluorescent lighting—it's all a bit much right after landing, but it's a thrill anyway. My thoughts are battling against each other, half longing for sleep and the comfort of known things, and half wanting to go exploring right away.

Before I can do either, I have to walk from the gate to customs, which takes nearly fifteen minutes of weaving in and out between slow-trodding people. Stretching my legs is a welcome change. At passport control I'm sent to booth 22.

"The purpose of your visit?" The officer squints at me like I could be a spy carrying classified information.

"Pleasure?" It comes out as a question even though I don't mean it to.

He eyes my landing card. "You've listed an address in Berkshire—Bracker's Common—as your place of temporary residence."

"Yeah, it's my friend's house. Wait—I mean my friend's parents' house." Coffee, coffee, coffee.

"But you're a student?" He asks this incredulously, like I've demonstrated such a lack of competence that he's amazed I'm capable of studying at all.

"Yes—at Hadley Hall," I say automatically, like the name means *anything* to the random Heathrow guard.

"So why have you listed the London Academy of Drama and Music?" he asks suspiciously.

"Because that's where I'm studying here." I sigh. "For the term."

The passport man calls over one of his government cronies and they confer about something. I start to feel my palms sweat (tasty treats!) wondering if I've filled out the wrong form or if my student visa is somehow illegal and I'm going to be deported. It would be so easy to turn around now—to go back to Hadley and settle into my routine there. Then I remember my dad's advice just to go do something different and how Mable told me to stop being so comfortable in my prep school world.

"I'm supposed to be here," I say.

Then, after all the questions, I'm suddenly stamped through and on my way to "baggage reclaim," where, yes, say it with me now, I get to reclaim my bags.

Or at least most of them; my dad's advice proved correct, and the bags he marked with an obtrusive Hadley crest slide out first. The ones I insisted were fine without such a noticeable tag are sadly stuck back in the netherworld of lost luggage (a word, by the way, invented by the English Bard himself, Shakespeare—never let it be said that I'm lacking in the area of trivial knowledge). So I stand with the last of the other Virgin Atlantic passengers, waiting at the carousel for my final duffel. At last, the machine coughs out my stuff and I pile it onto my little trolley. Lopsided, the thing is determined to wheel to the left, so I have to lean my (very tired) body into it to get it to follow the green line through customs and out to the international arrivals area, where I'm supposed to meet Arabella.

I can't wait to see her face, to link arms with her and have her guide me toward caffeine and give me a comforting hug. In front of me, there are various exclamations of early hellos. (In London it is nearly seven in the morning—back home it's about two a.m.—my mind and body are somewhere in between.)

"So good to see you!" "Hi, how was your flight?" "Vanessa!" "Mrs. Robinson!" "Taxi?" Of course, none of these greetings are meant for me. With a silly smile plastered on my mouth, I scan the crowd for Arabella's face. Then I spot her chestnut hair neatly coiffed. I go to tap her on the shoulder, but when she turns around, it's a total stranger. Um, oops.

"Can I help you, miss?" This from a creepy-looking man.

"Nope, I'm all set," I say confidently so he'll piss off, which he does.

But I am totally alone. The semifamiliar faces of my fellow passengers disperse, heading home with their friends and family, or to their touristy hotels, leaving me sitting on my trolley, wondering what to do next.

I could change money, get some coins, and call Arabella's parents. I could wait for her here and assume she's just running late (no surprise there), or just collapse in a heap, let the fatigue really sink in— or jump on the next plane home and be in my own bed by afternoon. Before that thought grabs hold of me, someone's hand grabs hold of my arm.

"What the—"

"Miss Bukowski, welcome," says a tweedy man dressed as a chauffeur circa 1940: cap, gloves, jackets, the works.

"Hi?" I say. Note to self: Stop speaking in questions. It's annoying and way too teenage-girly insecure. I may as well just walk around with my hands tucked into my sleeves à la every teenage girl on TV who tries to look coy.

"Miss Piece arrived earlier and has gone ahead," the man says. "I'm Lundgren Shrum—the driver."

"Oh, right. I kind of remember Arabella mentioning you. Thanks." Lundgren pushes the trolley for me and walks me to the parking garage, where I wait for him to pick me up.

I wonder if he's going to drive me in a limo or a regular car. Instead, Lundgren Shrum (will everyone I meet have interesting bizzaro names?) pulls up in an antique Volvo. It's purple, kind of like the car in *Pretty in Pink* (minus Ducky).

"Your cases are in the boot," he says.

"What?"

"Sorry, the trunk," Lundgren explains and opens the door for me. At least I can sit in the front and not feel totally Hiltoned out by riding in the back. Inside, the car is outfitted with modern amenities: a phone, a GPS (just where does Lundgren drive to that he needs one of those?), and custom fabric seats in burgundy and purple stripes.

We leave the airport environs, and Lundgren gestures for me to open the glove compartment.

"I thought you could use a little something," he says when I've unlatched the small door and revealed a silver Thermos shaped like a large bullet.

I pause for a second, unsure what to say. "I don't really drink."

He laughs. "It's not liquor—it's espresso."

"Oh, right. Thanks. I am so in need of that right now."

"Sugar's in the small pot just there."

We speed along the M4 (the motorway) as I sip my highly charged drink and then, despite wanting to look around at the billboards, the row houses, the funny-shaped streetlights, I nod off. Screw the fun of driving—I could so get used to having my own chauffeur.

CHAPTER TWO

♡

"Here we are," Lundren says, "at Bracker's Common." I wake up from my freakish dream in which I am trying to find Jacob in some huge body of water, but Lindsay Parrish (the pariah and piranha) is holding me back while Arabella sings "Midnight Train to Georgia," and I have an illegible note from Charlie saying he's waiting for me on the Vineyard. Man, even my dreams are exhausting.

"Miss Bukowski?"

I shake off my nap and rub my eyes, then do a double take. "Whoa." Bracker's Un-Common. Not eloquent, but an honest reaction to what I see in front of me.

Marked by two large marble dolphins on either side, the driveway curves through flat green fields. We drive under a canopy of umbrella pines, the kind I remember from *Winnie the Pooh* books. To the left, a lake that shimmers with morning sunshine, the steam rising from it. To the right, sculpted topiary, formal gardens. Oh my God, I'm in *Dangerous Liaisons* or one of those English historical movies where everyone skulks around and has nothing to do all day but write love letters and carry parasols. Sign me up. It's all so beautiful and historic—except for the security cameras.

"I'll take you to the front of the house and bring your bags round the back," Lundgren says.

"Thanks—and thanks for getting me from the airport. Sorry I fell asleep."

Outside, the cold air feels good, a refreshing wake-up call to the amazing sights and wealth around me. It's so weird to suddenly have another side of Arabella, to know where she grew up, to fit her into the context of this place. I can't imagine what her parents are like—possibly they sit on thrones and wait for their servants to fetch them arcane items like wigs and dusting powder. And—just think—they're supposed to be my local parents while I'm here. An enormous (and by enormous I mean seriously bigger than waist-high) Russian wolfhound bolts from the bushes and over to where I am, nearly knocking me over.

"Don't worry—that's just Mouse," says the woman at the massive entryway to the house. "She won't bite." She motions for me to come in, and I walk with Mouse following me up four shallow stone steps.

"I'm Love," I say and shake the woman's hand.

"I'm Shalimar de Montesse," she says. "Better known as Monti—or, as you might know me, Arabella's mum." The handshake turns into a huge hug, and Monti welcomes me into the museumlike front room. "Of course you can show yourself around later," she says and flails her hands to a hallway to the left, a flight of ridiculously large stairs to the right. "Up that way's the billiards room and guest suites—Arabella's loft is that way—library's to the back. Let's just go to the kitchen and get you something to eat. You must be starved."

Monti is totally familiar to me. Her eyes, in particular, are breathtaking, and it suddenly dawns on me that she's *that* Shalimar. Shalimar de Montesse—Monti—*the* Shalimar. As in that woman whose face is always done in Warhol-type art (the pink and green cartoon sort of things), the woman who ran (still runs? jogs?) with the Jerry

Hall/Mick Jagger totally cool crowd from way back when. The woman who broke Bowie's heart (prior to his finding solace with Iman), who led Clapton astray, who revived the club scene in post-punk London. Who posed half-clad with a cheetah in those black-and-white photos. Just as I'm thinking this, Monti turns around from her position under a blue and white chandelier, looking like some glacial goddess in her pencil-cut jeans and bat-wing cream-colored sweater.

"Yes, I'm that Shalimar—formerly. Now I go by Monti." She smirks. "Didn't Arabella say?" I'm unsure whether she means the name change or the fact that her mother's a major icon in the fashion rock world.

"No," I shake my head. "She kept . . . pretty quiet about her—your—family."

Monti nods. "Doesn't surprise me in the least. Arabella's never tolerated hangers-on. You know, the ones who just want to be a step closer to the ridiculous world of RAF."

"RAF?" I quickly run through a list of possibilities and decide that Monti probably doesn't mean the Royal Air Force.

"Rich and famous, of which we are certainly a part—but choose not to be defined as such . . ." She rambles on, her voice echoing in the cavernous hall, talking about how they've tried to raise the kids outside of the public eye (haven't we all?) and to teach them that having parents with big names might open a door but won't keep it ajar, and so on.

"Forgive me blathering away," she says, and for a second sounds slightly non-English. "You must be famished. Do come to the breakfast nook for a bite to eat." Casually she strolls me into "the nook" (nook = giant circular room off the kitchen with a rounded widow seat and an enormous antique table set with food).

During breakfast (toast served on little sterling silver racks, personal jam and butter containers, smoked salmon and eggs—a girl could take up permanent residence here. Forget Cornflakes) I expect the typical parental questions; age, academic standing, summer plans, likes, dislikes. Instead I get a barrage of brainy and cool ones:

Do you feel that you're defined by your origin?

Where haven't you traveled that you'd like to?

Do you believe in past lives or the circularity of life forms?

Have you ever really been in love?

Trying not to feel like I'm in ethics class à la last term at Hadley Hall, I do my best to answer all of these questions. I figure that if Monti's cool enough to ask them, I should be mature and mod enough to answer—except the last one I manage to breeze over, which probably means no—of course no. But then Angus Piece, Arabella's dad, who shows up in the middle of my rant about wanting to go to India, makes me go back to the in love question. Which is not what I want to be discussing with my friend's parents, especially after fifteen minutes of sleep and upon first meeting. Angus Piece—surely he's not *the* Angus Piece, the playwright? The one we study at Hadley Hall?

"Come on, Love, dish it out," he says, his accent Scottish and thick, so I have to go over practically everything he says twice to make sure he hasn't said something more banal like *Yum, salmon is good.*

"I'm not sure," I say and sip my coffee, taking time to butter my toast.

"Fucking hell," Angus smiles. "Kids these days know shite about love."

Blush from me, smile from Monti. "Don't mind his filthy mouth," she says and stands up near Angus. Then she full on makes out with him. Talk about breakfast entertainment. Pass the scones.

They look at me like nothing's happened, so I just focus on the food. Angus points to me. "Let that be a lesson to you, girlie. When

you find love, you'll know it—none of this 'I'm not sure crap.' "
Angus is tall with very dark hair and the same eyes as Arabella, and
he smiles at me, instantly reminding me of how much I miss her.
"Anyway, welcome, welcome. Our house, as they say, is yours. Just
don't mind your manners."

And so begins my uncommon stay at Bracker's Common. Monti
shows me to my gymnasium-sized room—a king-sized bed on the
far wall set between two floor-to-ceiling windows and covered with
a fluffy cream duvet trimmed in deep blue silk. On the other wall is
a dressing table set with various potions and lotions, all new. ("The
stupid fashion people still send me all that junk, as if I'm interested
in Burberry or anything so insipid," Monti says—yet she lovingly
arranges all the bottles in front of the bevel-edged mirror.) Then, way
over to the left side of the room is a claw-foot tub. A huge one, set
on a raised tiled platform. A silver tray that goes across the tub holds
Kheil's shampoo and Jo Malone bath gels and soaps.

"You just draw the room divider like this," Monti shows me,
pulling a faded blue sliding screen from one end of the wall. "And
then bathe in peace . . . or Piece . . ." She laughs and points to herself. "No pun intended."

"Ha." I smile. "This is incredible. Really." It's like I'm in some
funky Swedish castle. It's not ostentatious with gaudy golds, more
farmhouse chic, with an old-fashioned washing basin.

Monti smiles as she looks around the room. "I hope you'll feel at
home here, Love. Arabella has told us so much about you—and I
know what a good friend she's found in you."

"When will she get here, do you think?" I ask and can't help but
look longingly at the bed. It's the sort of bed that cries out to be
shared—ahem—but anyway.

Monti frowns for the first time, but still is the essence of glamour.
"That is a question I cannot answer. Obviously, we don't impose

rules on her—that's just hierarchical bullshit, the concept of time. But we do hope she exercises her choices and decides to make an appearance."

No wonder Arabella didn't tell me much about her family. Where would you even start? Monti leaves me to my palatial suite (my own sitting room, of course) and the tiny stocked library off of the bathroom. Of course I find a ton of Angus Piece's plays—all the ones I drew a blank on upon meeting him. He's the Scottish Sam Shepard or something like it—cutting-edge but well respected. While reading through one of the scripts that's in the tiny library I'm reminded of the Hadley Hall speech team's attempt at a dramatic reading of *You, Like Night,* one of the award-winning plays Angus wrote before I was even born.

I decide to save my luxurious bath for later and slide out of my clothing and into the billion-thread-count sheets of my giant, fluffy bed, and go to sleep, feeling like the princess and the pea (minus the legume). Only when I roll over onto a large brown envelope, which scratches my back, do I reenter reality. I pull the thing out from under me and look at the front. Addressed to Miss Love Bukowski, the return address is LADAM. A brief riffling reveals my class schedule. (My "provisional" acceptance was such that I didn't get to choose my courses, since they were pretty much all filled and I never had an interview to inform them of my "personal preferences." I'm trying not to assume that means I'm stuck with the shit classes no one wanted.) Also included are directions around the campus. My pulse speeds up just looking at the information. I'm excited, but in some ways I feel like I so quickly made the decision to come here that I haven't figured out what to make of it all. Or maybe I'm not supposed to have it figured out yet. I take a final glance at the term's schedule, the room I've been assigned to in student housing (note to self: Ask why every dorm room in every college/boarding school catalogue always looks like it was photographed in 1983 with horrible carpet and outdated sweater big-collar combos), and my welcome letter (which, unlike the ones Hadley Hall sends out, isn't filled with exclamation points. This one's just like *Yup, welcome. The work is hard. Go audition but expect not to be cast in anything*—um, sounds fun). I slide all the long papers (A4 size, not 8½ × 11) back into the cave from whence they came and curl myself up, determined to enjoy my winter break before dealing with more school.

When I wake up, the light in the room has shifted enough so that I know its past noon. Stretching myself out in the silky sheets, I have to do a double take when I survey the room again. Mable once described a palace hotel she'd stayed at in Finland during her traveling days, and I have to think it looked like this. I get my digital camera (thank you, Dad, for giving me a departing gift I'll actually use) and, still clad only in a T-shirt, bum bare for the world (world = no one) to see, I snap a few shots to email to Mabel later. Then I remember that Bracker's Common has no modern amenities such as DSL—or a computer for that matter. Angus Piece mentioned in passing that he still creates all his plays in a journal and then transcribes them onto a typewriter. Quaint, cool, and totally apropos of the *I'm such an eccentric* lifestyle to which he and Monti cling.

I stare longingly at the lovely tub but eschew the shower/bath combo for a walk around the grounds instead. My jeans are crispy from the dryer, but I wiggle into them and slip on a thin black turtleneck and boots and head downstairs to see if Arabella's "chosen to exercise her choices" or whatever gibberish Monti called it (basically, if she's shown up yet).

To the right, the hallway outside my room leads to the formal staircase I climbed on my half tour with Monti. Curiosity gets the better of me and I head left, checking out the library (complete with those sliding ladders for reaching the top shelves), the billiards room (where I feel like Ms. Scarlet in Clue. Except not the Asian stereotype dressed in red silk and smoking with a cigarette holder), and almost go down a whole other wing but decide not to. Probably weird Clive's (former English exchange student whose only redeeming feature is that he's Arabella's brother) bedroom is down there and I have no desire whatsoever to see him or his (no doubt desperately trying to be cool) bedroom.

So I wind up taking the back stairs, secretly hoping for a Potteresque adventure (not so much magic as, say, a hidden passageway and a hot sorcerer), but aside from being awed by the wealth and wonder (understated, tatty in that Anthropologie catalog way) there's nothing remarkable that happens on my way out the kitchen-side door.

Thoughtfully, the cloak room (oh, I feel so British when I say that) has a row of jackets in varying sizes and styles (Barbour ones, riding style ones in quilted navy and green) so I grab a shearling (if you're gonna go communal, you might as well snag the top pick, right?) in a buttery caramel color and feel cozy and chic as I crunch over the gravel drive and wander toward the lake.

In the pastures, cows graze freely, as if even they are well-to-do. I wish Arabella were here so I could gush to her, but it occurs to me that maybe that's one of the reasons she didn't want to arrive with me—so she wouldn't have to deal with my *oohs* and *ahhs*. Quite possibly, another reason is because she was rushing to a royal rendezvous with Sir Tobias Wentworth-Jones. Arabella is so obviously besotted with Toby I feel bad for even questioning slightly the reality of her relationship with him—but the fact that he's a famous face still gives their dating an odd sense of Hollywood glam that is completely out of my realm of normalcy.

I put my hands into the pockets of the borrowed coat and suddenly think of a camera filming this scene. I fantasize I look like a sexy Anne of Green Gables but then feel like a bit of an imposter—a coat that's not mine, a house that's someone else's, grounds that are so far beyond what I'd consider normal to live on . . .

"You look lost."

I stare at the guy in front of me—forget Anne of Green Gables, how about D. H. Lawrence, whatever that book was about the gorgeous gardener.

"I'm not lost," I say. Why must everything I utter sound so defensive?

"Just aimless wandering, then?" The mouth attached to the face of wonder says. He's like someone from a bygone era—tall and slim, with straight dark hair partially falling over his bright green eyes, chiseled face, hands that are—whoa—reaching out to me. "Asher."

"Hi," I say. "Nice to meet you. I'm Love."

He nods and must be one of the first people not to make a cutesy comment about my name or ask for an explanation. Then again, with a name like Asher, he must know what it's like to forever have complicated intros.

"I can show you down to the lakeside," he says. With a gloved hand he gestures and adds, "There's a secluded path that way—through the topiary gardens."

Secluded—warning, red flag! red flag!—I am not supposed to go with strange men (or boys) anywhere, but the many security cameras must ward off complete crazies, right? He clearly knows his way around, and judging by his commenting on all the flowers and trees as he walks, he's got to be the gardener—or one of them, since a place this large must have an entire grounds crew.

Asher starts off toward the path without pausing to see if I'll follow—which, of course, I do because (a) who wouldn't follow such a creature of beauty and (b) I was—seriously—heading in that direction anyway and (c) I have always harbored a secret handyman fantasy (not in the rerun classic *One Day at a Time* yucky Schneider guy way. More like Johnny Depp as a mechanic/guy with a trowel—or do I mean hoe?).

"You seem to know your way around here," I say for lack of anything interesting. "Do you know when the house was built?"

"The main house—presumably where you're staying—was constructed in the seventeen hundreds by some count and the addition is new."

"How new?" I try to picture contractors and Ty Pennington coming to knock out a new wing in one day or something.

"New as in eighteen hundred and one—the music and ballrooms were added on." Asher smiles and stops. "Ridiculous, isn't it?"

"What is?" We're paused at the entryway to what I presume is the garden path.

"All this," Asher says and sweeps his arms out like he's displaying a (loud voice) BRAND NEW CAR on a game show. Then he reconsiders. "But beautiful, too."

"Is that Alice?" I ask as we go under a trellis that is still covered in roses (winter blooms, Asher informs me).

"As in the girl who fell down the rabbit hole—or whatever the symbolism is there—yes. Angus Piece, master of the house, has a thing about topiary—God knows why." It seems odd to me that Angus—a man who likes everything to be au naturel—would want to impose shapes on nature. I say this to Asher and he nods. "Exactly."

Asher puts his hand on top of a tree-shaped Alice and lets me walk around the various clipped shrubs. Some are twirls of shrubbery (no *Monty Python* jokes here I remind myself—that would be way too Clive) that point up into the gray and darkening sky, others are characters like Alice, the bong-loving Caterpillar, and other non-Wonderland creatures like a flamingo. Or, wait, didn't the Queen of Hearts play croquet with a flamingo? Does it matter, Love?

"This is great." I smile at Asher. "Oh—a giant teacup!"

"Come here," he says.

When I go over to where he's standing, he puts his hands on my waist (gulp) and lifts me into said giant shrub teacup and I sort of perch there. "I feel like I've shrunken," I say. "Shrunken somehow sounds like a made-up word. It is shrunken, right?" The whole scene is so surreal and cool I wonder if I'm in the middle of one of those dreams that feel so true you wake up surprised to find yourself in bed.

"As opposed to shrunked?" Asher laughed. "I'm fairly certain it's just shrunk. Sort of present-past tense." Now I do feel shrunk. Nope, still sounds wrong. He leans on the shrubby edge of the teacup and looks down at me. "You can sit in there, you know. It's sturdy enough to hold you."

"Why, thank you," I say. "If I had more body image issues, I might take that the wrong way."

"Well, how refreshing that you don't—or at least aren't admitting them to me. Nothing less appealing than a girl complaining about her thighs." The last word hangs in the air between us, and I swear, I catch Asher staring at my thighs, which I don't mind at all.

"If you're sure I won't fall through," I say and gingerly stretch my legs out. When I'm fully sitting in the cup, I can't see out—I'm cocooned away.

"You look cozy," he says. The wind whips his hair around as he reaches into the cup. I'm sure, heart-poundingly positive, that he's going to touch the side of my face in some romantic gesture, but all he does is pluck a twig from my hair. My heart sinks just a little bit when he stops touching me and flicks the twig to the ground. Maybe he notices my face registering some look of disappointment, or maybe he's just acting on impulse, but Asher hoists himself up on the side of the teacup and climbs into it with me.

"There's room for two I assume?" he asks.

"Well, you shouldn't really assume anything," I say and then add, "Except that I'm continually making that mistake, so probably you shouldn't listen to me." If I could pull back with one of those crane cameras they use in movies, I would be able to survey this unusual scene. Me on the grounds of some castle in a country I've never been to before, sitting inside a giant green tree teacup with quite possibly the best-looking boy I've ever seen in real life, and very definitely the most thrill inducing. I like to call this MCA (massive crush alert), or Booty Signal (like a bat signal only, um, hotter).

There's an electrical current I can feel running its race through my entire body, coursing through my veins until I just can't sit still in the cup any longer, and I get up on my knees, lean forward, and am totally about to make a huge and, uncharacteristic leap and kiss him, but instead I fall over, landing on top of his shoulder as my hair gets tangled in the branches.

Lest I ever forget how klutzy I am. Lest I ever attempt to be more dramatic and romantic and cooler than thou. I'm just not.

"Here, let me, um, untangle you." Asher helps free my red hair from the greenery and then watches as I climb out. I pray he doesn't know I was about to plant one on him, that he just thinks I was getting up to leave our enchanted forest scenario.

"I should go back to the house," I say. Asher nods.

"See you around," he says, and I watch him walk toward the lake, where I assume he has his own handyman cottage or perhaps a cave decked out in leopard skin (faux, of course) or something suitably animalistic. No—wait—actually, he's much more the leather-bound-book type, I think (think = assume).

I walk off, too, back toward the cloak room entrance, and turn around a couple of times to see if Asher happens to be checking me out. But he's not. Or at least, I don't catch him in the act.

Inside, Monti is padding around in a chartreuse kimono with her butt-length blond hair twisted up in a complicated ropy knot at the nape of her neck.

"Would you mind peeling the potatoes?" she asks me while fixing my tea. All the mugs are either chipped or mismatched, adding to the rustic charm of the kitchen. A huge Aga stove (the kind that's always on), lavender of course, is in the center of the room, adding literal and figurative warmth to the space. Monti lifts up one of the left-side burner covers and slides the oversized tin kettle onto the black ring.

"Green or Lapsang?" she asks and opens a cabinet to reveal an enormous selection of teas.

"Lapsang, I guess," I say. "I'm not a huge tea aficionado—I'm more familiar with coffees." I don't know why I feel the need to tell her this, but I'm battling with loving the new life I'm seeing here and wanting to prove somehow that I do have knowledge, even if I'm not rolling in money. Obviously, explaining the difference between a latte and a misto isn't going to win me intellect points, but it's something.

"No problem," I say and reach for the paring knife. "Do you have a shape preference?" I mean for the spuds, but Monti considers what I've asked her like it's got a double meaning.

"I know I'm supposed to say circle, aren't I?" Brief pause where she waits for me to say something, which I don't. "But I am actually not a fan of the circle—it's endless, boring. Instant karma's gonna get me, right? Well, I guess I'd have to say trapezoid. Aren't they just so beautiful? Much more so than octagons, for instance."

She is so weird. It's like this is normal conversation—how's the weather, what's your favorite shape, that sort of thing—but I can't help going along with the quirkiness of the whole day (my whole term? Who knows). Monti suddenly puts her hand to her mouth and makes a little gasping noise. "Oops."

I wait for her to say something grown-up, like "Silly me. Why on earth was I talking about shapes? But instead she says, "I almost for-got." She gets up from the table, goes to one of the drawers (insert various clanking noises), and brings back two cookie cutters—one in the shape of a star, one a heart.

"Are we making cookies?" I ask. "My dad taught me how to make gingersnaps." Inane, inane, inane.

"Oh, no. I just thought these would be fun for the potatoes." Which is how I come to sit, looking out at the now slate-dark sky, making starch stars and hearts. Granted, Martha Stewart would ap-prove, and the effect will be cool I'm sure, but it's a funny thing to be doing. Monti tells me to immerse all the shapes in the bowl of ice water she's given me (so that the potatoes don't start turning brown), and they float and sink there while I clean up and wash my blue polka-dotted tea mug. Then, just as I'm thinking of making use of the bath (bubbles, book, and boy thoughts), I spot Asher near the foun-tain at the center of the driveway.

I casually (read: bolted like a bat out of hell—nod to Meatloaf) saunter (saunter = sprint) outside, but by the time I get to where Asher was, he's far enough ahead of me that I can follow him with-out him noticing but close enough that I don't get lost. I spy walk and finally catch up with him when it's nearly pitch-black outside. Hooray for the lanterns aglow on the paths—slightly creepy and slightly romantic.

Asher doesn't turn around but says loudly (for my benefit), "I'm just turning to the left now, so make sure to keep up."

I do. Then, when we get to a little gazebo, Asher goes up the stone step so he's standing under the dome. There's enough light from the far-off lanterns so that slim ripples glint from the lake's surface. The gazebo is tiny—an open-air circle (not a trapezoid) surrounded al-most entirely by water, attached to the land only by a long stone pathway and a step. One minute I'm staring at the lake, getting cold, the next Asher and I are deeply connected at the mouth, pressed up tightly together. Maybe five minutes go by, maybe ten—again, not going to estimate, especially since Monti and Angus Piece probably forbid time telling or anything "so banal" on the premises of their house.

But suffice to say the kiss—oh my God, the perfect kiss—lasts a long time, and when we finally do pull apart, Asher tucks his hand under my chin and brings it down the base of my throat, his cool fingers sending sparks through my whole body.

Then a bellowing, enormous *gong* echoes out into the night.

"That'd be their dinner bell," Asher says in a near whisper. It's like even he doesn't want to break our moment.

"I'm going to go out on a limb here and guess that means dinner's coming?"

"Wrong." Asher kisses me again. "Cocktails."

Ahem!

Even though I don't want to, I say a hasty good-bye and go back to the house in a trotting fashion—Jesus, two seconds in this country and even I'm moving like a horse. But a happy one.

CHAPTER THREE

♡

I'm scarcely inside the house when a glass of red wine is shoved in my face. Um, hello, did someone forget I'm underage? "Drink up, Love," Angus says. "A toast to the evening."

I take a quick sip and then see Arabella lazing on the chaise longue in the, well, what would be called a living room in normal circumstances but here is more aptly called a drawing room. Large windows go from floor to ceiling set with heavy silvery blue drapes embroidered with tiny vines. I wish for a second that my dad and Mable could see it all. Then again, I could get used to this world on my own.

"Bukowski! Where the hell have you been?" Arabella smiles, stands up, looking more incredible than normal—or maybe I'm just totally relieved to see a familiar face (as opposed to, say, a random hot guy's in a gazebo). She's got on deep maroon lipstick and her hair is coiled like her mother's, so she looks dramatic and casual at the same time, with jeans and pointed green heels that on anyone else would look like lizard feet.

"Piece—it's about time," I say but don't allude to any of her possible adventures lest she get in trouble with her parents. I can totally picture her sneaking around London's hottest spots with Tobias the

Prince. He's not really a prince. He's a lord. But still . . . a cousin or some relation—nineteenth in line to the throne or something.

She hugs me and whispers, "Yes, I saw him. Yes, it was fucking brilliant, and yes, you will meet him soon."

I'm about to burst with my own semi-sordid details of an afternoon of feeling like I wandered into an awesome miniseries, but soon we're hustled upstairs to change for dinner.

"You don't *have* to change, of course," Angus says as we're almost to the top of the grand staircase. "But feel free to—or not." Or have rules—or not. Or make sense—or not.

"I can't believe you grew up here!" I have to be allowed to gush a little now. Arabella sighs and brushes her teeth for probably the fifth time today—she's got a bit of a dental fetish, or at least loves toothpaste. I introduced her to Glide floss in the States and you'd have thought the woman had seen God.

"Bracker's? Yeah yeah yeah, it's grand. Fab, all that. But it's just like every house, really, once you get used to it." She spits in and rinses. "You know, good, bad, ugly, enchanting."

Somehow, this reminds me of talking with Charlie on the Vineyard this past fall, about happy families being all the same and unhappy ones being unique. I wonder where mine falls in that spectrum—or Arabella's. The Vineyard, America, Hadley Hall—everything on that side of the ocean seems far away right now. I could totally get sucked into life here—my own personal rabbit hole à la Alice.

"Well, so far, I'm going to have to say enchanting."

At dinner, the parade of funk, fun, and fabulosity continues. The dining room, which I hadn't seen yet, is long and rectangular. The whole table is up on a mahogany platform, so sitting at the table feels like being up on a stage—which I guess is the point, given the dramatics running through the veins of this family.

The huge windows are draped with burgundy velvet curtains; miniature topiaries twirl up toward the chandelier, which is set with real candles. The spirals remind me of my garden of non-Eden moments this afternoon with Asher and, while part of me hopes he doubles as a butler, most of me is relieved to find him absent from the rest of the night.

Shalimar de Montesse has her curtain of hair down, Angus Piece is dressed in what I would call a pseudo tux, but what Arabella informs me is a DJ (dinner jacket), and Arabella is in a blue slim satin sheath dress—you know, normal attire for a family dinner. The fact that everyone is barefoot in their formal getups saves me from feeling totally out of place.

"I'd like to make a toast to Love," Arabella announces and holds up her goblet of wine. "I'm so glad you're here—not just at Bracker's, but in England. I hope you settle in and have some fun."

"I'll drink to that!" This comes from the doorway. We turn and find Clive the annoying brother standing in sweats. A minute ago I wouldn't have thought anything about his clothes, but already I'm being Piecified—and the thought occurs that Clive is way underdressed. Possibly this is highlighted by the fact that I find him so grating.

"If it isn't Love the nighttime stalker," he says and comes to sit—blech—next to me. "Not climbing into any dorm rooms I take it?"

My defensive self kicks in right away. "I'm not a stalker."

Clive chuckles. "Could have fooled me."

"Oh shut up, Clivedon," Arabella says and dishes out the roasted star potatoes.

"Thanks," I say when she's served some to me.

"Give Love some of the heart-shaped potatoes," Clive insists, looking at the spuds. "She needs one."

"Oh my God, you total freak," I say. I swear the words fly out without much thought. I put my hand to my mouth and try to brush away my rudeness. "Sorry."

Angus pipes in (clearly he heard my Clive-jibe). "No need to apologize, Love. That's what we like here. Honesty. Even if belligerence accompanies it, right, kids?"

Arabella gestures at me with a spear of roasted asparagus and says, "Angus is a big fan of self-expression, in case you couldn't figure that out."

"Of course," Monti says, "we have to be thoughtful as well—honesty for the sake of cruelty is nothing to strive for."

Clive gulps loudly from his water glass and asks me, "So what brings you to our humble abode, anyway?"

"I'm heading to LADAM, actually," I say.

"Exhausted Hadley Hall already, have you?" he asks. I know he's just trying to get a reaction from me, and I wish I weren't responding in textbook fashion to him, but I can't help it. He drives me nuts and for no real good reason, except for the fact that he sullied my nearly perfect transcript with a disciplinary action. And it's not a case of movie annoyance that thinly veils a crush or major attraction. This is just full-on, straight-up eye-rolling annoyance. His orange hair (not red, orange—bright as a tangerine) and pimply skin wouldn't matter if he weren't the human equivalent of an asswipe, but he's just grating on all fronts.

But Monti begs to differ. "Oh you two are just like Mick and Jerry," she says. "When they first met they couldn't stop arguing over the silliest things, and now . . ."

"Now they're divorced, Mother," Arabella says, saying *mother* like it's a slur. I've noticed that she calls her parents by their first names except when she's digging at them—sort of the way parents say your full name when you're in trouble. Suddenly it dawns on me that I can probably count on one hand the amount of times I've said the word *mother* or *mom* out loud. If you count how often I've wondered about the reality of my own birth, there'd be plenty, but uttering the name is a rare occurrence.

"I think Mick and Jerry are just separated again," Monti says. "Or maybe not. But nevertheless, many great romances begin with bickering."

"The roots of passion are such . . ." Angus agrees, but his words get lost in the mouthful of lamb he forks up and eats.

It's Christmas Eve eve, but no one has mentioned the upcoming holidays. I'm not a huge proponent of the wreaths and stockings—we never really celebrated much, come to think of it. Dad and I always exchanged gifts, but not necessarily on Christmas Day or anything. I have vague memories of lighting a menorah for Chanukah with Mable, but I've never been clear whether that was due to being part Jewish or Mable's Christma-Kwanzi-Kah-Solstice kind of open spirituality.

Part of being such a small family, a twosome really, means that we kind of live by our own rules a lot of the time. Maybe this is part of the reason Arabella and I click so well. Even though our backgrounds are totally on opposite ends of the spectrum, we have that overlap, the nontraditional family. So the fact that none of the Pieces have mentioned the holidays isn't such a foreign concept to me. Except that they could full well fit Santa's sleigh and herd of reindeer in this room, not to mention give a bedroom to each elf.

"I'll be going on a winter walk tomorrow at dawn for those who might be interested," Monti says.

"I'm decorating my topiaries," Angus says with pride, which causes Arabella to stifle a giggle. I lock eyes with her and we explode with laughter. I'm also hit with that nervous post-illicit kiss (was it really illicit?) energy when I think of sitting in that teacup. Arabella looks at me and mouths "What?" She knows from my face that something happened, so I mouth "Later. I'll tell you later."

Clive watches our exchange and swigs a glass of wine, then pushes his chair back. It scratches the slate underneath. "I'm out of here."

He says it in a Hadley-dude kind of way that makes Arabella stop laughing and say, "Don't try to sound American. It doesn't suit you."

"Don't try to sound mature, Arabella. It doesn't suit you," Clive intones back. Times like this I am very glad to be an only child. Sure, the sibling companionship would be nice, but the fighting I could do without.

Full of wine and rich food, I help clear the dishes. Monti and Angus remain at the table as the candles drip down, signaling how late it is. I check my watch—midnight here, seven at home. I go to the phone room to call home (phone room = one of those red phone boxes set into a long corridor that leads from the kitchen to the pantry).

Inside, I'm not Superwoman, but deflated when I dial the international operator and think about Mable and my dad.

"I miss you," I say to my dad as soon as he's picked up.

"Well, hello to you, too," he says. "You sound more refreshed." I had phoned just to let him know I'd arrived but was pretty much incoherent.

"Yeah," I say, wanting to substitute *refreshed* with *drunk,* but don't for the sake of keeping the phone call on task. "How is she?"

"She's . . . she's right here. Hang on."

"What's it like?" Mable asks right away. She sounds good, not tired, not hoarse. She wants to know all about Bracker's Common and the family, and I tell her about Monti being Shalimar and Angus being the playwright, and Mable nearly chokes. "Are you serious? Did you ask Shalimar about the punk scene in London? Also, didn't she have an affair with Bono?"

"I don't know," I say. "But they're all really nice. It's just different and I wish you were here. It's hard to explain."

"Many of the best things in life defy explanation," Mable says.

Arabella knocks on the glass of the phone box and waves.

"I gotta go," I say. "Have a good night and Merry Christmas, Happy Chanukah, Kwanzaa, and all that."

Arabella undoes the latch on the door in front of us and leads the way into the music room. By room I mean hall, and by hall I mean auditorium. Not one but two grand pianos, a harpsichord (yes, I pluck played it and found out), a cello, and so on.

"Do you guys really need all the orchestral accoutrements?" I ask. It's not that they aren't deserving of all this stuff, and at least their money has bought good things as opposed to say piles of drugs, but it's . . .

"It's kind of . . ." I start, unsure how to say what I'm thinking without sounding bitchy or jealous.

"Oh, it's totally OTT." Arabella nods. She doesn't need to explain Over the Top. It's just obvious. "But it's not like they're uncharitable either. Some people buy islands or collect figurines . . ."

"You can't compare someone's Hummel collection with this estate," I say, half laughing, half incredulous.

"I'm not. I'm just stating for the American jury that my parents don't judge anyone else's money or status. You know they despise traditional displays of wealth, like Tobias and all his British royals, so they choose to spend their money on what they value—a nice home, instruments, that sort of thing."

"Isn't that contradictory? If they don't judge anyone's money or status, then they shouldn't care about Toby being loaded—or royalty."

"I guess," Arabella says, mime dancing by herself, complete with a curtsy and bow.

"I know. I know. It makes sense what you're saying. It's just hard when you're here—or when I'm here"—I take another look around the grandness of the room—"to remember what life's like outside it. And I'm not trying to say that I'm, like, this bastion of everydayness, being at Hadley and everything, but this is pretty extreme."

Arabella nods and takes her wine goblet over to one of the pianos and sits on the bench. Suddenly, she begins to play (play = show mastery of the instrument, hands fluttering up and down the keys, bare feet working the brass pedals).

"I had no idea you even knew how," I say.

"There's a lot you don't know," she says and smiles. *You, too,* I want to add, thinking about when I should explain my whereabouts with Asher the gardener, but deciding now's not the best time.

"Like she's a total wanker," Clive shouts from the doorway.

"Fuck off!" demands Arabella without pausing her playing for a moment. To my surprise, Clive obeys her commands, taking a small bow and exiting.

Arabella stops playing. "Is he not the *most* annoying creature ever?"

I sigh. "No offense, but yes." I almost never use the *no offense* clause because it basically means *I am going to offend you now,* but it's okay in this instance.

"At least he's only my half brother," Arabella states casually and shakes her chestnut hair back dramatically.

"What?" I ask. "How is that possible?"

"First off, anything is possible around here." Arabella looks me in the eye and smirks. "I learned that when I was eight and wanted a hot air ballooning birthday—and got it."

"Um, hello non sequitur?"

"Not really," Arabella says. "Come sit." I join her at the piano bench, and we play "Chopsticks" and then the ever-annoying "Heart and Soul" while she informs me, "I mention my eighth birthday because as I was about to climb into the ballooning basket, someone yanked my knickers down so my bare bum was on display for the whole party—Madonna was there, by the way, not that she had anything to do with the pants situation—and when I screamed, Angus patted me on the shoulder."

"And then?"

"And then he said 'Well, never mind, Bels. That's just Clive—your semi brother . . .' " She stops playing and stands up. "And that's how I found out Dad had been married before."

"My God—that's slightly traumatic."

"I know. When I was up in the balloon I kept looking down at Bracker's—we were directly over the lake and the topiary garden, which I'll show you later—and I just couldn't help but wonder what other secrets or surprises we were hiding down there."

I stand up and go to the window. The glass is outlined in lead and is cold, and outside I can't see much except for the lanterns glowing on the drive. Arabella stands next to me, her arms wrapped around her shoulders for warmth. I want to tell her I've already seen the topiary garden, but I'm still digesting the Clive news and how overwhelming it must have felt for her to suddenly have a sibling she never knew about.

"What else haven't you told me?" I poke her shoulder.

"Oh, nothing," she chides.

"Tell me!" I say. "Is Sting your uncle or something?"

Arabella raises one eyebrow like I taught her to do and I raise one back. We stay mirrored like that for a minute and then she breaks. "Come on. I'll show you something."

My adventures in Wonderland continue when Arabella and I climb a set of stone stairs up into a narrow tower. At the top is a "whispering circle," which is a sort of stone curved bench that arcs into one side of the cupola.

"See," my crazy English friend explains to me, "you can sit on one side and whisper really softly and the person on the other side can hear you."

"How Victorian," I say and take a seat on one end while Arabella sits far away on the other side of the arch.

"Exactly. I think lords and ladies or whatever used to sit here and confess their deep dark secrets without genteel society being able to hear." She points to a seat that's carved into the wall on the far side of the room. "That's the chaperone's spot—mixed company was never left alone, you see. Young women were assigned a governess or a chaperone to make sure they didn't get in trouble."

"Am I your chaperone?" I ask.

"No—I'm yours," Arabella says. "You're in my country and my house, so it's my duty to make sure you have fun but do it properly."

"Have fun or behave?" I ask.

"Both," she says.

We pose there, our hands over our mouths, overly demurely, and then Arabella whispers, "Say something." It's so cool because I can totally hear her as if she's just faintly spoken into my ear.

"Say what?" I ask.

"Tell me your deep dark secrets," she says.

"Like you don't already know everything—not that there's much to tell. Not yet."

"Well, I told you that Clive isn't my brother—he's just half. And Angus's prior marriage—his former wife—was this notorious wild woman. But that's a story for another time. And my mother—Monti—she's not really English. She's from Indiana by way of Newport, which is how she knows Lila Lawrence's lush mother."

"Oh, yeah. It's weird because I thought I heard your mom slip into an American accent today, but I didn't want to say anything, obviously."

"Anyway." Arabella tucks her knees up to her chest and rubs her arms again, probably freezing in her dress because the room is cold. "There's enough fodder in my family to fill a billion tabloids—not to mention my brother being the biggest mystery."

"Clive?" I ask. "It's nice that you refer to him as your brother, even if you kind of detest him and he's only genetically linked by half."

"No," Arabella says, "I didn't mean Clive." She stands up and breaks our whispering, her voice sounding even louder than normal after all our hushed conversation. "I meant my other brother."

"God—don't tell me there's another one like Clive?" I laugh.

"No. This one's nothing like Clive. I was talking about my full brother, whom I don't think you've had the displeasure of meeting."

"Oh," I say and sigh, incredulous that Arabella just forgot to mention another member of her family. "And who is this forgotten soul?"

"Asher." Arabella slides her bare feet along the cold black-and-white checked marble floor. "My brother Asher."

CHAPTER FOUR

♡

That's me: putting the ass back in assumption. Why I ever assumed Asher was a gardener is beyond me. Of course he's related. Of course now that I know he's Arabella's brother the resemblance is clear. Arabella is halfway down the tower stairs before I regain my composure and follow her. "Bels, wait a minute," I say.

"No—I'm freezing," she whines. "Let me just run to my room for a sec and then I'll meet you downstairs. It's probably time for hot chochie in the kitchen, anyway."

Hot chocie is just one of the many abbreviations I've heard since my arrival—presents are pressies, kisses are kissies, biscuits are bickies. Note to self: Keep list of English phrases and their meanings in journal. I start to head downstairs to wait for Arabella but feel like I need to tell her about my run-in with Asher, so I walk the maze of the second-floor hallways and try to get to her room. The trouble is that we came down the back stairway and I know my way around only from the front stairway, so I'm wandering around like Alice (which I kind of am, between the teacup kiss—kiss = snogs—and my wide-eyed amazement).

Each room is a different color, and I take a quick peek in as I go by. There's the yellow room, with its buttery curtains and cream-colored bedspread and worn-in tapestry on the wall. The silver room is austere: gray linens, throw pillows bordered in silvery rope, polished cement floors, and a floor-to-ceiling mirror anchored to the wall by a wrought-iron hook. The pink room—where Monti mentioned she likes to sleep when she needs to feel "closer to her inner organs"—um, okay—is a vision of warmth; since it's at the front of the house in one of the turrets, the room is round with a queen-sized bed oddly in the center of the room, not touching any wall. I don't think I've ever seen a bedroom where the bed just floated, but it works in this one. Deep rose silk drapes billow on the floor, two round couches quilted in velvety pink (not My Little Pony pink—antique, mellow pink) beckon me over.

I sit on one and take a breath. The lights in this room cast a pink hue, and I feel calm (and probably closer to my inner organs). Calm enough that I stand up and go to find Arabella to tell her I have giant crush on her brother.

When I finally get to Arabella's enormous room, she's changed into a skintight crewneck sweater that clings to her enough to make anyone envious and a pair of Hadley Hall sweatpants.

"You look cozy," I say.

"Much better, yeah. Where were you?"

"Oh, you know, wandering around. Taking the tour of all the guest rooms."

"Did you find the trap door?"

"No—where's that?"

"The purple room," she says. "You have to sort of bonk the book-shelf with your hip like this . . ." She demonstrates. "And then the wall spins."

"I definitely want to check that out. But listen, can I tell you something?"

Arabella sits cross-legged in a leather chair. "Sure. But then we should go downstairs. Monti gets cross if you miss the ritual." When I look confused she adds, "It's nothing big—just hot cocoa before bed."

"Yum."

"So what did you want to say? You're not upset are you? Everything's all right here? God, I didn't even ask about your phone call home—is Mable okay?"

"Yeah, yeah, it's fine. What I wanted to just say was that—in terms of your family and everything . . . obviously, thank you for having me and I am having a great time so far . . ."

"Piss off I said!" Arabella shouts and makes me jump. "Not you, Love."

I turn around and see Clive the Dickhead leaning on the doorframe, listening to our conversation. Arabella leaps up from her chair and slams the double door in his face.

"Sorry," she says. "He'll leave for an extra-long holiday soon and we'll be free of fraternal fuck-ups."

"Speaking of fraternal, about Asher . . ."

Arabella takes a tube of lip gloss from the mantel and puts it on without looking in the mirror. "Don't even get me started or we'll never make it to the kitchen. Clive's annoying as hell, but with him you know what you're getting. Asher's a different story altogether."

"Really? How so?"

"Look, Love. Asher and I share the same genes, but he's not like me." She faces me and sighs, puts my hair behind my ear. "He's moody. All he cares about is his camera and making sure his gallery doesn't fold."

"Maybe he's shy," I offer. Except with a certain girl in a certain garden. "He has a gallery? That sounds cool."

"Why are you defending him when you haven't even met him?"

she asks but doesn't give me time to answer. "He's this struggling photojournalist-slash-heartbreaker-slash-photographer-slash-hook-up artist who thinks he's entitled to whatever—or whomever—he wants."

Suddenly, I have different image of Asher. Not the rugged gardener, but the hot womanizer at a party. Somehow, I can't merge the two images. "So you're saying you guys aren't close?"

"Spot on." Note to self: Add this to the list of phrases. "Asher is interested only in himself. He wants nothing to do with me or my friends, and he's come very close to telling my parents about me and Tobias, which he knows would be a huge scandal."

"But he hasn't, right? Told them, I mean?"

"Well, no," Arabella says, considering. She leads me to the doorway. "But basically, Asher is to be left alone. It's what he wants, and you'd do well to just ignore him, which shouldn't be difficult since he's hardly ever here."

We're on the grand front stairwell when Arabella thinks of something and spins around to me. "Yeah," she says. "I'll introduce you to Asher—and then just forget him."

In the kitchen, Asher is nowhere in sight. Our mouth-to-mouth contact this afternoon is feeling further away—possibly I dreamed it? Angus and Monti serve hot cocoa in cylindrical glass mugs and pass around a bowl of fresh whipped cream.

"All right," Angus bellows. "Who wants to go first?"

Since I have no idea what he's talking about, I say nothing. I keep waiting for someone to clue me in on the Piece family rituals, but they don't. It's as if I'm just expected to figure things out as I go, which is fine, but a list of rules or a guidebook (that includes *Don't hook up with Arabella's brother*) would be nice.

Monti sips her drink and says, "As you know, I have the cover of

Celebrity Life coming up. And although I am the first to admit this is a silly, superficial wish, I just hope it goes well."

"That's not superficial, Mum," Arabella says. "It's your career. You should be proud. It's totally respectable to want it to go well." Arabella licks her spoon clean of whipped cream. "I want to be honest."

Massive pause as we all wait for Arabella to continue, but she doesn't.

"Care to elaborate?" Clive asks. He snickers until Angus nudges him and then says, "Come on, Bels, tell us more."

Angus shakes his head. "No, no. This is free-flowing release here, not a forced outpouring. Now, Love, what do you wish for?"

Oh, right, that's what we're doing. "Um, you mean long-term? Or now, for tomorrow?"

Monti flips her blond mane back and winks at Angus. "Oh, interesting!"

"Oh, no," I groan. "What have I revealed about myself? I wasn't sure about the rules of this."

"Oh, very interesting . . ." Angus lets out a big belch, and I swear I will wake up from this weird dream and be back at Hadley Hall, late for class. I dig my thumbnail into my thigh to check—nope, this is real.

"What Angus is trying to say," Arabella explains, "is that you're supposed to just say what you want."

"And *do* what you want," Clive says and makes it sound like what I want to do is jump into bed with him, the thought of which is enough to inspire bile at the back of my throat. "Why do you limit yourself?"

"But all I was asking was what the rules are," I say, defenses up. "I mean, this"—I gesture to the table, the hot chochie, the whole room, the whole thing—"this is bizarre! I don't know what I'm doing here. So for me to say what I wish for, or what I want to happen—I just can't . . ." Before I can unravel further, I clamp my mouth closed.

Clive the spotty slimer, Arabella the English rose, Monti the model, and Angus the playwright stare at me like I'm a freak of nature.

Monti pats my hand, and when I don't look her in the eye, she leans down so I can see her. Her lids are lined in white, her green eyes vivid. "Maybe you will. Let's hope you will."

Will what? I think, and then, in case I wanted this pseudoséance to be even freakier, it's like they've read my mind and Arabella says, "She means you will know what to do. You will know what to wish for, or how to act if you just stop thinking about it."

I have visions of the evening ending with handholding and aura reading, but instead it's surprisingly normal. Arabella washes the glasses in sudsy water, Clive sponges the table clean, good nights are said, and we all go to our respective rooms.

I'm tucked under the cushy fluff of the down duvet when I feel a crunch. I'm lying on the packet of information from LADAM, which, once I slide it out from under me, I feel the need to read. The Hadley Hall exchange program is through St. Paul's, which is a fancy private all-girls school (private is called public in England and public is called state—it's all confusing) and LADAM is a sort of offshoot of St. Paul's. Arabella is fully on the LADAM side of things, but you can take classes in either—with St. Paul's being more traditional academics and LADAM being exclusively dramatics and music with classes that range from Acting for the Screen to one just called Posture— seriously. In order to have enough credits that transfer back to Hadley, I have to take two classes at St. Paul's, which sound interesting. One is a Shakespeare lecture, and one is Expository Writing and Modern British Literature—aka Brit Lit—which Arabella recommended since it's taught by Poppy Massa-Tonclair (aka PMT, the anglo version of PMS). PMT is the British equivalent of Toni Morrison—except not African American, rather, Indian-English, very respected, major awards, and so on.

All of my classes are outlined in the packet, along with the honor code, which I have to sign. All the tests are take-home ones—exams, too—but you have to swear (swear = sign your name) that you won't cheat. By signing your name, you're also confirming that if you do cheat—say, use your textbook or go online to search for a forgotten fact—that you will turn yourself in. I fall asleep with the bright moonlight (I couldn't bring myself to close the heavy inside shutters on my windows) casting shadows across the papers and schedules, the map of the London underground, the date and time I'm expected at the dorms, and a picture of said housing, which looks, to be honest, like a motel circa 1960: boxy rooms with brown crocheted bedcovers, dusty vinyl-coated curtains, and a desk. I can't quite imagine myself there, singing, studying Brit Lit, working on my posture, but it's looming. The holidays will be over soon, and I'll have to leave Bracker's Common, with all its rituals and intrigues, and head to London.

Of course, when I wake up to a tray of strawberry crepes, fresh croissant, and coffee with steamed milk waiting for me outside my door, the student housing and London life seem very far away. I nibble at my food and run the bath. Sitting in the warm bubbles, I have a clear view out the windows to the Bracker's grounds. I can literally control my pulse by thinking of—or ignoring—the kiss with Asher. What do I wish for right now? That he'd walk in here and join me in the bath.

But no such luck. Plus, if he did, I'd freak out, never having been that naked with anyone before, and also worrying that Arabella would find us together and make me go home. And I don't want to go back home, or to Hadley, or any of the glut of gossip I left behind—the mess with Jacob and bitchy Lindsay Parrish, the constant fear of Mable taking a turn for the worse, my dad delving into my affairs (or lack thereof, but still), the everydayness of life back there. With a shudder and a smile, I remember that I don't have to go back—not yet. For right now, I'm here (here = bathtub in palace minus hot English boy, but here nonetheless).

The day is spent stringing flowers onto ribbons and slinging the ribbons from the ceilings, adding bows and holly, until the effect is that of a Shakespearean set. I studied enough of the Bard to know that a lot of his plays have magic in them, either a forest with fairies in which all guards are down, or a swapping of identities that causes havoc, and when the dinner gong sounds, I realize I've got a starring role.

The "theme for the evening" as stated by Monti as she tried on vintage outfits for her magazine shoot is "purity." Over lunch, it was agreed upon that we'd all dress in white for Christmas dinner and "arrive with pure thoughts." I'm guessing since Monti was dressed in a leopard G-string and halter top and drinking champagne, that she didn't mean pure as in no nookie, more like pure as in open to new thoughts, honest, which is a good thing, since I must confess that my thoughts have been less than pure when it comes to dreams involving Asher.

"Are you ready?" Arabella arrives at my room wearing a white tank top, white boa, skintight white suede flares, and white heels.

"You look like a slutty angel," I say.

"I feel like one, too." She smiles. "I got a phone call from Toby just now. He just got back from drinks with William."

"As in Prince?"

"As in, yes."

"Right," I say. "Sounds ordinary."

We laugh, and when I hold up a white loose-knit sweater to compare it with the white Oxford shirt I've got on, Arabella shakes her head. "Just borrow something from Mum."

She leads me into a room I've yet to see, which turns out to be one devoted entirely to clothing and accessories not currently being worn by Monti. The room is bigger than my living room at home and organized by color, so we head right to the white section.

"Tops are on the bottom and bottoms are on the top," Arabella explains. "and no, not just to be quirky—"

"I know," I say. "It's so the bottoms of the dresses and pants don't hit the floor, right?"

"Ah, you learn fast, Grasshopper," Arabella says in a faux-wise voice. "Just rummage around and I'll see you downstairs. But don't be shy. You've got an amazing body—if only you'd show it."

When she's gone, I slide into clothes I'd never think to try on in a store—not that I've been to many stores that carry couture. In Jimmy Choos and an Armani sheath, I'm ready for the white party in the Hamptons. In a cropped white fur coat and hip-hugging pants I'm ready for my Sundance close-up. Then I find a low-slung, but-not-too-low-cut skirt and a white turtleneck bodysuit, which, when paired, look very good. I complete the ensemble with white knee-length boots, and before I give in to the urge to try on clothes from the other color sections, I turn off the lights and head downstairs.

I pause in the middle of the staircase. The Christmas lights twinkle below; fragrant smells come from the dining room; music wafts up; and it feels good. It's one of those rare moments where everything feels in synch, and I feel pretty and calm.

Calm until, that is, I see Asher staring at me from the arch of the front door.

We lock eyes, and I go down the steps, hoping not to trip on the boots, which are a half size too big. I make it safely to the bottom, and Asher is right in front of me. The cold air from outside is still on him, on his clothes, his cheeks. This is it: He will grab me and kiss me right in front of everyone, his hands cold on my neck, on my body . . .

"Oh, look what the night dragged in." Arabella sighs and takes my hand. "Love, this is Asher. Asher, this is—"

"Love." Asher reaches his hand out and shakes mine. I don't want him to let go.

"Asher," I manage to croak out.

"Now you've met him. Now forget him," Arabella says and leads me away. I turn back, my heart beating way too fast, my hand still cold from his touch.

Christmas Eve dinner extends from night into the following early morning, with food, festivities, and gifts, followed by more food and—let me be very clear—a startling amount of alcohol. Bottles assemble like a small glass army on top of the sideboard. With the table skirted in white linen, the pillars of white candles, and white food, the room is a vision of tranquillity, except of course for Asher, who has chosen to wear an entirely black outfit.

"If white is the absence of color," he says, downing a glass of white (of course) wine, "I don't think that's purity."

"Go on," says Angus, seriously intrigued.

Asher stands up and wanders around the room as he speaks. "Purity—to me at least—has nothing to do with absence or abstinence or avoiding anything. It's more to do with openness."

"So where does wearing black fit in?" Arabella asks, annoyed. She passes the white asparagus to me, and I eat a spear while listening, even though my appetite seems to have vanished in Asher's presence. It's not like school-crush stuff here; I feel magnetized to him, completely taken with his physical being, his words, everything.

"Black is everything," Asher says. "All colors, all feelings." He looks directly at me. "It's a mistake to think that clarity is purity. The mix and confusion, the overwhelming nature of desire and despondency is pure."

Ahem! I know I'm not imagining his stares, the electrical current between us, because it's obvious. Or maybe I just want it to be so. We eat risotto and white truffles, monkfish with a white sauce, and have white chocolate fondue with marshmallows and white raspberries during the gift exchange.

"Oh, my presents are upstairs," I say. I excuse myself to go get the books I've brought for the Pieces, the Hadley socks I've brought for Clive, and realize I've brought nothing for Asher. I could give him the socks, but they were meant to be kind of a joke. Plus, they're white and lame. Oh well. I'll have to just explain and get him something later. My arms filled with the gifts, I turn the light switch off with my elbow and am in the dark room for two seconds when Asher appears in front of me and without saying anything slides his hands under my hair, tips my head back, and kisses me. Then, before I can even catch up to myself and the kiss, it's over and we're back downstairs, seated in the drawing room as if nothing's happened.

"Oh, thank you, thank you, thank you, Monti!" Arabella is saying gleefully. "Love, look!" She waves a large brass skeleton key in my face. I'm still in the kiss fog for a second and then snap out of it in time for her explanation. "This is our ticket to a hot term. Monti has the most incredible flat just off of the King's Road . . ."

"I thought you girls would like it." Monti shrugs and smiles. "Rather than the horrid dorms at LADAM." She turns to me. "Arabella spent so many nights out of the dorms last year we barely knew how to track her down—thankfully she's got that cell phone." Probably, Arabella was at Toby's, but of course I keep quiet about that.

"Those dorms build character," Angus says. "Everyone ought to have the experience of living the way real artists do, with shite accommodations, beans and toast to eat, and no money."

"Like me, you mean?" Asher says and cocks his head to one side, his dark hair falling across his forehead.

"I suppose." Angus nods. "A little hard work never hurt anyone."

"Just because I accept their money doesn't mean I'm any less of an artist, Asher," Arabella says. She looks to me to say something.

"I don't know. I mean, there is this supposed link of art and struggle," I say. Arabella looks pissed. By pissed I mean both the American meaning—pissed off—and the English—drunk. "But I think you should do what you want." Asher and Arabella both stare at me.

"What would you do?" Clive asks and actually has a normal tone for once, "if you had loads of money? Do you think you'd be more or less inclined to work hard?"

I sigh and squish a marshmallow between my fingers. "I don't know. I'd like to say it wouldn't change anything, that I'd still want to write music and earn my way up the rock-folk ladder. But at the same time, if someone clicked their fingers"—I snap for emphasis—"and just made me a professional musician . . . I don't know. It'd be hard to turn that down."

Nods all around except for Asher, who stands up, takes a final slug of his drink, and says, "Thanks for the gifts, everyone. Thanks for the food, Angus. Monti. I'm due at Heathrow in the morning, so I've got to run."

"Where are you going?" I ask.

Arabella butts in. "Some island? Where is it this time, the Galápagos or the Seychelles?"

"Neither," Asher says. "And why do you even care? You've got your cushy flat to run to and your even cushier boyfriend . . ."

Monti perks up. "Boyfriend? I didn't know you had a lover, Arabella!" I'm embarrassed both by the use of the word *lover* and that I'm stuck in the middle of a sibling skirmish. Arabella, meanwhile, looks panicked that Asher's about to spill the royal beans.

"No," I say. "I have a boyfriend—not Arabella."

Two—or twelve—glasses of wine too many, Monti slurs, "Oh, right, then. I see. A nice American boy?"

"Um, yeah," I stammer, lying in an attempt to deflect the attention away from Arabella, who mouths "Thank you." "His name's Jacob." Monti and Angus wait for me to say more, as if giving the name of my imaginary beau isn't enough. "And I miss him."

Arabella giggles and offers me a candy cane, which I promptly shove in my mouth to avoid further verbal fumblings. Asher clears his throat and looks at me. "Well, then, I guess that settles that."

I want to explain myself, to erase what I've said, seeing as I've just made it clear not only to Asher that I'm off-limits, but that I'm the kind of person who cheats on her boyfriend with a complete stranger. "Wait," I say.

Asher comes back and stands very close to me. Close enough so I can feel his breath on my face. It smells sweet and minty. "What?"

"I didn't get you a gift," I say. "But not because I didn't want to— I just didn't know you existed."

Arabella interrupts us. "Aren't you going to be late for your models?" she asks. Then she turns to me. "Asher likes to photograph nude women."

"They're not nude," he says. "And even if they were, who the hell cares?"

"I might," I say.

Arabella rolls her eyes. "It's not illegal or anything. He's a shoot assistant—you know, for catalog photographers. Bathing suits, lingerie, supermodels. Every straight man's fantasy."

Now it's my turn to smirk. "What a hardship," I say. "You really are struggling for your art." I don't mean it to be that sarcastic, but I can't help it. The thought of Asher galavanting (or whatever you do on photo shoots) with semiclad models on a beach makes my insides twist up. But he thinks I have a boyfriend, so there.

"Bye, everyone! Arabella—be good. And Love?"

"Yes?" I stare at his mouth.

"Have fun in London," Asher says. I'm about to say that I will, that I'm psyched, that I can't wait, but he says, "And say hi to your boyfriend."

Back in the living room, the white-dressed rest of us greet the dawn with Happy (not Merry) Christmas and hugs. Arabella tucks her feet under a cushion and hands me a woolen throw, which I put on my feet. The candles have seeped onto the tablecloth, Clive is snoring on his chair, and Angus scrounges for leftover liquor though he's still drunk and clearly the worse for wear. Monti, splayed out on the chaise longue as if she's just fainted there, looks glamorous despite her impending hangover.

"Hey," I whisper to Arabella. "No one spilled anything."

Arabella looks at her stain-free outfit. "The benefit of all white foods, I guess." She closes her eyes and mumbles, "I hope you had a good time—and I'm sorry about Asher. See what I mean? Forget you even met him, okay?"

"Okay," I say, and it comes out wobbly—which in my case has nothing to do with liquor consumption and everything to do with knowing that forgetting Asher would be impossible.

CHAPTER FIVE

♡

"Taxi!" Arabella puts her arm up and a black cab comes flying over, its brakes squeaking. She climbs in and lowers the window halfway. "Now, you're sure I can't convince you?"

"I'm positive," I say. "It's for the best."

"Okay." She breaths in deeply. "Good luck."

And just like that, I'm alone with a pile of bags in front of Gladwell Mansion, which—despite its name—is a complete shithole. It's also my dorm. Even though Monti's flat sounds awesome, and the idea of sharing an apartment with Arabella is undoubtedly appealing, there's a large part of me that kind of agrees with what Asher was saying. Not that I need to slit my wrists and struggle and be miserable to be an artist, but that I should—or want—to experience the real student life here. My life. Not Arabella's. So I lug my crap up the three flights of stairs to room 16A and find that it's connected to 16B, in which two girls are screaming at each other.

"Bitch!" one yells. "You lying sack of shite!"

"Whore!" the other shouts and is about to slap the first one when they notice me and go from screeching to completely friendly. "Oh, hi!"

Um, bipolar, anyone?

"Hi?" I say and it comes out a question because the vibe is so weird in here. I drop my duffel on the 16A side of the doorway.

"We're not total lunatics in need of anger counseling, by the way," the girl with a pixie haircut says. "We're practicing for our Stage Rage class."

"Yeah," the other one adds. She's tall with skin the color of instant coffee (ah, Mable would be proud of me for using caffeinated substances for my descriptions) and a pile of hair that's long enough to be tucked into her suede jacket. "After we finish telling each other to go to hell we're going to get a coffee. Want to come?"

I smile and say, "Sure. Can I watch you duke it out, though?"

"We love an audience," the pixie says. "I'm Fizzy." *I'm bubbly* I want to add, but she gestures to herself. "Real name's Gertrude, otherwise called Rude, Rude turned into Rizz and Rizz morphed into—"

"Fizzy, good to meet you. I'm Love."

"Oh, God, I'm Keena," the other woman says. "Not a sane name among us."

At the tiny coffeehouse three streets behind of the dorm, Keena stirs milk into her tea and says, "I know, I know I'm supposed to be on the American coffee kick that's sweeping the country, but I still like tea. Good, old-fashioned harvested tea—loose, preferably, in a bag if you must."

"Thank you for that rant and rave, Keena. And now back to our regularly scheduled program," Fizzy says in mock-news-broadcaster speak. To me she adds, "Keena's just a bit old colony for my tastes."

"Don't let my mother hear you say that." Keena laughs and Fizzy joins in. When I stay quiet, out of the joke loop, they look at me. "Oh, right—you don't know Keena's mum."

"Nope," I say and sip my coffee. It's not Slave to the Grind by any stretch of the imagination, but it's not bad. Especially because it's warm in here and freezing and rainy outside, especially because I'm not wandering around aimlessly, and especially because I am not alone wondering why the hell I've chosen to live in the dorms instead of the posh place Arabella's got six tube stops away.

"Her mother is Poppy," Fizzy says, thumbing to Keena.

Now I get it. "You're Poppy Massa-Tonclair's daughter?"

"The very one," Keena says with obvious pride—and deservedly so. Her mother has won every literary prize from the Booker to the Orange to the Pulitzer. "Out of wedlock, of course."

"Really?" I ask. "They never tell you that in the bio at the back of the books."

"I know." Keena shakes her head. "Actually, they used to—in the mid-seventies, when she first started writing. But then with the whole Thatcher regime and the political climate of the eighties in this country, it just wasn't as hip bohemian, so the publisher decided to make her bios more . . ."

"Mundane?" I offer.

"Right." Keena watches me drink my coffee. "So what's your deal, Love?"

"I'm not sure I have one," I say. "My life seems pretty mild compared to yours here. My dad's the principal at Hadley Hall, my school—which you might know from Arabella. And my mother's . . ."

Keena looks at me and waits for me to talk. Fizzy ruffles her hair—it's short and standing up on end, and she makes it flip direction just by running a palm over the top. When I don't say more Fizzy adds, "We've heard lots of good things about you from Arabella, of course, but she never mentioned you were quite so beautiful and reserved." Huh? That's how I come across? One: cool, because I've never been beautiful—pretty, maybe. Two: weird, because it's not how I see myself at all. Somewhat appealing and goofy—but not beautiful and certainly not reserved.

"Maybe that's not how Arabella sees me," I say. Damn the drama devotees for being so inquisitive.

"No," Fizzy says. "I bet she does—we just have that anti-American kind of slant, I guess. Shame on us for being so closed minded." Fizzy swats Keena's hand like she's scolding her.

"Yeah, I guess I thought you'd be pushy and loud, or a big old slag like everyone on American television. You do know what a slag is, right?"

"I believe I do," I say in my best upper-crust Brit—thank you Gwyneth Paltrow for showing me the way. "Slag is equal to slut and hag and can be said either seriously, as in 'Lindsay Parrish, the biggest bitch I know, is such a slag and she always will be for sleeping with my first boyfriend and trying to steal my supposed soul mate, Jacob.' Or, in a mock way—as in, 'Give me that last bite of biscuit, you slag.'"

"Hey, the girl learns fast," Keena says. "And if the example you gave was true, slag is definitely the proper terminology."

"Damn straight." I nod.

"Come on," Fizzy says. "Let's go back and unpack your stuff and go meet Arabella for dinner."

"At the Buttery?" I ask. In the packet of information there was a whole section on student life that read like it had been printed twenty years ago, which it probably had been. The Buttery, it stated, was the dining hall of the campus, but served tea with scones in the afternoon and dinner at long communal tables. It sounds glam, but when I walked through it, the tables had a sticky sheen, stray peas rolled underfoot, clinging to my shoes, and the place was devoid of any people or good vibes.

"Fuck no." Keena shakes her head and wraps her long multicolored scarf around her neck. "The Buttery is terrible. Honestly, you would be hard-pressed to find worse food anywhere. Trust me. I've spent a ton of time in third-world countries, and I'd take the beans or rice any day over that slop."

"Okay," I say. "How about showing me some favorite place of yours, then? A first night out in London? A pub?"

Keena and Fizzy look at each other and smile. "I think Arabella has something else in mind."

Loud, pulsating music courses through my body, smoke stings my eyes, and I can't hear anything. But I don't care at all: I am dancing with a prince. A real prince. Yes, that one that's always in *US Weekly* and *Teen People* with his collar up on the grounds of a polo club, or on a ski holiday with his dad (um, the would-be king).

Reality check: I am not the only one dancing with said prince. There's a group of us, including Arabella—looking like a fashion icon in a halter top that shows off her perfect skin and jeans seemingly made for her—swirling around together. Everyone moves pretty well—everyone that is except for me. I try to disguise my lack of dancing skill by smiling and nodding, hoping that enthusiasm will make up for the fact that I basically dance the way I did in seventh grade, feet shuffling side to side, every once in a while lifting my arms up and clapping when warranted.

"You like dancing?" Prince shouts. At least I think that's what he says. Could be *You like prancing; Keena's a man-see;* or *You look fantastic. Run away with me*—this last one is a bit of a stretch. I shake my head but smile and shrug. He mimes a drink, to which I nod and give a thumbs-up.

We've (we = the group, not my royal and me) claimed a circular table at the back of Le Temps, the supertrendy club that Tobias (to whom I've yet to be formally introduced) apparently co-owns (thanks to turning eighteen and getting access to his enormous trust fund), which is the only reason the doormen let us in. That plus the fact that we showed up with a prince (*the* prince?).

"So Arabella tells me you're here for a whole term?" the prince says, and I can actually hear him.

"True. I'm studying at St. Paul's and LADAM," I say. Chitchat with the British royalty. I can't wait to report back to Hadley. Chris will be so jealous—he has a thing for the prince, even though he knows the guy is straight. "What about you?"

"Oh, I'm in my gap year, like Tobias." I nod but don't really know what he's talking about. Sure, it could be his year working at The Gap, but I doubt they make that a requirement for the throne. "It's like a year out—you know, travel, have fun, help people, or whatever."

"And will you?"

"All of the above," he says, and I swear I catch him looking at my cleavage—for which I have Keena to blame, because she insisted I wear one of her mini shirts, which has a gaping V-neck. But the peek is fleeting and then he's back to interview pro. Unlike the typical American conversations, I've noticed that the Euros (and they are Euros, even if they're not the silly mean ones I met through Lila Lawrence at Brown University) have better conversational skills. Note to self: Master the art of small talk without making it seem small and boring.

"Hey, there you are, Love!" Flushed and out of breath, Arabella stands next to me. "I have someone I'd like you to meet. Tobias— Toby—this is Love Bukowski."

And he's just like his picture. Tall, blond, broad in all the right places and with a wickedly sexy grin. "Love, finally we meet in person. I feel as though I know you already."

"Good to meet you, Toby," I say, and we shake hands. He slides in next to me. I am the turkey in a royal sandwich. I suddenly lose my inhibitions and drape my arms across the boys. Arabella leans in so her face is pressed in tight near Toby's. "Look at me! I love this country!"

Then, two potentially disturbing events occur.

The first: While I'm still stuck between Princey and Toby, I look down and notice I'm drastically close to spilling out of the top of my top. Rather than sexy cleavage, I have a case of the Pamela Anderson blues. I try to wriggle free in order to subtly fix my breastage, but before I do, a blast of bright lights temporarily blinds me.

"Oh shit!" Toby holds his hand out, not in front of his own face, but in front of the prince's. "Who let the paparazzi in?"

"Never mind," the prince says. "It was bound to happen sooner or later."

"It's okay, Toby," Arabella says soothingly. He shrugs her off.

"I'm going to tell the doormen to be more careful." Tobias takes a sip of Arabella's water and then looks at me. "Sorry, darling. I hope you don't wind up as new meat for the press here."

Disturbing event number two: Just as I'm about to assure him that it's fine, that I'm sure we'll sort it out, I feel his hand on my thigh.

Possible explanations for this include but are not limited to: He thought my thigh was Arabella's, since we were seated on either side; he was flustered by the photo incident moments ago; he's a slag plus/minus an idiot and would dare to make a pass at me when he knows Aabella's my best friend. Or none of the above. I could be misinterpreting all the European, princely customs and need to relax.

"We should go, Love," Arabella says. "The last thing I want is to have my parents see paparazzi pictures of me . . ."

"Think they'd mind that we're out clubbing the night before school term starts?" I ask, trying to figure out if I want to tell all this to my dad or if it'll make him worry about my time here.

"They don't care about that. They'd just throw a fit if they saw me in the arms of the—in their minds—right-wing establishment."

On the way out, we double kiss good-bye our group of friends and talk as we wait for the tube. "I have Massa-Tonclair's class tomorrow," I say to a very distracted Arabella.

"Oh yeah?" she says. "You'll like her—even though she lives up to her nickname, PMT." PMT = English version of PMS. This I know after Arabella freaked out and chopped her bangs this fall at Hadley, feeling insane and crampy, then regretted it immediately. I nod, and Arabella bites the side of her lip. "Did you happen to see the guy who took that photo? Would you know him if you saw him?"

"No," I say and wish it wasn't such a big deal. But I know it is for Arabella, and I try to help her. "Except he did have a shape, I think, on his jacket. Or maybe a—yeah, now that I think of it—a star on the back." I trace a star onto Arabella's back to show her the size and location.

"Brilliant," she smiles. "You're a lifesaver, Love. That's the official press jacket from *Top Star,* a weekly celebrity rag that tries to catch everyone in compromising positions and then runs the photo with a tagline that's like BEAUTIES AND BREASTS or ROYALS REVEL IN RAUCOUS RAMPAGE."

"Oh my God, *you* saw my boobs, too?"

"People in Paris could see your tits, Love." Arabella cracks a smile. "But if you've got it, flaunt it, right? Anyway, my darling sweet brother Asher has a contact at *Top Star* and I'll just have to beg him for help. Which I hate to do, but . . ."

"I could talk to him," I say. My mouth has a power source all its own. Sometimes I want no responsibility for what my mouth says. "If you want, that is."

"Would you? Thanks, Love—really. He'll listen much better to you than to me. I owe you one."

Arabella is truly grateful, and I am truly guilty and yet thrilled at the knowledge that I will have a legitimate reason to call—better yet, see—Asher. Then I remember that Asher thinks I'm deeply involved with some boyfriend I don't have, and I try to script a conversation in which I explain that while there is a real Jacob, and we did start to date, that was almost a year ago and I haven't seen him in months and months and—most important—we are not involved now. Now I'm single.

Dear Dad,
I think this is the first email I've sent you since my internship in New York! Mark the date. Anyway, the pay phones are on the other side of the campus and are circa 1940 (they did have pay phones then, right?). I never have time to run over there, so I'm sending this and hoping you don't mind that I'm cc'ing Mable so I don't have to tell her the same stuff all over again.

Classes started a couple of weeks ago, but they don't go by the week. They go by how many hours your schedule crams in. For instance if your "individualised programme"—note the Anglo spelling—for some reason doesn't have enough of a certain class, you are doomed to run around trying to get that professor to work one-on-one with you until you've accrued enough time to qualify for credit. This is what's happening with me and my Brit Lit class.

Prof. Massa-Tonclair is just like I thought she'd be—very cool, very knowledgeable—but she seems to think her class is the only one for which I'm registered. Not to mention the fact that she thinks I'm this brash American. Or maybe that's

just my interpretation. But a lot of people here
think that until I prove otherwise.

    Example:

    Me: Here's the fifteen pages you wanted me to
write about the representation of the under-
privileged in modern fiction.

    PMT: Title?

    Me: Penniless, Proud, Pushed Aside, or Stigma-
tized

    PMT: Catchy. Now, read it aloud to the class
tomorrow and be prepared to defend it with specific quotes and journalistic references from
reputable news sources.

    Me: By tomorrow? Don't we have to read all of
<u>White Teeth</u> by then?

    PMT: You're a smart girl. Surely you can man-
age both.

    See what I mean? It's fascinating but totally
consuming. Plus, I'm friends with her daughter,
Keena, who has just as much work as I do and gets
it all done, so I can't complain about it too
much to PMT. Hey, maybe that's what people feel
about you and me at Hadley!

    Anyway, Arabella's busy being the lead in <u>Damn
Yankees</u> (not a rude jab at Americans, but the
play) and gets to strut her stuff. Maybe you'll
come see the show? I think it goes up in March.
My tryouts for the Choir (which, like everything
here, is not what it seems—it's not choral; it's

the elite LADAM singing group that gets to perform for the queen or whatever) are soon and I'm
nervous. There's nothing I can do to prepare except gargle and sing in the disgusting bath. (The
dorms have no shower—just one of those nozzle
thingies you can attach.)

Oh my God—I can't believe I wrote this much
without asking about you and Mable. Is she okay?
(Mable, if you're reading this, are you? Please
write.) Any news? Please, please, please tell me
if something bad happens—I will come home right
away. I have to go in a minute b/c my Stage Rage
class (not kidding—I get credit for yelling!) is
doing a fake public fight (Suffice to say teach-
ing techniques are not like Hadley!).

Please write back and tell me what's up—did
you go on your date? Anything interesting happing
at HH? Also, can you explain again where I go to
register for the SATs? I have visions of spacing
out on them and winding up arriving with ten minutes left. (I won't, really, but it's my current
nightmare.)

My name to you,

L.

Outside of the LADAM computer center, which is really just three
old Apples shoved into a dusty alcove, with hit-or-miss dial-up, the
sun is shining for the first time in a week. Even though I now have
only a couple of minutes to get to my class, I decide to walk. The days

are so short here and the weather is—like every clichéd London story—damp and rainy, and I need some fresh air.

The LADAM part of my curriculum is totally intense. Everyone here is convinced they're the next Jude Law or Cate Blanchett or Kate Winslet or other rhyming English actor, or they're determined to get discovered playing their angry rock in a slum bar and walk around pissed off and grimy to prove it. Not that I think there's anything wrong with being driven, but it's the drama kings and the continual feeling that all the students are perpetually on stage that drives me nuts. A simple "Do you have the time?" can turn into a one-act play where the glamour girl you've asked the easy question tilts her head, considers your missive, and then ponders it, dramatically checking her watch and saying—loudly for the back of the house—"Why, I do have the time! Indeed, it's half four."

But then, too, the classes and instruction are original and exciting. Rather than sitting in a standard classroom and discussing the obscure history of dentistry in Singapore (not that this isn't compelling reading, but it does wear thin after the tenth description), which I had to read last year at Hadley, I have Sex and Gender Portrayals (read: My first assignment was to dress in drag and act out a scene with Fizzy where she played a bisexual fairy). Instead of writing papers on great books for Brit Lit with PMT, I'm rewriting them in my Changing Visions class at St. Paul's—which is on the other side of London and a total hassle to get to from LADAM, but worth it. I am rescripting *The Scarlet Letter* (which I read at Hadley with Mr. Chaucer—glad to have it somewhat fresh in my mind) so it's set in the present day in a Wal-Mart type store, seeing how the plot or characters or dialogue change or don't. It's the first real creative writing I've tried—and I like.

I heft my bag onto my right shoulder but it inevitably slides off. What is the nature of the human body that I can keep a bag only on the left side? My left shoulder is capable of handling tons of weight, but even the lightest bag slides off the right one—like it knows it doesn't belong. Note to self: This is either interesting or proof I have spent too much time contemplating things rather than getting exercise and need to regroup.

"Miss Bukowski," says Galen French, who is not French but Irish, and my voice coach. "I see you're enjoying the weather."

I squint up at the murky but bright sky. "I hope the sun lasts. I'm heading over to Littleton Square."

"Ah, the infamous winter term faux fight! Good luck. May you draw many a horrified look from passersby."

"Thanks," I say. Galen—many LADAM teachers go by their first names—is a blend of old (as in Ye Olde) world—tweedy jacket and Oxford shoes—mixed with new—he knows every song ever, even obscure American songs like from the cds Mable gave me. "Listen, I feel like I should be doing more to get ready for the Choir tryouts."

Galen thinks for a minute and then sighs. "I'm not sure about that, Love. You're right to go ahead and audition, but I wouldn't have unrealistic expectations about the outcome. You're competing against final-year students and vocal superstars who have had loads more time to stretch their range."

I smile and nod and we say good-bye. I put my hands in my pockets and take a deep breath of January air. One thing I've noticed that's so different here is that the faculty members aren't constantly bolstering the students. At Hadley, we—or I at least—take for granted how interested the teachers are in having us succeed. Here, it's like they're along to guide me, but they're not invested—or maybe they just want to be realistic. I mean, how many people can really go on to be the next great thing?

At Littleton Square, several students are already shouting and gesturing wildly.

"No, no, no!" yells Patrick de Rothschild, our very campy, very chic Stage Rage teacher. "You're too exaggerated. Real anger comes from deep inside." He points to himself. "Not in the chest, in the stomach."

Keena sidles up to me and whispers, "Speaking of stomachs, I am so hungry. I bet if we're really quiet, we could sneak out and go to HEL."

"What?" I whisper. "Did you say go to hell?"

Keena giggles. "No, not like that. Come on. I'll show you."

And just like that, I ditch class for the first time, even though it was fun. Keena subtly takes a couple of steps backwards, just enough so she's at the corner of a large stone building (behemoth ancient buildings are everywhere in this town), then suddenly disappears. I meanwhile pretend to focus on the scene in front of me (read: three students bickering, onlookers gawking, and Patrick de Rothschild tapping others on the shoulder at will and saying things like, "Now, you've just been slapped for no good reason—go with it!"). While I ever so casually lean on one of those cylindrical red post boxes, I listen to the shouting and wonder if I'd have it in me to scream publicly were it not for a good grade or going yellular on my cell phone back home. For a split second, I blush, remembering a certain incident of cell yell back on Martha's Vineyard, and how my disappearing summer boy, Charlie, scolded me for that display. Ah, good times.

When I'm safely away from the Stage Rage crowd, I slink into a small side street where Keena is waiting.

"Finally," she says and undoes her bundle of hair from its rubber band and lets it spill onto her shoulders, only to gather it up a millisecond later. She watches me watch her and says, "I know, I know. I have a hair-playing habit. Drives my mum crazy—but then I guess all mums are like that." She smiles.

"I don't know," I say. I'm never sure whether to casually drop the bomb of my mother's no-show in my life thus far or brush it aside.

"Is yours more laid back, then?"

"You could say that," I say and half laugh. My hair falls in front of my eyes and I bite my top lip where it itches in the middle. "She's not really in the picture at all."

Keena gets right to the point. "Anymore or ever?"

"Ever." I say the one word as a complete sentence and wish I had more to say about it, but I find myself sighing as usual. "Listen, there are a million journal entries here but the basic gist of it is that she . . . left." This is the first time I've ever said that out loud. "From what I gather—and I'm only just really beginning to gather all this information because my dad's been really secretive about it, probably to save me from feeling like shit, leading to emotional scarring and irreparable damage—it seems like she had me and left me with my dad."

Keena's eyes are wide and round like a cartoon character's. "Wow. That's pretty instense." She reaches her hand out and gives my shoulder a squeeze. "Well, I have enough mum for the both of us—Arabella, too. You can borrow ours."

She means well, but it's an offer that I could never take her up on and she knows it. But then she adds, "Besides, my mum"—she puts on a deep authoritative voice—"the revered international author, thinks you're a force to be reckoned with."

"She'd be horrified that you ended with a preposition," I jab, and Keena grins.

"A force with which to be reckoned. Fine, you really are meant to study with her."

Keena goes back to playing with her hair and then swats her own hand away as if PMT is there to criticize her. Despite the fact that it sucks when people pick at your habits, I wish I had my dad, or Mable—my mother, even—around to pick on me.

We keep walking, over a zebra crossway (aka black-and-white-striped crosswalk except cars *have* to stop or they get a ticket) and under a little archway until we're in a small enclave.

"I thought your mother figured me for some rude American," I say.

"A Damn Yankee?" Keena jokes. "No. She likes you. Even if she has a funny way of showing it."

"Yeah, like criticizing my first paper and ripping my modern method debate to shreds?"

"Yup, like that." Keena nods. "So what do you think?"

All around us are potted plants hanging from silk ribbons. Bright pink cyclamen create a floral cloud above a wooden bench covered with peeling aqua paint. Tucked behind a long swag of swirling ivy, I can just make out the letters *E* and *L.*

"This is HEL," Keena says and manages to find a semihidden door underneath the overgrown foliage, which would never stay so green and lush in the winter back home.

"How it'd it get its name?" I ask and scan the inside for a table. HEL is about the coolest café I've ever seen. The whole thing is under a bridge, I guess, so the ceiling is curved and the walls are painted brick. The decor is like something out of *The Prisoner,* that mod sixties show, with bubble chairs, tables made from thick Plexiglas circles that stem up from the splatter-painted cement floor like mushrooms. Very Wonderland. Keena goes up to the counter, which you wouldn't know is a counter unless you'd been here before— you write your order on a slip of paper, clip it to a wire clothesline, and turn a handle on the wall, which makes the whole thing snake its way along until it reaches a hole in the wall that leads to the kitchen.

"Looks like Jackson Pollock was here," I say to Keena when she's halfway back to our pod table and point to the floor.

"He was, actually," comments a woman with coiffed silvery blond hair and eyes rimmed in liquid liner who has appeared from nowhere.

"This is Love," Keena says, her voice musical and animated. "She's visiting us this term from the States, in case you couldn't tell."

"Hi." I shake the woman's hand and she holds mine for a minute. I expect a Monti moment, with aura reading or some other whacked-out thing, but instead she just smiles. "You look familiar."

I shake my head. "Oh. Okay. I've never been here before, though."

The woman shrugs and sits with us. "I'm Clem." She pauses, possibly for dramatic effect, possibly to consider again where she could have seen me before. "Clementine Highstreet."

I raise my eyebrows. "And I thought I had an interesting name. I swear, since I've been here, I've met more people with—"

Clementine interrupts. "That's my stage name. Oddly enough, I chose my career name because I had an Irish setter. A bright orange thing I called Clementine, and I first lived on High Street."

"What's your real name?" I ask, suddenly realizing I'm having this conversation with a complete stranger. It's as if all my inhibitions and regular ways of functioning have melted away and I have to relearn how to be in this place.

"You wouldn't believe it if I told you," Clem says. She snaps her fingers in the air and instantly a server wearing a Pucci-print apron rushes out and slings a thin-crusted pizza in front of us. Ah, real food. The Buttery is—as promised—revolting, so I'm glad for a change. "Mergatroid Hicks. And let me tell you, when I was discovered, that was the first change I had to make."

Keena leans forward. "In case you didn't know, Clementine Highstreet was like *the* hot thing in the late sixties."

"We call clemetines satsuma's here, you know, but that doesn't sound mod, does it?" Clementine laughs and fiddles with her hoop earrings. "Plus, I always had a thing for that American song—'My Darling Clementine.' It's sweet and sad and soulful . . ."

The lightbulb goes off in my dim head. "As in 'Like the London Rain'?" I ask. I always tell myself that if I were to meet a famous person, you know, be seated next to them on a plane or something, that I wouldn't gush. And under no circumstance would I quote their movies back to them or sing their songs, which must happen all the time. But since meeting stars rarely happens (Monti is the exception, but since she was more a model/icon/muse, there wasn't much to imitate, unless I happened to bed down with a Rolling Stone or something), I don't have the practical implementation of this theory. Which is why, as soon as Clem nods, I burst out singing her song:

> *Yeah, yeah, the London rain falls down to the ground*
> *Spilling all around, if you've never seen the sun,*
> *You can't just blame the moon*
> *time goes slipping by, rain ends all too soon*
> *You and I were time away from time*
> *You never know what will happen until you fall*
> *Like the London rain*
> *Thoughts collide on the pathway to your mind*
> *In the barrel of my heart, love collects*
> *Like the London rain . . .*

Keena is clearly mortified. Being around famous people is like knowing people are really rich. You're not supposed to talk about it. It's just something everyone knows and can tell by the private jet or the designer clothes or the impulse buys or the multiple houses. You're not supposed to reference the fame, the music, the moneyed heritage, the film or whatever. It's just supposed to lurk there, a silent shared knowledge. Like we're all so cool and on the same level that we don't need to acknowledge it. Leave it to me to not only talk about it, but do the flashing lights, horns honking reference.

But to my surprise, Clementine sighs and says, "If I had a pound for every time someone sings that bloody song into my face, I'd be filthy rich." She laughs. "And I do, in fact, have a pound for each time—"

"Sorry," I say.

"No need to say sorry. People try and act so cool these days. Back in the mo'—that's moment—you'd get students and mums and bankers coming up to you on the street, singing and asking for auto-graphs and trying for a quick feel. Or singing the song as if they were the first in the world to have discovered it."

I raise my eyebrows. "Was it really that crazy? Like in all the movies and swinging sixties and seventies? Or is it all blown out of proportion?"

Keena slides a piece of caramelized onion pizza my way and I gratefully accept it.

"It was even wilder." Clementine's eyes are round and wide. "More sex, more drugs, more, more, more—everything was more."

I'm about to ask her to tell me more, more, more, but I take a way-too-big mouthful of cheesy glory, and when I'm wiping the oil from my chin, I look up to see a familiar figure in the doorway.

"Asher Piece, get your bum over here!" Keena cries.

"Daaaarrling!" Clementine trills. It occurs to me that Clem and Monti probably ran in the same circles (or slept there) so she must know Arabella and Asher.

Wearing worn jeans, a blue-and-white-checked button-down with the cuffs undone, and a navy blue—cashmere?—sweater and looking very Anglo-comfy sexy complete with tousled hair, Asher walks over to our table. He leans down to kiss Keena on both cheeks, then Clem gets three kisses for some reason, and I get—none. Despite my lack of mathematical prowess, I do know that four comes after three, and I think about complaining. Instead, I manage, "Hello, Asher," and try to stifle the building goose bumps plus crush-induced nausea (plus caramelized onions) and the sinking feeling I get when I remember Arabella's wishes: Even if he were interested (which he clearly isn't) Asher is (according to my best friend and English host and the sister of my loveject) OFF-LIMITS!

"Love," he says with nary a glance in my direction. He reaches into his bag—a leather satchel sort of item—and pulls out a large manila envelope, which he hands to Clem. I expect him to produce a semi-nude photo from his catalog shoot in St. Tropical, for him to brag about his island pursuits, swimsuits, or lack of suits, but he doesn't. Maybe he's not the kiss-and-tell kind of guy. For my sake, I hope he isn't. "The details are all there," he says to Clementine, who appears to know what he's talking about. "We need to leave by half three—Lundgren Shrum will pick you up—just so we get there in time for dinner."

"Have Lundgren drive *you*. I don't need to revisit *that* ancient history. *My* driver will get me there in plenty of time. Not to worry," Clem replies. I'm curious to know what kind of past she has with Lundgren, whom I met all of once, during my sleep cloud post-Heathrow. Clementine stands up, managing not to disturb the Plexiglas table, and hugs us all good-bye. "Love, I do hope to see you again," she says to me. Then, softer, she says, "Though I'm sure I have before—in another life, perhaps?"

Um, okay. Whatever. "Sure. See you soon," I say.

"You're not coming, are you?" Asher asks me with something that sounds like dread.

"Where?"

"Oh, you must!" Clem smiles as she walks away, a blur of polished teeth and classic-scented perfume. "Do come to Bracker's Common this weekend. We've got the *Celebrity Life* shoot—you know, all the has-beens from the real era of rock 'n' roll . . . myself and Monti included."

"Maybe," I say to her. "I have a bunch of work, and I know Arabella's away with—" I stop myself from saying Toby's name and look busy by buttoning my jacket, wrongly I might add, and then fixing it. "She's just got a lot of work, too."

"I'll bet she does," Asher says.

"Monti would love it, I'm sure! I won't accept no for an answer," Clem says and gives a wave.

I stand up. Keena clears our pizza tray and waits for me by the door. Asher, who has barely acknowledged my presence, leans down, his lips to my ear. I can feel his breath. "I won't take no for an answer, either."

CHAPTER SIX

The next day, my chills have yet to fade. Just remembering for one second the tone of Asher's voice, the way his mouth was so close to my ear, is enough to make everything else fall away. But, of course, everything else is still right here.

Here being my grotty (love the London lingo) room in my crappyesque and crumbling dorm. Not crumbling as in castlelike and cool, more as in rotting plaster, presumed asbestos, and moldy carpets, the odor of which no cleanser can full of bleach nor incense can mask.

"How can you live here?" Arabella sniffs and perches herself on my bed like it's the only safe place to sit without fear of contamination—which, to be fair, it might be.

"Don't be such a snob," I say. "It's real." I sweep my arms around, trying to show her the finer points of communal student living. "For starters, it's right by half my classes . . ."

"Yeah, but the St. Paul's ones are closer to the flat," Arabella contests.

"Hey, I figure that living here gives me a better feel for the struggling artist's way of life."

"Whatever."

"Oh, good comeback. You spent too much time with Chris at Hadley."

"Oh, speaking of which, I got an email from him. I think he might possibly—maybe—have a boyfriend. Or at least a crush. Long distance, though. Shame."

I want to find out who the lucky guy might be but suddenly realize I haven't heard from Chris and he's supposed to be one of my best friends. "How come you got an email and I didn't?" I ask and then laugh. "Oh my God, could I sound any whinier? Pathetic."

"The only reason he emailed me was to find out why you haven't emailed him. I'm not going to get in the middle of your *Will and Grace* fandango, but will you just write to him already?"

I flop next to her on the bed, which sends up a cloud of dust, making me cough and causing Arabella to wave her hand in front of her like someone's at the mercy of digested cabbage or beans. "Gross. May I reiterate how revolting this place is."

"Yes, you may," I tell her, then get up and open the tiny window. All the students keep containers of milk for their tea and coffee wrapped in plastic supermarket bags and dangle them out their windows, so when I open mine, I can see a whole row of Sainsbury's bags blowing in the breeze. It's a creative—if unsightly—answer to the lack of refrigerators. "I would have emailed Chris but the dial-up here takes forever, and by the time I get back from St. Paul's, the computer center—if you can call it that—is locked."

"Yet another reason to abandon ship and come live with me."

"Stop!" I say. "If you ask me too many times, I'll either stay here to prove a point or pack up right now and leave."

After I say this there's a giggle from the next room.

"Don't forget us. We're close by. Aren't we selling points enough?" Keena yells from 16B. She and Fizzy can hear everything because the walls are so thin. And I can hear everything—including Fizzy's late-night exploits with a stunning variety of musicians, actors, and Sloanes (the upper-crust boys). Long-haired drummers, classical singing baritones, even an opera singer, have given their silent hello to me in the morning when I'm up early to get across town to my Brit Lit class.

"Right!" I say louder for their benefit. "Plus, Keena and Fizzy are the ones who make this place tolerable!"

"Cheers!" Fizzy says, her way of saying thanks for not dismissing the entire student hall experience as grim.

"Well, anyway," Arabella says and links her arm through mine once we're in the relative fresh air of London traffic. "I wish you'd come live with me." She pauses for a minute and then, without looking at my eyes adds, "It's free, you know. I wouldn't charge you or anything."

I'm at a loss for words. Just when I think I understand people's personal issues with money—the lack of it or the astounding mass of it at Hadley, the upper-crust royal old-guard show of it—something comes up that reminds me I live in (or at least vacation nearly full-time in) the world of extremes. Either the scholarship kids at Hadley talk about how the dorms and institutionalized food is better than their home lives, or—now—Arabella's unintentionally (I assume) pointing out that if it weren't for her, I wouldn't have the choice of living anywhere but the filth and squalor of the dorms.

"It's not like it's that uncommon," Arabella is saying when I tune back in. "Tons of people rent flats for the whole time at LADAM. Boarding school is the norm here—people don't all go to college—and living on your own isn't that massive."

"But you're not talking about boarding school," I say, defensive as hell. I start to cross the street and Arabella yanks me back. I have yet to master the look-in-the-opposite-direction skill required to avoid being squashed by a double-decker bus. "You're talking about playing house—living like an adult in an apartment and food shopping and paying electricity bills . . . except not."

Arabella tosses her hair off her shoulders—her haughty gesture—and pouts. "Look, all I meant was that I'm lucky enough to have this flat at my disposal, to live in for as long as I want. I know it's silly and it's a luxury and all that. I just want to share it with you."

We leave it at that because we're at our class, but while Arabella sheds her coat, scarf, and shoes, revealing her boot-cut brown yoga pants and skintight light pink ballet top, I stand still in my winter clothes, hiding from something. It's not that I want all the wealth. If I could snap my fingers and have a wish granted, that's not what it would be. It would be to make Mable healthy. I try to keep myself in check with all this, but it's getting harder and harder to remember life outside of all the Hadley Hall/London elite ways of life.

I'm shaken from my monetary moodiness by Sally Yarmouth (who has, thankfully, lessened her name—real moniker = Lady Sallicious Vermeer Ponticle Kara Yarmouth. It's breathtakingly annoying and posh and—if you were inclined—enough to make you long for a hyphen or an umlaut or something to set your name apart).

"Disrobe!" Sally Yarmouth commands me. I'm the only one without dancer gear (what Chris calls flouncewear).

I strip down to sweatpants and a double-layered tee and get the fisheye from half a dozen dance-a-bees (the dance-major equivalent of the drama queens). The DABs, as a collective, are pro-ana, starving, and thus have an abundance of arm hair—one of the side effects of being anorexic—and generally mean. They have two modes of dress: the flowy, fairylike ones keep their ringlets cascading down their backs, wear floral skirts over their leotards, and have a healthy supply of leg warmers that they wear earnestly. The other dancers, the nonflowies, are modern, lean, with bunned hair and broad shoulders, slightly andro, sexy, too, I might add but very closed off from the other students. They take their meals (if you can call sipping a cup of water or nibbling carrots a meal) together, work out together, and walk in clumps from dorm or flat to classes. And they all—every one of them—worship Sally Yarmouth because she was not only the prima ballerina with the London Ballet Corps, but also danced with Alvin Ailey, Martha Graham, and anyone else you can think of, all the while being a titled debutante.

Plus, she's gorgeous, with big tits and a tiny waist, and a hot sir or duke husband who comes to class with her and sits watching us (perv!).

"And we're becoming the ground, breathing from our bellies, pressing our hips into the floor . . ." Sally croons. Apparently, after her years as the prima, she spent time in an ashram and found her soul, which she then feels the need to inflict upon us.

I try to do all that. I try to be the ground or press my hips down. Really. But my mind races each time I come to Body. That's the official name of the class—just one word. "Are you going to Body?" someone might ask. Or, "I'd love to not eat with you, but I can't be late for Body."

I sometimes make bad poetry out of the BODY letters; Barfy Odorous Dumb Youth; Belittling or Delicate Yarmouth; But Oh Don't Yelch (yelch = yell and belch combo, which happens frequently at the student pub here). I'm not at my poetic best, but it does waste class time while keeping me still enough that Sally Yarmouth and her man duke think I'm so relaxed I'm sleeping. Once she had him kick me with his ankle boot.

Arabella lies next to me, following instructions, but pinching me when Sally Yarmouth's not looking. I try to stifle a laugh, and the resulting sound is a cough.

"Might I remind you," Sally intones right above my head. If I look up, I have a clear view of her nostrils. "That if one is feeling ill, that coming to Body puts everyone at risk. It's simply not fair to jeopardize the health of the dancers." *The dancers* comes out like they're her brood, and I'm clearly not a part of it.

"I'm not sick," I say, forgetting that sick in England means vomit, and ill means sick. "I'm doing fine," I add, but we both know that's not entirely true. In the movie version of Body, this is where the sound track would kick in and there'd be shots of me falling on my ass as I try to dance. As the movie sound track progressed, so would my dance and yoga/pilates-breathing self. Soon I'd be jumping and pirouetting or alouetting or whatevering with such grace that Sally Yarmouth would kick herself in the butt (literally— she can do this easily) for doubting my potential as the next best ballerina.

Instead, I follow Sally Yarmouth's directions as we all arch backwards until we hit the floor and everything appears upside down.

"That is a colossal waste of my time," I say to Arabella when we're back at her flat.

"I know. But, I have to say, I kind of look forward to it." Arabella clicks the automatic kettle on the kitchen countertop and readies two mugs for tea. "Don't you find it relaxing?"

"No." I hoist myself up on the counter, letting my legs dangle onto the washer/dryer, which is built in underneath. "The dancers stress me out. They're so judgmental, which then makes me judge them back, which bums me out. I don't like to do that. Plus, I have other work—real work—that I have to get done and it's like . . ."

Arabella pours the water and adds a teaspoon of sugar to hers. "You know what's interesting?"

"Tell me," I say. We take our tea to the living room, a large, vaulted-ceiling room with cozy overstuffed couches, tattered Oriental rugs, and a piano. Warholesque images of Monti in Day-Glo colors adorn the walls, holiday cards from Sting, Madonna, Moby, those Keane boys, Mick et al, are placed casually on a Victorian-style letter board. They will wind up in the trash soon, just like the ones sent to Bracker's.

"Well, you say that your dream is to be a singer, right?" Arabella asks. I nod. "But all the training classes are the ones you loathe."

I think for a second. "Lying on the floor and becoming a tree . . ."

"Trees don't lie on the floor," Arabella corrects.

"Fine. Maybe I just think that it's less to do with all the side stuff like Body and more about just being focused."

"But everyone trains. You know that breathing is essential for having a good voice and being able to sustain a song."

"I never said I wanted to be the next classically trained diva." I sip my tea. She has a point, but I'm not ready to concede.

"All I'm getting at is that for someone who claims to . . ." She swallows and takes a minute to figure out what she wants to say. Or, she knows what she wants to say but thinks it will hurt my feelings. "You have a great voice, okay? But are you sure you have the drive to go down this road?"

"I don't know," I say. For some reason, tears well up in my eyes and I sink back into the comfort of the couch, the warmth of the flat, the cozy closeness and quiet. "I'm self-aware enough to realize that I make fun of a lot of the things I'm supposed to revere. But I feel like an asshole lying on the ground focusing on my inner core, you know? I feel more in tune, more . . . I don't know . . . engaged when I'm talking or thinking about something."

"Like with PMT?"

"Exactly. I love that class. I know more already with her than I ever would on my own. Brit Lit at least demands my mental energy and, even though she is overly critical and challenges every damn thing I say, at least I'm getting something out of it."

Arabella nods and shrugs. "I guess it's just something to think about."

"Yeah," I say. "Especially with the tryouts for the Choir."

"Oh, shit. Is that today?" Arabella asks.

I look at my watch with a sudden jolt of panic. "It is." I've been trying my hand at playing cool, like the whole Piece family. They all seem to walk the earth as if the planet would stop on its axis for them if they needed a minute to tie their shoes or something. "Actually, I gotta go."

Arabella stands up and gives me a kiss on both cheeks, a gesture that is now so familiar from being in this country that I don't even think about it. Hugs are gone—double kisses are in. "I won't see you until next week!" Arabella grins. "I'm so excited."

"Tell Toby I said, 'Hi, handsome.' Or however you say that in Dutch."

"Begroeting, goeduitziend," Arabella quips. She seems to know useful lingo in so many languages. Then her smile fades for a second. "Did you ever talk to Asher about that paparazzi thing?"

I'm suddenly nervous, like she might know about my seeing Asher in HEL (heh). "No, I haven't. And he's going to Bracker's this weekend for your mum's photo shoot."

She perks up. "Oh, you must go! Please? Please?" She pokes me and makes her sad baby face until I give in.

"I was semi-invited anyway," I say, hoping this sounds like a viable excuse. "By Clementine."

"Ah, the photo spread extraordinaire . . . Should be a riot. Literally."

"Okay, okay. I'll go to your house without you. It just feels weird."

"Don't let it—you're one of the family now," Arabella says. Um, yeah, but I want to jump your brother. "Just don't let Asher try any tricks on you."

"What's that supposed to mean?" I ask when I'm halfway out the door. Arabella stands with one leg balancing on the other, her hand above her head, the tree pose in yoga.

"Among his other useless talents, my brother happens to be a big womanizer. Just so you know." She looks at me with narrowed eyes for long enough to make me wonder if she knows about the teacup encounter. "I hate every girl he's ever brought home. He has complete shite taste in women."

Feeling good, Love! I think about commenting, but realize it would just sound like I'm defending Asher when I would really just be defending myself, so I just say, "Be careful with Tobias. Don't get caught in another celebrity scandal."

"It's just Amsterdam," Arabella says. "And for only a couple of nights. But thanks for keeping my cover."

"Sure," I say. "I'll tell them you're working on a project with Keena and spending all day and night toiling away."

I'm not going to blame my entire Choir audition on the letter I receive via the Mailroom Minder (the sweet old guy who moves slowly, inspiring guilt and an overly thankful me). I really don't have time to read the whole thing, just the first couple of lines in Chris's beautiful, neat handwriting, but I'm too curious and happy to hear from him to wait.

Dearest Love,

Greetings from the depths of winter at Hadley Hell. I mean Hall. Just when you thought the school of scandal couldn't get worse, it has. I'm sure by now you know there was a fire in the dorms—Fruckner House is no longer. New construction begins in the spring, after the ground has thawed and ashes have cleared, but for now the devil herself had taken up residence in

the most unlikely of places. Yes, the one and only Lindsay Par-
rish, homeless after the middle-of-the-night blaze of gory (I
write gory because a certain senior was caught in the elevator
stance—that's going down for those minds not in the gutters—
and had to stand outside naked in the snow waiting for the fire
department). Anyway, the point I'm trying to make but failing
to is that the inhabitants of Fruckner have been dispersed all over
campus—tripling up in the other girls' dorms, farmed out to a
couple of day student families, etc. But since Little Miss Bitch
Parrish just can't make do with the temporary housing, her
trustee mother has called in yet another favor and she's living at
your house with your dad. Yes, you read right.

Fruck me. I'm frucked.

"Are you ready? Please come this way."

Sliding the pages back into the envelope, I shove the whole mess
of messages back into my pocket.

I try to breathe from my belly as I've been instructed.

"Love Bukowski?" The head girl (not kidding) calls my name
and motions for me to stand front and center. When I for some
reason don't exactly hit my mark and stand a half inch to the left,
the head girl says, "Millie, please show Miss Bukowski where to
position herself." *Up your ass?* I want to say but don't—both because the thought of that in reality is not something I'm interested
in and because I know they'd never let me audition and because
my mood is altered by Chris's dire news. Lindsay Parrish is living
in my house? With my stuff? With my dad? Is she like a single
white female stalker who will steal my identity but have a better
wardrobe?

Millie, still in her St. Paul's formal uniform (blazer, skirt, knee
socks, hair bow, beret—natch), fixes her hat so it doesn't threaten to

overtake her face and puts her hands on my shoulders. "Here." I shuffle my feet. "No, just there."

"Is this right?" I ask quietly. Millie nods and takes a seat at the table with the head girl. (Her actual name has slipped past me in a plethora of double-barrel names and English cutie-pie boarding school nicknames.) I feel like I'm on trial or in some lame movie where the audition is really tense and the girl thinks she won't make it but then amazes everyone with her talent and fresh ideas that ultimately convince the pole-up-the-butt judges that she's a rising star.

"What will you sing for us today?" Head Girl asks. She has perfect posture, which reminds me to put my shoulders back and stand up tall. The result of this, of course, is that my rib cage is open and my voice stronger, but also that my boobs look just that much bigger.

Of course I thought a ton about which song to sing—it's the kind of thing where not only do I have to pick something that shows off some vocal range, but also since the words and original artist will no doubt be subject to criticism or commendation, the song has to withstand both my rendering and the judgment of it. Looking at the Choir panel, I erase my settled-on song, figuring that Jolie Holland is too obscure for them (hell, she's somewhat obscure for me), anything from Mable's discs is bound to be too American, and any Ella/Louis/Nina Simone/Chet Baker is too done.

Something palatable, something bland but sweet. " 'Ice Cream,' " I say.

> *Your love is better than ice cream*
> *Better than anything else that I've tried*

Sure, it's cliché now, but it has decent vocal potential and doesn't require a backup band to sound good when singing it. To my surprise, the Choir seems to like my voice.

"Thank you," they say and take some notes in their St. Paul's binders. "If you just wait in the hall, we'll give you the results soon."

Soon = forty minutes later.

I follow Millie back into the audition room and use my useless breathing exercises from Body to try to center myself. Some girl rushes out of the room, clearly dealing with failure fallout after being told she didn't make the cut. Dressed in crisp school uniforms are two young ladies smug enough that I know they've joined the ranks of the Choir. If I'm correct, that means there's only one more spot. For me?

"Miss Bukowski," Head Girl says. The English people who don't know me (that's most of them) pronounce my name the way Arabella did when she first met me, Bee-yoo-kowski. I'm getting used to it, but it's still slightly unsettling.

"Yes," I say.

"We are delighted . . ." Head Girl smiles at Millie, and Millie gives me a real smile, showing me she's on my side. My heart soars. "To offer you a place on the wait list." My heart comes tumbling down, with my pulse still raging and my hopes dashed. "Obviously, you are very talented. We just felt, as a collective, that your sound is very—"

I decide to stand up to the task. "American?" I offer.

"Well, yes."

Millie clears her throat and tries to console by saying, "It's not that being American is bad—that's not at all what we're trying to say. It's more—"

Head Girl, annoyed by Millie's cavalier attitude toward her captainship, butts in, "What Millicent means is that, while we welcome your audition and enthusiasm, we're not quite sure if the Choir is the best spot for you right now, given the intense competition."

"I understand," I say. I don't expect to win everything. I don't need to have everyone's approval for my self-worth, but it's times like this

I feel like I could crumple up and slink into the corner and watch everything go by. I'm already writing all this into my journal—I can picture how I'm going to describe the whole scene.

"But take heart, Love. Spaces do open up sometimes at midterm—and we'd be happy to have you as an alternate should you accept."

Possibly, they want me to deny the alternate place. It could be they expect me to be so crushed or conceited that I can't deal with being second (or third or fourth) choice. But after thinking for a (Millie) second, I say, "Thanks. I'm thrilled to have made it this far. I look forward to the potential opportunity of singing with you."

Sure, it's the speech I've said aloud in the shower should I ever bump into Simon Cowell or Randy Jackson or Paula Abdul while getting a smoothie in L.A., where of course spontaneous tryouts for *American Idol* occur, but it seems fine. I leave the room feeling on the one hand disappointed about being wait-listed, but on the other hand, confident I sang as well as I could and that I can't help but stick out a little bit. Plus, there were thirty-six people trying out for three spots.

The word *wait-listed* inspires anxiety that could only be related to college. TCP (the college process) at Hadley starts in infancy basically, and I am semi on my own here in terms of setting a summer tour of my reaches, safeties, et al. Back in my former life, I'd be visiting Mrs. Dandy-Patinko every other day, obsessing about the details of extracurricular activities and teacher recommendations, but in London I am blissfully unaware of the constant pressure for Ivy.

I wait for a red bus to take me all the way across town, back to the dump I call my dorm. When it arrives, I show my frequent traveler card and sit down, ignoring my propensity for motion sickness in favor of finding out what other news Chris has to share.

You don't need me to tell you that addressing the situation with Lindsay Parrish is something that has to be dealt with pronto.

Just convince your dear dad to kick her out. Maybe she can stay at the Ritz and hire a driver. No, that wouldn't work—she'd need supervision. Ohhh, they could give her one of those ankle things that monitors her every move and jolts her if she strays too far. But Prada doesn't make those ankle cuffs, so she probably wouldn't agree to wear it. Oh, well.

In other less shitty news . . . Mr. Chaucer agreed to write my college rec. letter. I'm thinking of applying early decision to Stanford but I'm kind of worried that I might regret it. Dandy-Patinko says she thinks I'll get in and that it'd be the right place for me, but I also get the feeling she's basing this on TGF (the gay factor) on the West Coast.

What else. Snow, blah, blah, blah. I want a boyfriend. Hooked up with a hottie in Chicago over break. Don't know why I'm just telling you now—it still feels weird to talk about it, I guess. I'll avoid the nitty-gritty but tell you I wouldn't mind another trip to the windy city. Road trip this summer??

I look up from the letter to make sure I'm not missing my stop. As soon as I get back to the phones on campus I need to call home and talk to my dad. Mentally going back five hours, I figure he'd be in the middle of his day, probably talking trash with the other faculty members at their Thursday-morning meeting, so I'll have to wait anyway. Passengers get on the bus and the driver lurches the vehicle forward. I have no idea where we are, only that we're around halfway to school. My bus and tube route knowledge is limited; when I stray from my usual places, I get lost and it takes forever to backtrack to familiar territory.

As I'm thinking this, I suddenly think that maybe that's my problem. Maybe I'm too comfortable doing my little exchange-student thing and treating this like a Hadley Hall in London experience rather than a totally separate, fun, potentially wild or eye-opening deal. Right then, I pull the overhead wire that alerts the driver to stop at the next place, and I get off the bus still clutching my letter.

Feeling proud that I've stopped following the path of normalcy and banality, I wander around for a minute, dodging traffic and weaving among the throngs of people. Down a U-shaped lane, I look in the shop windows, check out the menu at a cool-looking bistro, and pause by an art gallery. It's small, tucked back into the side of a mews house. Mews houses used to be old stables back when horse and carriages were the norm, and they are my favorite kind of house here— even more than a place like Bracker's. The ones on this street are painted all different colors, and the effect—especially at this time of day—is amazing. I feel transported. My footsteps echo on the cobblestones, like this is my street and I really live here.

Then I walk under an archway and just as suddenly as I found the quiet haven of my little street, I'm in a loud burst of noise, spicy smells, drumbeats, and loud voices. All around are vendors selling fruit and vegetables on those little carts with handwritten signs stating the price. Other stalls have gauzy Indian shirts, beaded skirts, Irish lace, and jumbled masses of old watches. I pick through a couple, still looking around me. I notice a street name tacked to the whitewashed building and it registers as a place Arabella mentioned to me; it's the part of town she and her family used to have a flat when she was younger.

"Want one?" The watch-stall guy asks. He's got a thick accent—Scottish maybe—and shows me a pocket watch. "This would suit you."

"It's lovely," I say. "But I don't really need it."

"Oh, come now," he jibes. "There's got to be something you need here."

I smile at him and shake my head. Just behind him I notice a well-lighted window on the garden level—which is the London way of saying basement. I crouch down to peer into the space and see that it's a gallery with enormous—wall-sized—photos. Slowly, so as not to seem rude—I never know how to tactfully end the bartering/salesman thing—I back onto the curb and look for the stairs down.

"That way," the watch man says and points behind a black gate.

I take the steps one by one, just enjoying my newfound freedom in this city. I so needed to break away from the noise of my dorm life and the routine of trekking from one place to the next for my classes.

I push the door but nothing happens. I pull the door and nothing happens. I'm about to leave when there's a buzzing sound that unlocks the door and I go in. The room is almost bare, but warm—both in temperature and in tone. The floors are wood painted a rich caramel color; the few chairs are a mix and match of old bar stools and ladder-backs. Nothing takes away from the impact of the walls—each one has just a single image on it. Rather than a crying child or a black-and-white pouty image of a girl being ogled, these are very simple. The first one has a cup on a table in the center of an open room. I stare at it, transported, because the photo itself is so big, it feels like I am part of it, that I could reach out and touch it.

"See anything you like?" asks a voice—the gallery owner, probably.

Without taking my eyes off the wall, I say, "This is incredible. It's like I'm in it."

"That's the exact point I'm trying to make."

I look away from the image and over to the other side of the room to see Asher Piece with his hands in his pockets, hair falling onto his forehead, caught in a half smile, staring directly at me.

He waits for me to talk, but even with my mouth open—which I realize it is and quickly shut it—he volunteers, "I wondered when you'd find this place."

My shoes sound loud in the empty space as I walk over to another picture. This time, the cup is even closer, as though the viewer has stepped into the photograph and is reaching out to touch something. It's a totally beautiful image but also really jarring.

"These are powerful," I say, but what I want to add is that they are messing with my sense of reality. That *he* does. That just being in proximity to him makes me feel off-kilter.

"Thanks," he says. "Want to sit down?"

"I have to go soon, I think," I say and wish I'd bought that pocket watch so I could use it as a prop.

"You do?" He walks closer to me.

"Yeah." I look at the floor, suddenly transfixed by the grains in the wood so I don't have to look at Asher's face.

"Is this because I behaved like such an intolerable martyr and stormed out at Christmas? Or because you have that boyfriend . . . Jacob?"

Now I click into action and remember how let down and guilty and humiliated I felt then. "Yeah, actually, it is. Why do you think you have the right to just breeze into a room and act all charming and English and everything—I mean, obviously you're not acting—I know you're English—but you're so . . . and I don't even have a boyfriend. Jacob *was* my—I'm not even going to get into that with you." I'm flustered and talking a mile a minute, but Asher stands there and takes it, listens to what I have to say. "And you didn't even bother to tell me you're Arabella's brother? How screwed up is that? Like, hello, let's make out and then find out—"

"Hey, hold up there. You kissed me, first of all, before I even got the chance to tell you. Besides, it's not shocking news. I mean, what the hell else would I have been doing at Bracker's, just wandering around seducing young redheads?"

"You didn't seduce me, for the record," I say, defensive as ever. "I don't know! Maybe I thought you were the—"

"The what?" Asher cracks a smile.

I can't help but start to laugh, realizing how ridiculous I'll sound admitting this out loud. "The gardener?"

"Dear God, you Americans are so trapped by the British films and literature you read at school." He backs away from me and takes a seat on one of the old bar stools. He links the heels of his shoes on the rungs and sighs. "Yes, that's me—Lord Lascivious wandering the grounds, looking for innocent young girls on which to prey."

"I'm not—" I stop short of defending my girlhood and my innocence and then reconsider. "I never said you were lascivious."

"No?"

"No." He's staring at me, and I can't tell if he simply finds my Amercanness amusing, he wants me, or he wants me to leave. So I walk to another wall and check out another picture. This time, the shot is of another cup, a grainier image in black and white, very very close up so at first I can't tell exactly what I'm looking at. Then it hits me. It's the teacup in the topiary garden at Bracker's.

"Is this . . ." I turn around and ask him a question without really asking it. He nods. I walk over to where he's seated on the stool and stand there, waiting for him to talk or tell me what he's thinking but—he's a guy—that's an impossibility.

"I'm thinking I need to kiss you," he says.

"I thought all guys kept their thoughts to themselves," I say and take a small step toward him. In the mother-may-I game, this would be the equivalent of a baby step.

"I'm not every guy," he says and, right as the words are coming out, pulls me between his legs, keeps one arm on my waist, the other at the back of my neck, and kisses me. I'm still holding Chris's letter, my bag is on my shoulder, my scarf half wrapped around me, and all of these slide to the ground. I press myself into Asher's body, feeling the heat from him and wanting to— He interrupts my thoughts by kissing me so deeply that I can't think, can't do anything but be in the moment with him until:

"Are these for sale?" a plucky old woman in a Chanel suit and two-tone tassled heels asks, completely ignoring the fact that she caught us practically ripping each other's clothes off in the middle of the gallery.

Shaking off the mind-melding make out, Asher, his hands on my ass says, "Why, yes, in fact, they are."

As ladylike as possible (ladylike = demurely trying to readjust my shirt so it covers my belly, picking my dropped items off the floor without my jeans revealing too much butt), I collect myself and stand off to the side as Asher crosses his legs (ahem) and stays seated, explaining his artistic motivations to the lady. I note that he never once mentions cost, and neither does she. Ah, the silent subtleties of the superrich.

"I'd like this one," she says and points to the teacup topiary one. Dashed are my hopes of hanging it back in my room at Hadley. My room, which is currently and cruelly inhabited by Lindsay Parrish, I suddenly remember with horror.

"Oh, that one's just been taken." Asher smiles at me and stands up. "I am sorry."

The woman thinks for a second, and I'm just about to say he shouldn't have even thought I want it—him—it—both, but Chanel says, "Never mind. I'll take the other one. You'll need to install it at my daughter's house by Monday morning at seven. Will that be possible?"

"Of course, madam," Asher assures her and gives me a wink. Already, we're both, I'm sure, thinking about the weekend ahead. Today's Thursday, which means tomorrow I head out to Bracker's for a blissful three days . . . with Asher. Asher rings up the sale, and when the lady is on her way, walks me to the door.

"Until tomorrow?" He smiles and kisses me again on the mouth. I have to push away before I find myself too hot and bothered to leave.

"I guess so," I say. Then, because I can't ignore the facts, I add, "I just worry that Arabella's going to be really upset with me."

"Why?" he asks. "It's not as though she specifically forbade you to date me, right?"

"Actually, she did," I say, but am totally hung up on the fact that he said *date* him, which semiclarifies what it is he and I are—or will—do together, and puts my fears of just a hookup at ease for now.

"That's ridiculous," he says. "She has no right to decide whom I go out with—or whom you do for that matter." He turns the tables so fast I have to stop thinking about the kiss, the possibilities ahead so I can focus. He goes over to the desk in the corner of the room and pulls something out of the top drawer and marches over to me with his hand outstretched. "Here," he says and hands me the envelope. I open the little metal clasp and slide out the negatives inside. "I knew you needed these."

"Oh, thanks, Asher—really," I say when I see that he's secured the snapshot taken at the club with me and Arabella sandwiched between royals. It's so cool, though, that I wonder if maybe I should send it to Mable. I decide to tuck it away in my journal and add it to my pile of *I have to tell you*s for later.

Asher goes right back to where we left off. "I mean, aren't you just the slightest bit offended that she—Arabella, your friend—is picking, or ruling out, your next boyfriend?"

"To be honest, I never really thought of it that way." I tuck the *boyfriend* reference away to snack on later and go on. "I sort of assumed you and she had all these issues and that since she knows me really well and . . ."

"Look." Asher takes his hand and puts it on my face. "I want to get to know you more and be with you—in whatever way that happens—but I want to know that you're not hiding. It wouldn't be right."

"So I'm just supposed to confront her and tell her that I . . ."

Asher shrugs. "Ideally, yeah. I don't let anyone control me. I do what I want when I want to, and I won't let my sister of all people tell me otherwise." He pushes his angry tone aside and holds my hand. "See you soon."

I want to see him soon. I even want to see him naked soon, seriously, but I just don't want to deal with calling Arabella and talking to her. I couldn't now, anyway. Even if I went to her flat, she'd be rushing around packing for her fabulous weekend away in Amsterdam with Toby and then she'd leave in a huff and I would feel like crap all weekend. If I call her it'd be worse because you can't talk about stuff like this on the phone—she'd think I felt like it's not a big issue, and it clearly is for her. Then I think about something Asher said. If he won't be controlled by anyone else, why should I? Just because their weird sibling sufferage makes them have competitive tantrums doesn't mean that Arabella should control Asher and that he should control me. So I decide to hold off on telling her and get ready for my own wild weekend.

CHAPTER SEVEN

Outside, a clock rings, the sky is silvery blue, just about dark, and inside my la la's are falling flat. No, not those lalas, I think as if Chris were here to giggle with me.

"No more flat *la*'s," Galen French orders and plays a scale for me yet again. "Listen." He la la la's himself to near breathlessness, his deep Irish brogue hidden in the perfect pitch.

"The Choir said I sound too American," I say out of nowhere.

In mid la, Galen smirks. He sits at the piano and plays some tune I don't know and speak sings to me. "You know that's a bunch of bullocks . . ."

"I do," I speak sing back. "But what can I do?"

"Don't repeat words for starters . . . and then forget the Choir. Focus on yourself, your voice, your energy. You have a lovely voice." He stands up. "But you expect everything to come easily—a very American trait . . ."

"You shouldn't generalize," I sing like a heavy-metal rocker.

Galen goes for operatic. "Most generalizations eventually turn out to be truths. Regardless, I'd like to see you put as much effort into your vocal range as you do with Poppy Massa-Tonclair."

I stop singing and ask, "How do you know what kind of work I do with her?"

Galen stops touching the piano keys, stands up, riffles through some sheet music and hands some to me. "PMT—yes, we're all aware of her menstrual moniker—and I are friendly." He points to the sheet music. "Let's end early tonight. It's late and I want a pint and a good curry. Kindly study those sheets I gave you and at least try to hit some notes next week, okay?"

I blush at the critique, though I'd say it was fair, and at the word *menstrual*. Even though I am pro-woman and once sang the praises of maxi-pads on the radio in my past life in Boston, hearing it from my vocal coach is off-putting. Of course, Galen's mention of PMT makes me wonder if he's friendly with her or friendly with her with a wink. Maybe Keena knows—she is PMT's daughter, after all, though they keep their distance during term.

"Have a nice pint," I say and know I could join him, but I don't. It's common practice for LADAM students to socialize with their teachers, even in intimate settings like dinner parties or bars or pubs. I still find this odd. Keena does it all the time, and Fizzy's had lunch with Sally Yarmouth (note: Sally Yarmouth did not eat as she was on a tea-only fasting regime but did tell Fizzy about her love of marsh-mallows and men with facial hair) a couple of times. I just don't want to know that much detail, maybe. Or maybe I'd want to with PMT, but it might make me more nervous. Once you open up the well of family history or personal info, you can't go back. So if I then wrote a paper on the nature of parenting as seen in modern fiction or something, PMT would probably interpret everything I wrote through the lens of my absent and perpetually perturbing mother. Plus, rumors (or, to be oh-so-British *rumours*) abound regarding bed-ding down with the faculty. Not that the rumors have proved true as of yet.

*   *   *

Back at the Bat Cave, which the dorm resembles, I push past the chain-smoking throngs in the hallway outside my room and climb—literally—over a guy who's passed out on the floor looking none too well.

"Do you think he's okay?" I ask some stranger and point to the drunkard.

A couple of people shrug, while one girl bends down and wipes the soon-to-puke boy's brow like she's auditioning for the role of Nurse in that Hemingway book. "I've just rung the porter, who will ring the nurse, and I'll tend to him in the meantime."

"Okay," I say. "Let me know if you need anything." Not that I have the necessary medical degree to care for the guy, nor the interest in being puked on, and I definitely don't want my already-grim room to turn into the infirmary, but I feel like I have to offer. It's the least I can do considering I have no real interest in hanging out with the rest of the masses in the hallway. At some point, they'll migrate to the student pub and then come back here and stand in the vicinity of my doorway until four in the morning, when they'll either slop to their own rooms, hook up in someone else's room, or wander around banging on the doors until some friend or fellow partier lets them crash.

If the scene looked like more fun, I'd be game. But the truth of it is that Arabella was right: Keena and Fizzy notwithstanding, most of the students I know or have at least a nodding relationship with, have off-campus housing. They rent flats—even crappy ones with someone sleeping in the living room—or have trust funds and own their own, or—like Arabella—have ones on permanent loan from their parents.

The more I deal with nights like this, the more appealing living with Arabella sounds. The apartment is awesome, the location is central and chic, but it's not just the fact that I'd feel like I'm skirting around the reality of being a normal student. On top of that is the fact that if I really want to date Asher (which I am sure of) and he really wants to date me (which I am mostly sure of), I can't have Arabella know (which I am definitely sure of).

Basically, the situation sucks.

In my room, I take out my weekend bag and begin to fold clothing to take with me to Bracker's. Even the shouts of *"Fucking Hell,"* *"Hell-ooo"* and *"Oh, he's been sick on my foot"* don't distract me from my thoughts of the next few days: me, Asher, celebrity photo shoot, good food, great bed, incredible stories from Clementine about her rise to stardom and the music industry.

Then a knock at my door: I open up to see that yes, in fact, the passed-out boy has vomited on the carpet and some girl's foot and that the ancient mailroom master has a message for me.

"For you, miss," he says and sticks out a shaky hand with a note. I swear the man is so crinkly and sweet I could cry. He's been part of the school since it started as a place for the wealthy and titled to send their kids who couldn't quite hack it in the traditional boarding school circuit or who had exceptional promise for the stage—I guess not much has changed on that front.

"Thank you," I say and fight the urge to hug him like a grandpa. He looks at me and waits for a minute, which makes me wonder if I'm supposed to tip him or something. I've never actually seen him outside of the mail room, which is this tiny box with floor-to-ceiling files and air that smells like melted wax and leather shoes.

He looks at me for one second longer and says, "I'm sorry."

I look at the note and realize it's actually two taped together. The master writes down everything word for word that the person says to him on the phone.

Message for Miss Love Bukowski received via telephone at six fourteen in the evening:

Please could you tell her Shalimar de Montesse regrets to say the photo shoot has been postponed due to flooding in the ballroom. We've rescheduled for Bank Holiday weekend and can't wait to see her then. Ciao!

Fine. Disappointing, yes, but not tragic. Plus, Bank Holidays are long weekends here, which means I'll have even longer to enjoy the luxuries of Bracker's.

The next note is altogether different:

Message received via answer phone at seven oh one in the evening:

Please have Love call home when she gets this message. This is very important, but if you could use your discretion in telling her . . . I don't want her to worry or to interrupt her classes, but her aunt is gravely ill and will require surgery. But just don't tell her that. If you could just say that she should call home, I will do the rest. Thank you.

I don't even bother to lock my door or get my coat. I just run to the phone corridor, where thankfully there's an empty one. I pick up the massive avocado green receiver and get the international operator, who finally connects me to my dad's office at school. The whole process from message to now feels like an hour.

"Dad? Oh my God, tell me what's going on. I need to come home. Tell me."

"Love, slow down," my dad says. Just hearing his voice is reassuring and comforting. I start to cry and a couple of passersby nod at me. It's a common sight around here to see the dramatics of the pay phones—boyfriend groveling for cheating, some dancer crying to her mother, students speaking foreign languages while the tears stream down their cheeks—we're a very emotional group, I guess.

"Please tell me what's happening. The message sounded horrible," I say.

"Did he just repeat verbatim what I said?" I can almost see my dad shaking his head. "I never should have done that. I should've just told him to tell you to call home. Oh, well." Dad sighs. "Anyway, first thing's first—you're not coming home."

"But, Dad," I say and cry harder.

"Mable's okay. I'll be honest with you—that's what you want, right? She was responding quite well to the treatments, but the doctor is conservative and just feels that it would be prudent at this juncture—"

"Dad, quit it with babble—just say it."

"She's having a mastectomy on Tuesday, first thing in the morning. They expect a full recovery and that this will really head her in the right direction."

I take a deep breath and think of Mable. I think of driving with her, singing cheesy songs and sharing sweet potato fries at Bartley's Burgers in Harvard Square, how she held my hand when at age seven I broke my leg sliding into home plate, how she picked me up when I was drunk last year and spoke to me without lecturing. I picture her wide smile and the ringlets of hair she no longer has, the way the sunlight used to bring out the gold hues, the strawberry blond on the top.

"I miss her," I say. "I want to see her."

"I know you do, sweetie," Dad says. I can hear him clicking, unclicking, and then reclicking his pen, one of his habits. "That's why we're planning a visit to see you when Mable's in the clear."

"Really? That would be so great," I whine. "I am so whiny right now, sorry. I just feel like I need you and Mable and there's no one here for me to even talk to about this and . . ." Dad laughs a tiny bit. "It's not funny, Dad. This is huge—"

"I'm sorry, Love. I'm not laughing at you or the gravity of the situation. But you know Mable. She's determined and upbeat and trying really hard to be positive, so she needs us to do the same."

"I know. I will. Or, I'll try to, anyway. But I still wish I had someone to talk to. Arabella's away all weekend."

"That's a shame," Dad says but sounds like he doesn't get how alone I'll be. "I did send a package over to you, though, so you should check and see if it got there."

I shake my head even though he can't see it and bite the skin on the side of my thumb where it's flaking off. "I doubt it did. Mail takes forever and I just got my messages, so it's unlikely . . ."

In the background, I can hear my dad's secretary paging him. "One minute," he says to her and then to me he says, "Just do me a favor and check for it. At the front gates?"

"Mail doesn't even get delivered there, Dad. You don't know the way this place works. It's just a step above horseback—"

"Just do it, okay?" Dad says. "I love you. Mable's expecting to have a call from you in her hospital room on Sunday. She's lying low until then. But call her at noon our time."

"Your time, you mean?"

"My time," Dad clarifies, and the words highlight that we're miles and miles apart, time zones away.

"I love you." I hang up and wipe the drying tears off my face and realize how cold I am. Central heating is still touch and go here, and the doors are always open to the outside, so the hallways are glacial. I'm about to head to the warmth of my room when I remember my dad's package. So—to humor him—I head outside to the front gates. I can tell far from away that there's nothing waiting for me, no cardboard care package, no poster tube filled with a print to hang in my dismal room. In the lamplight, there's just the shadow of a lump.

Upon closer inspection, I find that it's a canvas bag. Just as I'm about to investigate it further, I am scared shitless by a voice. "Don't even think about touching that piece of luggage until you hug me."

With a jolt I remember my self-defense class in gym sophomore year; go for the eyes, kick the groin, scream, run like hell. I'm about to take off when I focus harder and see that the face in the foggy night looks familiar, the curve of the chin, the slightly femme stance.

"Chris? What the . . . What're you doing here?" I ask.

He laughs, then emerges from the shadows and hugs me. "I'm your package!"

We laugh. "You're my package?"

"Not that kind—the care package kind." We're still hugging, and Chris talks into the top of my head. "Your dad knew you'd be really upset, and I was planning on surprising you at some point anyway, and he couldn't come over, so we just—"

"Collaborated? Thank you. Thank you." I relax into his familiar hug, and just when I think I'm about to cry about Mable and all my fears, I don't. "I'm so psyched you're here! Come see my room—but don't *Queer Eye* me, okay?"

"I'm not making any promises I can't keep," he says.

Back in my hovel, Chris and I have rearranged my bed, hung two flat sheets up in the windows for curtains, stuffed my laundry piles in my minuscule closet, and the room still looks like hell.

"I have some bad news for you," Chris says.

For a second it doesn't seem like he's joking and I get that zing of panic. "Not more bad news—I can't take it."

"This place is beyond help." Chris holds his arms out like a saint, which he is in my mind. "No quick paint job, no gelp is going to work." Gelp = gay help.

I flop down on the makeshift rug we've laid on the floor—really it's an oversized towel. "I wouldn't mind it so much if it weren't noisy, smoky, *and* disgusting. Two out of three would be fine." Chris slides down from the bed and sits next to me. I look at him. "Maybe I should move in with Arabella."

"What's stopping you?" he asks.

"A solid combo of guilt, stubbornness, and fear of further suckage into the world of money. I don't want to live better now than when I'm thirty and on my own."

"I can see that." Chris nods. "But right now's right now."

We look at each other and crack up. "Wow, that's deep," I say in mock reverence.

"Put it in your journal," Chris says.

Chris, originally a native Londoner, drags me to the tube, and we spend forty minutes catching trains and wandering around before arriving at the restaurant he's been talking about.

"Voila," he says. "Osteria Basilica. My favorite."

The place is packed with late-night diners, the windows fogged, the heat comforting and enveloping as we step inside. We don't have a table booked, but Chris seems to know the guy, who asks us to wait a second before squeezing us into a two-top by the kitchen. We are practically lap dancing with the next table, but the coziness and good smells relax me.

"I can't even tell you how good it is to be with you—someone who knows me and just—"

"Oh my God, there's Gwyneth and Chris Martin with their fruity baby." Chris pretends to scratch his top lip so he can point to the right of him, where said celebrities are chowing on bruschetta.

I am transfixed. Even though I try to take my eyes off the flaxen hair and scruffy beard (on the Coldplay guy, not on Ms. Paltrow), I can't. Chris slaps the back of my hand. "Stop!" he says.

I divert my gaze for a moment but then, magnetized, look back. So far they haven't noticed my persistent stare, but it can't be long before they bolt or glare back.

Trying to get my attention, Chris talks rapidly. "So, um, anyway, news from Hadley—what can I tell you? Did you get my letter?" I nod. "Did you deal with your dad and the Lindsay Parrish debacle?"

Still sneaking a peek I say, "No. I was too upset about Mable's mastectomy to even remember to address the issue with my dad. I'm so going to have to call him back, though—she can't live in my room."

"She's not in your room. She's in the guest room, I think—at least that's what I've heard. But it wouldn't stop her from nosing through your things. Please, for the love of all things Hollywood, stop looking at them. Jeez, you'd think you'd never seen a blond famous person before." Chris shakes his head and bows his chin to his chest in shame.

It's no use. I keep looking—it's out of my control. So much for being aloof and cool like I am in my imagination. Chris tries again. "Okay—I didn't want to tell you this way, but I can see it's time to resort to drastic measures . . . I have news that didn't make it into my letter. Last weekend was the winter carnival."

"Can't say I missed eating slushies and freezing my ass off," I say, still staring. Gwyneth pierces a tomato with her fork and eats it with grace. Note to self: Learn to eat vegetables without dropping them in my lap.

"Well, you didn't miss much on that front. But what you did miss . . ." Chris turns my head so it's facing him and not Gwynnie (I feel so connected to her that I allow myself the familiarity of a nickname—someone help me, please). "You missed Lindsay Parrish making a spectacle of herself, hooking up in the middle of the snowfest with . . . Jacob."

All eyes forward on Chris. My mouth is half open to object, but Chris cuts me off.

"And before you say something inane like *not my Jacob,* I'll tell you, yes, your Jacob, your kind of sort of boyfriend, quiet sweet Jacob from Mr. Chaucer's class. In short, Lindsay got further with him on the quad than you did in several weeks and a near trip to Europe with him."

"I don't know what to say." My pasta arrives, and I eat some of the tangle of thick noodles without once glancing at the table that had held my attention for so long. "Are they like a couple now? That's sick. I mean, the girl is the embodiment of all things Jacob detests."

"You mean, what he *did* detest. You haven't seen him in over half a year, Love. He was in Switzerland for God's sake . . ."

"So, what, doing Swiss things makes people suddenly become superficial idiots who jump on the—"

"She is hot. You have to give her that." Chris eats a mouthful of his entrée, an unidentifiable morsel of meat, and gestures at me with his fork. "What exactly were you expecting to happen while you were gone?"

I shake my head. "Not this. That's for sure. I mean, I figured life would go on without me, obviously, but not him. In my mind it's like he just stayed static—you know, at Mr. Chaucer's table in English and he'd be . . ."

"Waiting for you when you got back?"

I blush. "Even though he was at Cordelia's house with Lindsay when Arabella and I left to come here, I just assumed Jacob would see Lindsay for who she really is."

"I guess you perceive her differently than he does."

I push my plate away and wipe my mouth. "Or she's just using him as a bitch slap to me."

"Either way," Chris says, "it's not like you guys have any hold on each other, right? He was off doing the European thing and you were ensconced with those Vineyard boys, anyway, so what are you complaining about?"

The Paltrow-Martins have left the premises and I didn't even notice, too wrapped up in Hadley Hall gossip.

"You're right, of course . . ." I'm immediately transported, however briefly, back to Martha's Vineyard and can easily picture boat boy Charlie's wry grin and preppy Henry's sweet face. "I haven't given much thought to those boys."

Chris narrows his eyes and studies my face. "Wait a minute," he says and smiles. He knows me too well to let anything slide. "Here I am feeling sorry for you and your pathetic insistence on rehashing the still-unresolved if not unrequited lovefest with Jacob when it's totally clear!"

"What?" I say and sip my water to hide a creeping grin. It's been hell keeping all thoughts on this front hidden, so knowing Chris is about to pry open my web of delightful deceits, I'm nervous but elated.

"You have a hottie here, don't you! All this fuss about poor you and Jacob betraying you . . . and you have a boy of your own. Is he a Brit? Tell me all."

I breathe in deeply through my nose and hold my hands in front of me in overzealous yoga meditative pose. "I cannot say. I am a supremely evolved creature with no need for dishing details."

"You are so full of shit," Chris says, slaps a credit card down on the table, and motions to the waiter. "Let's go get wasted and you can tell me everything."

A mere hour later and I may as well be reporting live on *Entertainment Tonight* about the status of my quasi-relationship to all of trendy

London. Chris buys a round of vodka jelly shots served in mini martini glasses for all the well-heeled heiresses and Euros who surround us. My American heartache is clearly amusing. Each time I finish one or start to pout about Mable or Jacob (for some reason I cannot shake the image of him kissing Lindsay), another shot appears in front of me.

"That's enough." Chris waves away the next shot. "I need her to be coherent enough to tell me the rest."

"He's so hot," I slur.

"Jacob?" one Euro asks. It's loud in here, so we shout practically everything, or read lips. I shake my head, but too vigorously, so I feel nauseated. "Not Jacob. Asher." His name sounds funny in my mouth. Asher. Ask her. Ash, er. "His name sounds drunk."

"No, sweetie, you do." Chris laughs. He sits near me, protecting me, enjoying the club Icon and its scene. He's getting checked out right, left, and especially center, and loving it.

"The thing is, he's Arabella's brother, so I can't. Or she doesn't want us to."

One posh listener interjects, "But if she's really your best friend, won't she understand?"

Even in my liquored haze, it makes sense. Kind of. "Maybe," I say. My stomach is starting to churn and I have to focus on Chris's eyes in order to keep from spinning. "But couldn't you also say that if I'm really her best friend, I wouldn't even think of doing the one thing she begged me not to?"

Later, tucked into my bed with Chris asleep on the floor, I can hear Fizzy and her latest conquest having a grand old time in the next room. Keena must be home at her mother's house. My head hurts, my belly has that puffy post-drinking gross feeling, and I lie on my back with my hands on my hips, looking at the dancing shadows on the ceiling. Right now, Mable is in her hospital bed at Mass General. I wonder if she's okay, and for a second I have that telepathic thing where you know the person you're thinking about is thinking about you. I know I'm supposed to call her later on, but I can't wait.

I pull my down coat on over my pajamas, shove my feet into my boots, and go to the phone booths yet again. Note to self: International cell phone would be lovely—find sponsor. After being routed through the operator, using my calling card yet again, and getting hung up on not once but twice, I'm finally put through to Ellison 414.

"I knew you'd call. I just knew it," Mable says. I know she's grinning by the way her voice rises at the end of the sentence.

"Stephen King moment?" I ask. It's our code for the times when we know we're thinking the same thing.

"Completely. I wish you were here. I'm watching bad TV and drinking high-calorie protein shakes."

"Yum, sign me up!" I say. As soon as we're talking I feel calm and centered, but also far away from her—so much has happened that I normally would have told her.

"How is Poppy Massa-Tonclair?" she asks. Leave it to Mable to ask the right question first. "I can't believe you know her now. I have every single book she's ever written—even an anthology she edited—on my shelf at home." She says at home like it's a place she hasn't been to in a long time. "What's she like, anyway?"

"In a word, incredible. She knows every writer, every poem, every essay and novel—and she's kicking my ass into gear."

"Maybe you're the next Poppy!"

"Yeah, right," I say. "That's me—putting the list back in journalist. All I do is write lists, not epic works of fiction."

"We'll see," Mabel says. Then, since she can tell what I'm about to say, stops me before I launch into it. "Let's not, okay? We're not going to go through the what-ifs scenario. There are too many possibilities in this lifetime—we're much better off just dealing with what we have in front of us, the reality of the situation at hand—or breast."

"I can't believe you can make fun of yourself like that when you're stuck in the . . ." I burst into tears. "I'm sorry, Mable, I know I'm not supposed to get upset—and that you want me to . . ." I can't talk through my tears. "But you're like the one person that I have who . . ."

"I know, Love. I know." I can hear something in the background, probably a nurse or a resident coming to examine or poke her with a needle.

"Is that a doctor?" I ask.

"Yes," she says. "Dr. Green Day. I switched to MTV."

"You're channel surfing while I'm crying my heart out to you?" I laugh.

"No, my butt rolled onto the clicker." I can hear the music faintly and Mable's breathing. "Miles came to see me."

"Miles your ex-fiancé?"

"No, Miles the road measurement. Yes, my ex-fiancé."

"What did he say? How'd he know where you were?"

"Your dad spilled the beans."

"Heh—funny coffee distributor humor. So, what'd he have to say?"

"He still loves me," Mable says and sounds happy about it. "We might get married."

"What?" My voice is loud, echoing in the empty middle-of-the-night hall. "You're engaged again and just telling me now?"

"It's not definite or anything, but will you be my maid of honor again?" Mable asks.

"Of course I would—that's great—great!" I'm bursting and know that I'll wake Chris up to tell him. "When's the big day?" I love using clichés like that at times like this.

Mable's voice drops slightly. "Oh, we don't know that yet. It depends on everything this week. You know how it is."

I want to say that I do, that I know how major surgeries go, or how the outcome of this one will be, but I don't, so instead go for the ever-brilliant, "Oh."

"But let's hope for the best, okay?"

I nod, even though it's a gesture she's blind to, hang up, and trudge back to bed.

Here's a brief (read: non-all-inclusive list—all-inclusive would require my own personal secretary) list of places visited with Chris during my day of Touristy London Crap (his title, not mine). I've been so busy going to class and being a regular student that I've bypassed some of the typical traps, and I'm glad to have Chris around to make me go out.

1) The Tower of London (old, crows, those Beefeater guys in costumes that make you want to do stupid things to get them to laugh until you realize every tourist ever has done the same thing).
2) Hard Rock Cafe. (Am I a JAB—jaded and bitter—to think that it's just not a big deal? I've been to the one in Boston and this is the same thing but with mad cow beef potential and more Sex Pistols paraphernalia than I need with my fries.)
3) Picadilly Circus (lights, camera, action).
4) Trafalgar Square—read: me and Chris posing on lions looking cheesy but having fun . . . until Chris got shat on by a pigeon and got pissed off because I couldn't stop laughing.
5) The Tate (coolest art around).
6) Abbey Road. (How can you pass up a chance to imitate the in-

famous walking across the street à la John, Paul, George, and Ringo?)

7) And so on and so on . . .

"You have completely exhausted me," I say to Chris and flop down next to him on a bench in Hyde Park.

"That's a shame," he says. "Actually, it was kind of the point."

"What do you mean?"

Chris hands me a pen. I study it. "Lovely," I tell him.

"Hey, it's Britain's finest."

The pen is shaped like a guitar and has the Hard Rock logo on it. "Does it really write?"

"You'll have to try it, I'm not sure. But I got it for you so you could go back to recording your thoughts on paper." He shakes his head. "Don't look at me like I'm daft. You know you haven't been writing in your journal much—you told me that. All I'm saying is that you'll wish you kept a better record of everything that's happening so you have something to look back on when it's over."

"Is that why people write, do you think? Or is it to try to make sense of what's happening at the time?" Chris doesn't respond, which is okay, since the questions were more for me anyway. I watch the sky darken. In the distance, a couple of people are trotting by on horseback (Note to self: Do not leave London without trying this). "How'd you get to be so smart?" I ask and poke him.

"From watching you, Dad," he says in his American after-school-special voice.

"Speaking of dads," I say. "I gotta find a phone and call mine."

"On his new cell?" Chris asks and stands up. He's decked out in the tackiest tourist stuff we could find (and that he could waste his money on); polyblend sweatshirt swathed in the British flag, sweatpants that read *I heart London* with the heart over the crotch, and a glittery hat that uses rhinestones to spell *God Save the Queen*.

I smile at him and say, "Can it really be only a couple of months ago that you were in the closet?"

"I know. So little time, so much change." He twirls for my approval. "But don't judge me on this outfit alone—you know I'm still half Lacoste."

"I know, I know. Believe me—you're still very Hadley."

"Aren't we all?" he says and points to my cuffs. The Hadley Hall sweatshirts have wrist bands that rip off very easily, and the students who have been there for a while (pretty much everyone but the freshmen) tear them off. The guys tend to throw them out, but they make decent hair ties, so the girls keep them around for that purpose. Without even thinking about it, I've started to fray the cuffs of my current shirt (an Arabella castoff, Juicy, if truth be told) in order to have the stretchy teal cuff for my hair.

"Have I really become so used to the moneyed life that I'm ripping hundred dollar sweatshirts just to get a hair band?" I ask, annoyed at myself.

"It's like stealing a car for its parts, right?"

"Is it? Look, there's a phone box—let me get in touch with my father. Wait here."

Chris nods, hands me my dad's new number (how weird that my friends seem to know more about my dad's current day-to-day than I do), holds my bag like a good nonboyfriend, and leans against a wall to wait for me.

"Dad?"

"The one and only," he says. "I'm using one of those earpieces."

"Welcome to the mobile age."

"I don't know why I waited so long." He pauses. "Maybe it's because I was afraid no one would call me!" He's joking, but the connection isn't great, plus there's background traffic noise, so this suddenly seems sad—like he really wouldn't have had anyone to justify the cell phone purchase. Or maybe that he did it so that Mable would always be able to reach him. Anyway, calls like this are like email—it's hard to read the tone.

"I would always call you," I say.

"I know, I know. And now . . ." He beeps his horn and I can tell he stops himself from swearing at some bad driver for my sake. "Now I have a solid couple of numbers on my fast-dial menu."

"Me, Mable, who else?" I laugh. Dad laughs, too, but doesn't tell me. "What, do you have some new woman in your life?"

He avoids my questions. "Anyway, enough about this thing. How's it all going there? Did you get the package we sent—ha ha?"

"Thanks so much, Dad. I don't know how you pulled it off, but it worked. I was totally shocked to find Chris at school. And it helped—helps, I mean—having him here with me this weekend. Not to mention it was a good break from my lectures. I swear I know more about Nelson, knights, and Brit lit than I ever could have fathomed."

"Great, listen, about Mable . . . Unless you hear otherwise, assume everything's fine on Tuesday. I don't want you planning your days around calling home."

"I'm trying not to assume much, these days," I say but don't get specific. "It seems like every time I do, I'm wrong anyway."

"True enough—but I'll leave a message with the porter just so you know the operation is over and done with."

"I miss you," I say and sound like I'm thirteen but don't care. I wouldn't want him here for the whole time, but it'd be nice to grab lunch and then have my freedom again. "Oh, and what's the deal with Lindsay Parrish living in my room?" I know Chris said she's in the guest room but it sounds so much more dramatic to say my room, like she's invaded my headspace, which in a way, she has.

Dad puts on his administrative tone. "It's not that bad, Love. You make it much worse sounding than it really is. She's in the guest room for another couple of weeks—a month, tops—while they reinsulate Fruckner . . . and she's on good behavior."

I don't pry about that last comment, but I'd like to believe my dad has her on a short leash. I'd like to have her on a leash, come to think of it—but that's considered hazing and a surefire way to get kicked out of Hadley. But a girl can dream . . .

"Make sure Chris gets back to Heathrow tomorrow night. I excused him from swimming practice and classes on Friday so he could get to you, but he's expected back at the dorms by late check-in." Late check-in exists primarily to annoy the dorm parents, who have to wait up for the wealthy boarders who have gone off to sun themselves or party somewhere for the weekend. It also exists to bust people who take an additional day off after a weekend of visiting their off-campus amours.

Which, by the time I'm off the phone, Chris apparently has—an amour, that is.

"Let me get this straight," I say as Chris and I walk to the bus. "In the time it took me to do a transatlantic dial, you got a date?"

"Pretty much, yeah," he says and runs his fingers through his hair, tugging on the sides like he always does for some invisible, but in his mind crucial, lock adjustment. "Don't judge me, Love. I'm like a gay spokesperson at Hadley with tons of responsibility and no action. Not that it's bad for my college apps to have a Head of Gay Student Union or whatever."

"Yeah, maybe I should start a club or something. Can I just say how much I dread filling out those things?" Essays and transcripts, recommendations and scores—it's enough to cloud even a great day.

The red double-decker bus, a dying breed of bus now, arrives and we climb to the top floor and sit at the front. I feel my body swaying slightly at we move through traffic, but I like the sensation of feeling tall, looking down at the noise and hectic Saturday pacing on the streets. "Do you regret coming out in front of everyone?" I ask.

"No, not at all. It's a huge relief. But at the same time, it's like I got put into this position of gay power that I never really wanted to have." Chris sighs and half smiles. "It's not bad, per se, but I feel sometimes that I'm being scrutinized."

"We all feel that at Hadley. It's small, incestuous, and a breeding ground for gossip."

"But this is more than that. You could date or hook up with someone, and after the initial buzz, no one would pay you much attention, right? But say I actually manage to find a guy who's ready to . . . get involved with me, you know it's going to end up a whole school debate."

"Yeah, I could see that. Like let's all support Chris in this overkill kind of way to show that we are *so* okay with the gay thing."

"Exactly. Or that a hookup has to mean everything."

"And what, pray tell, are you hoping for with . . . what's his name?"

"Alistair. My man of the moment." The bus stops, and Chris points to a dark redbrick building with arched windows. "That was my first home. No memories of it whatsoever, but that's where I went after being brought home from the hospital. Anyway, Alistair's American, if you can believe it. I'm like the only person in the world who would travel three thousand miles to meet someone I could potentially go out with."

"Slow down, guy. You talked to him for all of ten minutes."

"I know, I know. Just let me dream, okay? You're not mad that I'm deserting you after dinner?"

I shake my head. "I have a bunch of work to do. Plus, I'm just getting into exploring on my own. Arabella's so busy with *Damn Yankees* practice and the royal boys that I have more time on my own than I thought I would."

"Well, let's go back to your cave and then get ready for a silly trendy meal. I want to take you to Apothecary."

"It's not some new-age vegan place, is it? I'm too hungry to eat beans."

"No, it's *the* hot spot right now, built into an old apothecary, so the waiters are dressed like they work in a pharmacy or something and the drinks come in beekers or pill bottles. My dad's got an account there."

"An account?" I stand up when the bus pulls over to the side and we hustle down the stairs before we miss our stop.

Chris shrugs like he's talking about the weather. "Dad's a dignitary, but aside from that, the restaurant gave a select few patrons the right to have an account, a house charge. So our dinner's on him. Which is good, because the portions are tiny and the bill winds up being huge." Chris runs his hands through his hair. "Then you can explore or do your homework and I will have a nice—albeit brief—shot at love."

CHAPTER EIGHT

♡

Dinner is basically three courses of pill-shaped weird food. Fish pâtes and frisée salads served in old-fashioned vials, drinks in test tubes set up on stainless-steel racks. It's the sort of place that will probably be really popular for all of two months and then close, when comfort cooking comes back into style, or people decide to eat at hunting-lodge-themed places.

"This is nuts," I say and drink from one of my iridescent test tubes. "But I like the lights!" The whole room, lined with floor-to-ceiling card-catalog-style shelves and old metal counters, is illuminated by lights made out of old glass medicine bottles.

"Try this," Chris says and holds out a forkful of frozen lemonade.

"Tart and tasty," I say.

"Just like us," he says.

"Speak for yourself," I say and hand him my room key. "Listen, you take this in case you need it. I've got Arabella's spare set, so I'll just sleep there and meet you back at LADAM for breakfast before you head back to Heathrow."

Chris holds the key to his heart like I've given him a rose. "Thank you, Love." The he gets serious. "Not that I'm going to use it for anything other than sleeping, of course. But it's nice to have just the same."

Chris goes one way, heading out into the London night for his date with Alistair the American, and I start walking. Pretty soon, my feet get me to an area I think I recognize. To my left is a bustling street, a movie theater with a bright red neon sign, and to my right is a more residential neighborhood. I dash into the movie theater with no intention of seeing a movie, just craving popcorn, and go for the sweet kind they sell—regular popcorn with sugar melted on it as a sort of glaze—in a word, delicious. Especially after my medicinal meal before.

I walk along, crunching and munching, eyeing couples out on their Saturday dates, arms around each other, and then I'm back on that street of rainbow mews houses, which look pale and pretty in the lamplight. Of course, I love this place, but it also registers as not entirely coincidental that I've wound up right near Asher's gallery. I could stop by. Or I could not be a big stalker and play it cool. Surely there's a line in between? I mean, if all had gone as planned, I'd be with him at Bracker's right now. In light of this, a casual drop by (are there intense drop bys?) is indeed in order.

The watch guy is nowhere to be found. All the stalls are packed up, which gives the street a ghostly feeling. Or romantic—it's all about perspective. If Asher swooped me up and kissed me, it'd feel romantic and ethereal. Without the kiss, the lack of other people makes it a tiny bit creepy, as if a vampire could appear at any moment.

Down the cement steps, onto the small entryway, I stop to smooth my hair and consider glossing my lips. On the one hand, shiny is good. On the other hand, sticky is not. I decide for a quick lick of the lips to give the appearance of shine. Then I mentally slap myself for being so girly and annoying.

I'm about to ring the doorbell when I notice something: One of the walls is empty. Then I recall the Chanel lady who bought one and think that probably Asher's using his non-Bracker's weekend to get it ready to deliver. However, when I put my hands to the glass so I can see all the way in the room, I know he's also using his weekend in London for other purposes.

I'm a total idiot to believe something too good to be true could in fact be true.

I shake the ink down on my new pen from Chris and write more in my newly purchased, pocket-sized orange journal as I ride the tube home—not to my home, my crappy dorm room from which I've been self-evicted, but to Arabella's flat, where she doesn't even know I'm staying.

Obviously, Asher's not that into me or he wouldn't have been pawing the brunette in tight jeans and heels. This is not one of those scenarios where I saw him with a girl but didn't catch him in the act and then I confront him and he's all oh, that's my sister (clearly not) or something equally lame. I know this because I did catch him in the act and had the privilege of watching him slink his arm around the waist of Jeans On Heels and plant a full-mouthed kiss on her. I even caught a hair toss with a giggle from her, which was so nauseating I had to leave. And then go back, of course. I'm not going to pass up an opportunity to spy on him. But then nothing else happened. She touched his chest, he pointed to one of the walls, no doubt wooing her with his art, and then I got the hell out of there just before he turned out the lights and they exited.

With bus scum (invisible, but present grime that coats my whole body after a long ride next to the coughing couple) still adhered to my hair, night film already threatening to overtake my teeth, and weary tourist-trodden feet, I stumble up the stone stairs to Arabella's flat and fumble (even in my haze I'm aware that stumbling and fumbling rhyme and don't constitute an interesting lyric of any kind) for the keys. The brass ring Arabella gave me is an antique oval, with a barely visible Shalimar engraved on the wider side. Two keys dangle from the thinner side, one a regular key, the other a skeleton key.

Inside, the flat is as expected: cold, empty, and dark. I flip on a couple of switches—mood lighting I suppose—pull the curtains closed, crank up the temperature, and take my clothes off, leaving them on the floor. Then I head to the stereo. It's from when Monti originally bought the flat, mid-1970s, I think (based on the original shag rug in the master bedroom that has no doubt seen plenty of action. Or Mick-action. Or Rotten-action). Choosing between records, I opt for T. Rex. I'm about to put it on the turntable when I see a bright orange album sticking out from the stack. Sure enough, it's Clementine's first album, done in that sixties font of half bubble writing, half script, hot pink on an orange background. Bragging words across the top read "Contains the Ever-popular 'Like the London Rain'!"

I can't resist. The needle scratches, drags, and then starts. The first two songs go by pleasantly enough while I get ready for a long bath. Since there are no showers in the dorm, only baths with a shower handle, I'm used to getting clean this way. Plus, Arabella's bathroom has a double-sized tub, Jo Malone candles and scents all around it, and one of those wide faucets that makes it seem like you're in a tropical waterfall. I fill the bath and step in just in time to hear Clementine burst out with

"Like the London rain you make me fall into the sky,
here I'm wondering why, you tell me, baby, can't we try?
Time goes slipping by, rain ends all too soon.
You and I were time away from time.
You never know what will happen until you fall like the London rain
But when I find you falling it's never meant to be.
Next time you'll be falling falling heading back to me.
But I'll be heading up.
Back to where the rain slips into clouds, you just may find me there.
You'll come running, I'll keep walking, flowers in my hair . . ."

Except for the flowers in my hair part (which definitely calls to mind a girl on a maxi-pad box in a flowing dress who just happened to stick a gardenia behind her ear before getting her period and heading off to Woodstock), the song is remarkably cool, with a backbeat that reminds me of Fiona Apple. As if it were made now but produced to sound mod. The record ends and I finish washing myself off, actually taking the time to leave the conditioner on the ends of my hair. Note to self: Living in a climate that is damp does work in my favor in terms of skin and hair.

When I'm done I dry off and make my way to Arabella's room to find some pajamas because of course I managed to forget mine back in my room (aka pit of despair). Luckily, Arabella has no shortage of comfy clothes from which to choose, loving the vagabond-chic look. She has no shortage of any garments, actually, so I pick a pair of what she calls tracky bums and which any American would call sweatpants and a worn-in navy blue henley top. It's times like this that the bed literally seems to be calling out for me. It's times like this when my whole body is so excited to slide between the high-thread-count sheets it's not even pathetic. It's times like this, at eleven o'clock on a

Saturday night in someone else's flat that the doorbell rings as the door opens and my dreams of—well, dreaming—are dashed.

They are replaced, however, by a gaggle of gorgeous boys (gaggle = four) and a bevy of beautiful women, Arabella included, who reek of smoke and wine, but who are all cheerful and bursting with bags of takeaway food (takeaway = take out—who knew two continents would be separated by so many adverbs?).

"Darling!" Arabella says, exaggerated but winking so I know she's not a total prat. (Prat is like loser, but not. It's somewhere in the lines of dickhead but in this case a nicer, sweeter way of saying I know she's kidding.)

"What happened to Amsterdam?" I ask as the whole haven of hotties push through the door and begin assembling an impromptu dinner party.

"It was undone," Tobias says. It's an expression he apparently uses all the time, which has begun to filter down to Arabella. Undone = lame, not happening.

"What he means," gorgeous boy number one—very tall, sandy blond waves of hair, bright blue eyes, manwich build—Says "is that we got kicked out of the first hotel at five this morning and there wasn't any room at any of the other hotels."

"Any of the proper places," one girl adds, kicking off her heels and sitting down to smoke. She's a mini Elizabeth Hurley, dark hair, high cheekbones, very English.

"It's the Dutch jazz fest or something," another woman says and kisses that tall hot guy on the cheek. I've found that the flirty kissing aspect of Arabella's circle of friends makes it sometimes hard to tell who likes who and which couple is on or off.

"We could've found a suite anywhere, if we'd wanted to," Tobias insists, adding an eye roll to imply that obviously, they have enough collective clout—or he does individually—that finding a fancy hotel room wouldn't have been hard if they'd pushed.

Arabella pulls me into the kitchen where it's just us and hot boy number three or two—some prime number (heh). She mutters under her breath, teeth clenched, "Not sure if you realize, but you're in pajamas—mine, I might add—so if you want to borrow anything . . ."

Hot Prime Guy spins around, holding a tray of curries and chutneys, and says, "I think she looks lovely as is, frankly." And then in a cloud of steamy turmeric, is gone.

Arabella raises her eyebrows at me. I grin. "Okay, tell me who he is," I say. "But I'm not changing. They can like me or leave me."

"Or bed you." Arabella laughs. "And don't think I'm skipping over the fact that you're here and not at your dorm and technically in violation of the Hadley Hall rule book since my parents are not aware of your whereabouts."

"Crap," I say. "I totally forgot about that *in loco parentis* thing. Do you think they'll say anything?"

"Hell no," Arabella says. "You know that if it were up to them, we'd all be emancipated minors at age thirteen."

"Long story short . . ." I start.

"From you? Seriously? I never get the short version—I didn't even know you were aware of the meaning of the word . . ." Arabella sticks a finger into my ribs and smoothes my hair down at the back. "Your hair looks good when it's wet."

"Thanks," I say. "So my dad gave me really bad news—oh, before I even get to that, the Bracker's weekend got canceled . . ."

Arabella bites her lip. "I know all about that—" Her tone had just a hint of bitchy scent, probably because she's still—even with me—territorial about all things Piece.

"Let me finish. So that was called off and I rang my dad," I say.

Note to self: Have started to use words like ring, rang, prat. Need to remember I am *not* a Brit. "He then informed me that Mable's getting a mastectomy the day after tomorrow, so I freaked out . . ."

"Naturally—God that's really rough. Never mind. Let's be positive and just plan on her getting through it with bells on."

"Let me finish! But thanks. Even if I pretend to not be thinking about it, I am. Just so you keep that in mind. So then Chris showed up, total surprise, but a relief and laugh."

"Oh, I want to see him! Where is our boy toy? He owes me an email."

I check my watch and tilt my head. "My guess is that he's either asleep or getting some right about now."

"Rock on." Arabella nods. "Leave it to Chris to journey all this way to find someone."

"That's exactly what he said—and the guy's American, no less!" I take a deep breath. "Anyway, I gave him the keys to the grotto and figured you wouldn't mind if I camped out here since you were supposed to be going Dutch and all."

"You know you're welcome anytime, Love." Arabella studies my face and wrinkles her brow. "What else?"

"Then, for icing on the cake, Chris tells me Jacob hooked up with Lindsay Parrish."

"Your Jacob?"

I nod. "I'm still in denial. And that's not the end of it. Just when I thought I was recovering nicely from news and surprises and a day of tourist traps and trendy eateries, I saw . . ." I catch myself midsentence but nip the pillage in the bud before I get kicked in the ass. Or in the Ash-er.

"What'd you see?" Arabella has her just-between-us tone. "Go on, tell us." Us, we, the royal we, etc.

"Nothing. I don't even know what I was saying. Nothing."

I'm saved from further drilling by the just-the-way-you-are boy, who introduces himself as, "Nick. Nick Cooper."

"Wow," I say. "A regular-sounding name!" I smile at him and he, Arabella, and I head for the living room. Someone has swapped Clementine's record with Donovan, and "Jennifer Juniper" plays while a buffet of Indian food is assembled.

"A regular name for a very irregular bloke," Arabella says so Nick can hear.

"I'm sure you know by now to take everything this one says with more than a single grain of salt." Nick thumbs over his shoulder to Arabella.

As I scoop chicken tikka masala onto my plate, Arabella gives me the lowdown. "I won't bother you with the details of everyone's pasts and presents, but just so you know, Nick's the one I would've set you up with."

"I never asked you to fix me up with anyone," I say and grab a floppy piece of nan bread.

"I know—that's why I said *would've*. Don't be so offended—it's not like I'm suggesting you need fixing up, but he's a great guy."

"Not one of your exes, is he?"

Arabella winks at me. "No, not yet!" Then her smile fades and she whispers in my ear, "Speaking of which, Toby and I've had a huge row, so if things seem tense, it's because they are."

I don't have time to respond before Toby bounds over, interrupting our whisperfest. Part of me thinks he's jealous of me—not my stunning good looks or enormous talent, or lack of royal title, but that my friendship with Arabella is fairly effortless. The times I've seen him with her he's been working hard at giving the appearance of being casual.

"Love!" Toby has his social (read: loud and very BBC) voice in use. "Do come and join us. Regale us with tales of Americana."

This is an empty asking, though, because as I sit down, it's the typical did-you-know situation that would happen with any group of old friends—who's slept with which ex-boyfriend, who was spotted in Marrakech, and so on.

"The spa there is utterly incredible," Mini Elizabeth Hurley says. She's so pretty and smiley every word comes out like she's giving check pluses on a test.

"Jnane Tamsna, you mean?" Tobias asks.

"Of course," the tall blond guy says. It's as if they're speaking gibberish, but before I can judge too harshly, I have to remember Arabella's trip to Martha's Vineyard with me. We went to preppy Henry's house where a U.S. equivalent game of prep school geography and summer house–hopping ensued, which is just like this conversation.

Tobias leans down to me (like the hired help, I seem to have secured a place on the floor, eating with my plate on the coffee table while everyone else is a tier above me) and explains, "It means 'big garden'." Um, gee, thanks.

"Wasn't it created by Meryanne Loum Martin?" I ask, pulling the name and fact recall from thin air. Just my luck I'd read about it in a recent *Tatler* magazine at Bracker's, and luckily my ability to remember seemingly useless facts does come in handy. Everyone's impressed and Arabella smiles with pride like I'm a toddler who has taken her first steps (toward name-dropping). Nick looks at me out of the corner of his eye while chewing a bite of curry, nods, but doesn't say anything.

Later, when we're clearing up the dishes and Mini Hurley's making out with the blond guy and another couple is off in Arabella's room doing god knows what, Nick says to me, "You know, at my house we have a rule about that."

"Dish washing?" I ask while letting the plates soak in warm, soapy water. I'll have to clean them tomorrow—even though it's technically already tomorrow and I have to meet Chris in a mere six hours to say good-bye before he leaves for Heathrow.

"No, name-dropping," Nick explains and grins. "Mum always thinks it's elitist and yet can't help herself, so to rid her of the habit Dad invented a rule whereby if anyone drops a name over lunch or dinner—or breakfast, too, for that matter, although we're usually too tired or hungover to have it happen then—you just fling your spoon onto the ground."

I laugh. "That sounds like a good plan," I say. He stands next to me at the sink, our legs touching while I put the rest of the dishes in and he dries the ones I've already cleaned.

"Arabella told me a lot about you," Nick says without facing me. "It's a pleasure to finally put a face to a name."

"But not drop it," I say.

"Right."

Fast forward in my head to meeting Nick's mum and dad, to name-dropping and spoon throwing at his glorious city digs or country estate. Visions of me telling Chris and my dad I, too, have a semi royal to call my own. Nick flicks a handful of soapy water on my face and I can feel the suds sliding down my cheek. With a quick move of the wrist, he grabs a towel and swabs my cheek and chin. Who knew how sexy clean could be. I am my own soap ad.

It's only when I look into his eyes that I realize I've been picturing this whole scene with Asher. Not picturing it, living it. That I've mentally substituted Asher for Nick and now, presented with the reality of it, I see its falseness.

"I need to go to bed," I say. "Sorry, it's been really nice meeting you." Then I think that sounds too suggestive, although if Asher's busy tonguing some girl in his gallery, there's nothing stopping me from having a romp with Nick. I add, "It's nice meeting all of Arabella's friends."

"Ah, playing it safe," Nick says. "I respect that—wouldn't want to actually let me know how you feel, right?" He has a perfect smile. Maybe I should reconsider. It would be easier, anyway, being a couple with one of Arabella's friends, rather than her off-limits brother.

Her off-limits brother who is standing at the doorway of the kitchen as I contemplate a short-term future with Nick Cooper. He's cute, witty, seems interested, kind, and safe. In mid bend-to-kiss, Nick looks to the side and says, "Hello, Asher. How's it going?" They shake hands and Asher nods, the silent guy *fine*.

"Don't let me interrupt," Asher says directly to me and turns on his heel and leaves.

Bum-bum-bahhhhh! I can hear the dramatic drum play in my head—talk about a bodice-ripping romance saga right here. If only Arabella could tell me what to do. No, she'd just tell me to hop in bed with Nick, which I would never do. The tension is palpable, and Nick Cooper—lovely boy who came into my life for a brief and shining moment—bids a fond farewell (perhaps not fond, but a good-bye nonetheless with a shoulder squeeze and double kiss that lingers just a tad longer on the last cheek for emphasis).

Finally, I am alone with my mixed-up self. Before the wondering, the daydreaming, the whirl of new and nuanced nighttime near misses can start, Arabella's yelling at Asher.

"You can't just bloody come in here and expect a meal—or lend your crap attitude to my party. It's my flat!"

"It's Monti's."

"Why do you have to insist on calling her that? Just say *Mum*, it's not like calling her anything else makes her any less related."

"You do the same thing. Shut up and go back to your posh pathetic party. I only came to get my lens."

"Next time, don't leave your shit here."

"But you live here," Asher says, getting the last word in while Arabella raises her hand to thwack him on the shoulder. Toby stops her just in time, but Asher is more annoyed by him than Arabella's griping. "Don't control her."

"He doesn't control me!" Arabella's voice is at dog-sonic level, which only proves that Asher is kind of right, and Toby does control her somewhat, and she knows this, which makes her pissed her off at everyone, including herself.

Asher walks by the kitchen on his way to the guest room. Quickly, I follow, leaving Arabella and her friends in the sibling fallout.

I watch from the guest room doorway while Asher rummages through the large closet, tossing aside old luggage, a few stray hanging bags, a box or two in search of his lens.

"Do you want me to help you look?" I ask.

He doesn't respond. I go over to the closet and scan the insides in case I'm suddenly gifted with lens-spotting abilities. "Do you want me to help?"

"No," he says. "I just want . . ." He pulls me into the closet, presses me up to the wall behind the door, and kisses me hard. I kiss him back, and when he pulls away to look at me, asking if it's okay, I just pull him back and kiss him more. Then I push him away.

"We can't," I whisper. "Someone's going to find out."

"You're right," he says. "But I don't care."

"But I do." Then I look at him. I can't help myself. His lower lip is slightly wet from our kiss, and I need to feel it again, so I lift my face up to his and he does the smoothest maneuver I've ever experienced—his arms around my waist, he slides me onto the carpeted floor, dodging the boxes and detritus around us, and gets a hand under my shirt while never once breaking the kiss.

"I'm impressed," I say into his mouth when we pause for breath.

"Oh, you like that, do you? I've won awards . . ."

"I'll bet," I say. I fight off mental images of him with anyone other than me. Then I have an RJ (reality jolt) and say, "Wait a second." I push him off me—he's lying half on the side of me, half off.

"What's wrong?" He is genuinely concerned, like he's upset me or did something I didn't want him to, of which he's definitely not guilty right now.

"No, it's not this." I point to him and then to me. "It's before. I saw you at your gallery. I don't even care if you think I'm stalking you but—what's her name?"

I expect denial. I expect him to play the dumb guy who says or does anything to get what he wants, but what he says is, "Honestly? Her name's Celia and she's my ex. A very sad, confused ex, I should say."

"So you always get it on with your exes when they show up at your place of work?" I pull my knees up and rest my chin on them.

"Yes," Asher says, sarcastic in voice but even-keeled facially. "I'm a male escort, actually. She paid me to make her feel wanted, and I reassured her that she's still desirable and . . ."

"Fine." I stand up and look down at him. He's too appealing to resist, so I have to look away while he stares up at me from his position on the floor, one hand on his stomach, one hand behind his head. "You obviously find this all terribly amusing . . ."

"God, you Americans are so lacking in humor."

I stand above him, one leg on either side of him. Taking a breath, I allow myself to look down only on the condition that I don't give in and kiss him. My willpower lasts for less than three seconds and I am back where I was, mouth on his, his hands on my back.

"Love," he says into my ear, "nothing except that one kiss happened with her. I think you know by now what my intentions are."

"No," I whisper back. "I'm just a classless American—you'll have to clarify."

"You—"

Noise from the hallway makes me jump like I've been shocked. (Once, as a kid on a dare, I touched an electric fence—same kind of reaction.)

"It must be here somewhere!" I say way loud and back out of the closet shaking my head.

Mini Hurley and her mate are standing watching us. I don't think they saw anything, but they could have. It's up for speculation, anyway.

"Found it!" Asher comes out of the closet with a bag held up trophylike in his hand.

Hurley and Hunky lie down on the bed and we leave them to it—seems like they've got enough stamina for everyone and want to make use of each room in the flat.

"Where was it?" I ask Asher in the safety of the hallway.

"The what?" he asks and gently traces a heart shape onto my back as we walk.

"Your lens," I say.

"Oh." He stops and pulls the back of my pants so I have to stop lest they fall down. "I wasn't missing a lens—that was a load of bullocks. I went to your dorm to find you and Chris told me where you'd gone."

Arabella interrupts. "What're you still doing here?" she asks.

"Just leaving," Asher says. Then, to me, he adds, "And that's *my* shirt, by the way."

I look down at the blue henley I'd chosen out of all of Arabella's tops and can't help but feel it's kismet, if clothing can be considered such. "Do you want it?" I threaten to take it off then and there, which Arabella thinks is cool and defiant but which Asher thinks is hot as hell.

He licks his lips and says, "No. You keep it."

"Out." Arabella pushes Asher playfully until he's almost to the front door. Toby is near snoring on the couch in the empty room. "Don't pull any of your crap with my friend, okay?"

Asher shrugs her off. "I was just offering to do Love's head shots for her."

I perk up. "Really?" I've never had head shots before. When I did voice-overs back in Boston, the radio station asked for one and I handed in a poor-quality black-and-white eight-by-ten of my Hadley Hall face book photo.

Arabella concedes. "He's not a bad photographer, to be honest." She pauses and sighs. "Are you going to do it with him?"

I blush. "I'm thinking about it, yeah." The three of us stand in the draft of the open door.

Asher doesn't waste any time. "Fine—I'll stop by sometime and we can do it then."

Do it. Do it. He must know I've never done it. Head shots or otherwise. But I catch my breath, heart racing and say, "Sure—I'd appreciate that." Like he'd be doing me a favor.

He leaves without a double kiss and Arabella bolts the door. "Good riddance." She goes over to Tobias, pulls a blanket from the back of the couch onto him, removes the wineglass he's still clutching in his hand, and motions for me to join her in the kitchen.

Outside, the clock chimes four o'clock and I know I'm going to wake up feeling worse if I sleep than if I just stay up until it's time to meet Chris first thing.

"Want to walk back to LADAM with me and have breakfast with Chris?"

"Are you going to the Greasy Spoon?" Arabella asks.

"We are," I say. The Greasy Spoon, so named for its typical English breakfasts of eggs and beans and toast and sausages, is a no-frills, cozy place near school. The booths at the back are a perfect place to memorize lines or read or alternate underlining critical theory texts with spoonfuls of cocoa. "That way he can just hop on the train to the airport afterwards."

Arabella makes a sad face. "I would. I want to . . ."

"Let me guess. Tobias would be upset to wake up and find that you're not here."

"Don't be a bitch," she says. "You know you'd do the same thing." I look at her and raise my eyebrows. "Fine, maybe you wouldn't."

"I'm not being bitchy—I'm being honest. Chris is here all the way from Boston and your boyfriend you see *all the time* is wasted and asleep and you're too afraid to leave him for all of an hour?"

"It's more than an hour, Love. You've got to factor in the Sunday tube schedule and then getting a place at the Spoon, and . . ."

"Whatever. Let's not get into the math and physics of it. I just thought it'd be nice to have you along. I know you miss him."

"I do. But things are rocky with Toby right now, and I don't want to make them any worse."

I hop down from the kitchen counter where I've been perched and stretch. "Do you want to tell me what's going on?"

Arabella shakes her head. "It's the same old, same old. We have this bad pattern set up. He starts to pay less attention to me and I poke at him until he finally notices me, but then I'm so frustrated that I treat him poorly, so then he acts like a dickhead." I nod. "It's just a down cycle, that's all."

"Sorry. I hope it gets better."

"It will," she says. Then, like she needs to prove it to me and to herself she adds, "It will." Arabella switches off the lights and we go into her room.

"Don't mind me," I say to her after we've brushed our teeth and are sitting on her bed. She's snuggled under the covers and nearly-asleep. "I have a lot of reading to do for PMT's class."

"Sounds good," she mumbles. "Hey, you think anything will happen with you and Nick Cooper? He's never interested in our group, but—"

"What's that supposed to mean?" I ask, bookmarking my page with my thumb.

Arabella pulls the duvet up to her chin so she's almost covered by it. "No, nothing bad. Just that I thought you'd be pleased to know he's like the least incestuously involved with our lot of friends. And I could tell he liked you."

"Oh." I'm not sure what to say without either lying or sounding too interested in Nick, so I say, "He's nice and everything and maybe at another point in my life I'd have been really psyched to get to know him, but there's something I need to . . ." Then I notice that Arabella is solidly, soundly asleep. So much for a confessional or cover-up. I'm spared both. And the truth is, if I hadn't met Asher, I'm sure I would have gone for Nick Cooper. But I did meet him, and I can't undo that.

At the Greasy Spoon, Chris tells me Alistair the American is joining us for breakfast, that he definitely has a crush on him. Alistair waves to us from outside the front window and sits down.

"Oh, here," Chris says, remembering something and hands me slip of paper in the porter's shaky scrawling script that reads:

Please tells Miss Bukowski that she has a confirmed place in the Choir.

After the round of watery orange juice cheers and congrats, Chris tells me, "The bad news, is that some girl named Millie's dad got made redundant." Translation: got fired. "Therefore he can't pay the school fees anymore. Therefore Millie's out of St. Paul's/LADAM and off the choir."

"Thus giving you the chance to take her spot," Alistair says. He pours more coffee for me and for Chris, going so far as to add a teaspoon of sugar to Chris's and stirring it for him.

"Actually, I've got to run," Alistair says, slugging back his coffee. "But I'm sure we'll get a chance to hang out at some point. In L.A., maybe?"

I make a "he's crazy" face to Chris. "When am I going to L.A.?"

Chris kicks me under the table. "Our road trip, you know?" He takes a sip of iced water. "Love, don't be shy. Tell Alistair our plans."

Thank God for drama improv and other near rhymes. "Right, well, as you know, being American and all, there are just so many colleges to look at and you can't tell what a place is like without seeing it . . ."

Chris overlaps with me. "So Love and I are in the midst of planning this big college tour, as I think I mentioned . . ."

Alistair nods. "Sounds good. I'd be happy to show you both around Santa Monica anytime. If you're looking at UCLA, that is."

Another kick from Chris. "Oh, I am," I say and nod vigorously. "It's in my top five."

"You made me a huge liar," I say to Chris after Alistair's gone.

"Oh, you're already lying to Arabella. What's one more?"

"Not fair," I say and stab a piece of fried egg with my fork. "Was it really necessary?"

"I didn't want to come off as a desperately seeking long-distance love kind of person." He chews his food. "Also, it is possible—I mean, we do *have* to tour colleges. We could take a trip together."

"Yeah, um, I'm sure my dad would go for that."

"Why not? I'm, like, the perfect chaperone for you," Chris says, scooping up a piece of egg. It wobbles as he gestures with the fork. "My parents don't care where I wind up as long as it's impressive." Chris shakes his head. "Serious pressure. I guess it's better than just signing the check away."

The multiple dollar signs of tuition loom ahead. "I'm going to have to get some aid or a job—or both," I say. Then I think about my dad. "I'm sure my dad sees the college tour as a real father-daughter experience. Plus Mable—maybe she'll come, too, and . . ."

"Fine," Chris says. "I get it. You'll have the all-American experience of picking exactly the right place to spend the next four years of your life with your perfect unit."

"Hardly perfect," I say, not so much complaining as stating the obvious yet again. "It's not like my parents have been married for twenty years and we're all piling into the minivan to check out the Ivies."

"Close enough," Chris says.

I eat the rest of my breakfast and fold an empty sugar packet into thirds, then in half. "Blech. I don't even want to think about TCP. It all feels really far off."

"That's only because you're here. I swear we get reports and stats from Dandy-Patinko and the college counseling office every day. It's enough to make me want to forget the whole thing."

"Do you know what your top choice is yet?" I ask and then, like I've sworn in the middle of a class (Harriet Walters did last year, she said *fuck* in the middle of a history class and then managed to gloss over it, but it was big news for a day or so)—"wait. Ignore that. Ignore me. I'm in serious danger of getting sucked into the whole prep school pit of potential placement."

"Not to mention the fact that if I don't hurry up I'll be late and in mucho troublero."

"Nice Spanish," I say.

"I take Russian, what can I say?"

We say good-bye, hugging, outside where the rain (the London rain) has started to spit down at us.

"You look exhausted," Chris scolds me.

"You, too," I say back.

"Well, this was a quick trip. I never got over my jet lag and it's already time to head back." Then he looks at my face, searching for details. "Think we'll be lucky in love?"

"Who knows," I say. "Part of me wants to come back with you—"

"No, you don't. Enjoy yourself. Hadley's got nothing going on right now. Aside from the midwinter slush and sex quests, there's only college shit . . ." He pauses, reaches for his carry-on, and adds, "I almost forgot to give this to you. Your dad would be mad."

I hold a heavy envelope with my name and class year (class II— senior year I'll finally be a class I) on it. "Let me guess. More college prep?"

"What else? Note the silly quiz that tells you *Cosmo* style whether you're meant for a small liberal-arts school or a rowdy big ten."

"Nice. Listen, Chris, thanks for schlepping all the way over here. And for comforting me."

Chris shrugs. "I feel like I didn't do enough, really. And I feel guilty for last night."

"Well, don't—especially not about last night." I can't help but smile. "And with all the other crap—Mable and everything—I'm not sure how much more I can talk about it. It's scary and I'm worried, but talking about it doesn't seem to make it better. It actually just makes it worse." My eyes fill up with tears. "I'm tired and sad you're leaving and it's raining."

"How poetic. I fully expect to read a tome from you at some point."

"You will—LLS."

"What does that mean?"

"Oh, it's leftover from fifth-grade camp. It's code for Long Letter Soon."

"Good."

I watch him heft his bag onto his left shoulder, his carry-on in his right hand, and wave as he walks to the tube stop, down the stairs, and out of sight. I stand for a second singing Clementine's "Like the London Rain" in my head while the real thing falls around me, and then head home.

CHAPTER NINE

♡

Home = an acronym *hell on my emotions*.

My door is ajar (like the lousy Dixie cup riddle my dad used to ask me: When is a door not a door? When it's—say it with me—ajar. But in that version there wasn't a random Goth girl looking through anyone's personal belongings). Goth barely raises her eyes when I come in. She just takes one of my Frank Sinatras and leaves.

"Bring it back when you're done!" I yell after her.

"Will do!" she agrees.

I've never met her before. The attitude here is that we're all in the same proverbial boat of angst and art and therefore should commune as one, with unlocked doors (which Chris clearly took liberty in doing), unspoken arrangements of long-term sweater and CD sharing, and the right to crash, drunken or otherwise, on the floor or bed of your choice.

All I want to do is write my paper for PMT and do my vocal exercises for Choir practice tomorrow in peace. Instead, I will do both at Piece's.

"I'm out of here!" I announce to no one in particular except yet another drunken artiste in dark trousers with Robert Smith–style hair and charcoal-rimmed eyes (not in a sullen, I'm a French-style in-génue married to Johnny Depp; more in the I drank too much Foster's and wound up stealing someone's palette to ridiculous effect).

If truth be told, I guess part of me wants to be like this. I want to feel loose and mellow and mutter "Yeah, sure" or "Whatever suits you" or the ever-popular "diamond days" (like cool, but cooler). The trouble is, I'm not. Maybe I'm too Hadley or maybe it's just innate, but either way, I want my living space to be somewhat clean, slightly private, calm enough to work in.

So I, as the English say, do a runner. Do a bunk. Well, kind of. Really when people say this it's more like skipping out on something without paying or whatever, which in a way I am. Part of me feels guilty, especially when I bump into Fizzy and Keena by the front stairwell.

Our voices echo as they chide me. "No, don't tell us—you've finally decided to give in," Keena says.

"Say it isn't so." Fizzy tugs at her hair.

I ignore them for the moment and comment. "Hey, are you using the tanning bed or something? Your skin is browner than it usually is."

Keena shakes her head. "I'd never use an artificial sun source—don't be daft. But I did jet off to Majorca for the weekend. I swear the slightest exposure and I go from half Indian to mostly."

"With your mum?" I ask her and Keena looks caught off guard, then shakes her head.

"Did you notice we were gone?" Fizzy squints at me and tugs on her frizz.

"I wasn't around much. My friend, Chris . . ." They raise their eyebrows. "My very gay, very good friend Chris came to visit rather suddenly and we just . . . well, I . . ."

"Never mind," Keena says. "Are you headed to Arabella's?"

"I think so," I say. "Don't hate me for it, okay?"

"Can you even do that? I mean on your exchange?" Keena asks, suddenly channeling her mother, PMT's, authoritative voice and manner.

My bag slides off my shoulder and I slump a little, thinking. "Good question. I guess it's up to the Pieces, since they're my *locos*."

"Oh, just do it. Who cares?" Fizzy says. She braids and unbraids the tassles on her scarf and moves toward the hallway. "I've got to finish my paper—it's a dog's dinner at the moment."

I clear my throat and nod. "Mine's a mess, too." I start down the stairs and then turn back. "Actually, I just got an idea. Would you guys be up for a study break at Pizza Express this week? Nothing too time-consuming, just to get some time together."

"Don't worry, Love. We won't forget you here." Fizzy pats my back.

"Sure," Keena says. "Pizza sounds good." Then she remembers something. "But not on Tuesday. I've got . . . That night doesn't work for me."

"Not Tuesday. Fine," I clarify as I'm walking down the stairs, away from my past life in the dorms.

"We'll see you there." Fizzy cups her hands in front of her mouth like a megaphone, though with her tiny stature nothing is mega.

"Yeah," Keena says. "And you can tell us what it's like to live in splendor."

On the way to the flat, I detour to HEL (the good kind, Clementine's coffee shop).

"What does HEL stand for, anyway?" I ask her when, without so much as an invitation or nod, she sits down at my swinging table and begins to chat.

"The real deal is that it used to be *Hello, Darling*. It sounds so naff now but at the time was considered very hip. Then people started called it *Darling,* or *Darls,* by which point it had become this—what's the term you use now—mosh pit of a scene. A veritable who's who of everyone in rock, magazines, music, or fashionable hangers-on."

"It's funny, because *Hello, Darling* sounds so sweet and cute."

"Well, right, my point exactly. So then everyone wanted to be hard and rough and punk, so darling was out and it was all, *Meet you at Hello.*" She laughs. "This was way way before Jerry Maguire and the *You had me at hello* bit."

"I'm sure . . ." I sip my foamy coffee and delight in the café life here. It's as close to Slave to the Grind as I can get, and just being here must register with my inner being as a calm, safe haven. Note to self: Dependence on caffeine and café comfort is a tolerable habit, provided I can keep up with the costs of coffee. This one's free, though, since Clementine won't let me pay for anything. "So now it's HEL—with one 'L'?"

"A lot of time has passed. In the eighties it was HD, but then people thought that meant hard drugs. So . . ." She stands up and pulls me outside to the sign. She gathers up her bat-sleeved ruby-colored top and climbs onto the bench so she can reach the sign. "If you brush aside the ivy like this . . . see? There are two *L*'s. But one got smothered in the plants. I think HEL is here to stay. Unless these ivies grow more and then it's just HE."

"Is darling under there, too?"

"No, no—this is the second sign. The first one is in the Hard Rock Cafe—haven't you had the privilege of dining there and seeing it?"

We sit in the chilly air until Clementine's hands go pure white and she complains, "It's too cold to sit here—come back inside."

"I did go to the Hard Rock, but I didn't see the sign. It was kind of crowded."

A server brings us a fresh round of hot drinks, plus nibbles of spanakopita, Greek triangles of spinach and feta that are so good I find myself making a meal of them.

"Are we on for a redo of the Bracker's weekend?" Clementine asks.

"So I hear. But I haven't been in touch with Angus or Monti, but I need to call them."

"Leaving the dorms, are we?" Clem smiles.

"How'd you know?"

"I don't blame you for trying. It's a good thing to put yourself out there, but it's not worth the hassle. Real art . . ." She pauses. "Is there real art anymore? I don't know."

I crunch and chew and watch her face for signs of what's okay to ask. She has the palest blue eyes I've ever seen, and they are almost perfectly round, so she seems like an aged doll. Then I remember her record cover for *Like the London Rain*. "I listened to your album this weekend. Is that lame to admit?"

"It's a great thing to say. You must be the only one in Britain to have it. Oh, wait. It's the one at the flat, isn't it?"

I nod. "It's so good—you know that already—but you were so young. Your picture on the album looks like it's from when you were seventeen or something."

Clem's voice gets quieter and she puts her coffee cup on the Plexiglas table, which sways in silence. "I was, Love. Sixteen. I lied and said I was seventeen—and the truth of it was that I did turn seventeen right after we cut the first single, which wasn't "Rain" but "Didn't You Always Know a Good Thing." It wasn't released as a single in the States, but it went to number three in the charts here." She looks at me. "It's pathetic. Twenty years later—more than that—and I still remember every note, every review, every business fact and figure."

I love the way the English say figure—not *fig-gure,* but *fi-gah*. It sounds so glamorous. "Do you miss it?" I make a gesture with my hands and hair that's supposed to show the glamorous life but makes me look more like I'm in a shampoo ad.

"Didn't you ask me that once before?" She studies my face. "Swear I've known you in a past life—or seen you. Anyway. No. I suppose, in my odd ways, I'm trying to tell you that it's a horrible, horrible business. They plucked me—literally—plucked me from nothing and made me into this little starlet."

"It doesn't sound all that bad," I say. "Not that I'd know, but you lived a dream . . ."

"And that's what you're left with. Me, Monti—every other used-to-be. We're a clan you don't want to be in. Once you're not doing the thing you got famous for, there's not much else. Except the money."

"Where would you be if you didn't find fame and fabulousness?" I ask.

"I've thought about that a lot. A lot. And you can't know, of course, what the different paths of your life have meant."

"Right. Didn't Milan Kundera write something like that?" I think for a second and say, "That you can't know what to want because you only live once? You can't compare your life now with any life you had before, and you can't make your future life better." I bite the inside of my cheek, hoping I don't sound pretentious.

Clemetine puts her hand on my shoulder. "Quite right."

I've noticed that *quite* over here is more akin to *exactly*, whereas at home it's more like *sort of*. Note to self: Add it to my growing list of slang translations to remember. Further note to self: Actually write down said list in journal rather than let it roam freely in the vast expanse of other trivia in the mosh pit of my brain.

"Enough about me—I'm just an old bag of air. What about you—Miss Love."

I cross my ankles and bring my legs back under the toadstool chair. "You mean what do I want to be when I grow up?" I say it like I'm five years old and then try to answer her without being entirely sure of what to say. "Easy answer? A singer."

Clementine's mouth twists as if she's licked a lime. Fruit on fruit. "How about the not easy answer."

I can feel my defenses rising, even though this is supposed to be friendly chatter, so I try to be calm and laid-back. "The uneasy answer—not uneasy like *nervous*—but the longer answer is that, unlike everyone else I know, I'm becoming less and less sure." My mug of coffee is cold now, the spanakopitas eaten, and my Sunday-afternoon gloom and doom has set in. "Why is it that I feel like I've known my whole life what I want to do and who I want to be, but now that I'm actually getting closer to it, I'm not sure I want it."

Clementine leans toward me. "Have you been offered a recording contract or something?"

Blush cough combo. "No, not like that."

"Oh, good. I was going to have to send you back to America—can't have you waste all your talent on actual singing."

"You've never even heard me—how do you know I'm talented?"

"Your reputation precedes you—I am an honorary member of the Piece clan, like you. That, plus I got to hear you sing my song, remember?"

More blushing. "Again, feel free to tape my mouth shut."

"It was a lovely rendition. But now I've gone and interrupted you. Go back to what you were saying."

"It's just . . . When I was six I used to have my dad tape all these songs from the radio so I could memorize them, okay? And then I'd perform them for him and my aunt Mable—who's probably my biggest fan." Pause for me to shove the teary worry back into my throat so I can explain. "And I love singing."

"Do you write your own stuff?"

I nod. "I do. I try to. Not the music, though. I'm not skilled enough—I haven't taken much theory or composition. The lyrics are my forte—and I wouldn't want to be one of those singers who . . ."

Clementine wrinkles her nose conspiratorially. "Who sings someone else's songs, you mean."

"Shit—sorry. I know "Like the London Rain" wasn't yours. But that's not what I mean. That was a different era . . ." Now I've made her sound old and unoriginal—the hits just keep coming.

"Don't be sorry—you're in the right. But you should know that I *did* have my own stuff, and I thought I *was* recording it. But they made two tracks—nearly a whole other album of my songs, my real songs, but never released them."

"Is that why you stopped?" I have to get going, but if I don't milk the conversational cow for all it's worth now, I might not have the chance again. If Arabella were around she might be bored with it or I might feel—I don't know—inhibited from talking freely. Only about this. I'd tell her anything else (oh, um, except for my sordid scandal with her brother), but for some reason it feels funny to think about mentioning all my doubts to her when she's so sure of her own path to stage and then screen fame.

"You know what? It's not! Can you believe what a sad sack I am? You always think that you'll stand up for yourself and not let the high-ups run you down or control you, but the fact is—or was—that I was desperate. I got shown a world I'd never even thought about being a part of, with jets and fancy feasts and fame, and then suddenly I couldn't live without it." She sighs and for one second I think she might cry. Surreal. "I never learned how."

"Maybe that's part of the problem. It's like you have to start so young to get anywhere, but then by doing that you don't know how to live a regular life."

Clementine stands up and offers two hands to me. I hold hers and she pulls me into the back room of the café. All over the walls are push-pinned photos of celebrities at HEL. "This is what I'm left with," she says and points to the pictures. "Memories and my café. Not that I'm complaining. I live quite well from the royalties—unlike many of the others who got ripped off along the way, I was too scared to spend much. I took the free offers and banked the lot I made."

"Smart." I glance at the wall where Burt Bacharach has Clem on his knee, where Monti and Mick are arm in arm, where Duran Duran is giving the camera lens the finger, where David Bowie in nearly all of his incarnations stands willowy with his hands on his hips, where those Keane boys are smiling, coy. I stare at the photo of Bowie with Natalie Portman for a long time, wondering how they met or why and what the story is or was.

"Bowie fan?" Clem asks and moves some papers around on her desk.

"Big-time," I say.

"A voice like sandpaper and glue," Clementine says and looks to see if I know what she's talking about, which I do.

"Song for Robert Zimmerman," I say. "Bob Dylan, the king of all lyricists."

"That he is," Clementine says and points to the man in question on the wall captured in photo with his eyes closed. "Off you go, now." Clementine shoos me out suddenly.

"I've used up the well of wisdom?" I ask as I back out the door.

"This well's never dry. But you have work, and I have . . . a café to run. Now, I'll see you at Bracker's for the long weekend, right?"

"Right—Bank Holiday Weekend. Who could forget?" I smile at her and reach for a couple of pound coins, which, when I offer them, she makes a face like I'm overly flatulent, which I'm not. At least not at present.

*   *   *

En route to Arabella's (Arabella's = Monti's = mine) I retrace the conversational highs and lows. Enlightening, yes. I could be discovered and swept up instantly in an *Idol* moment. But disheartening, too. Even though the industry has probably changed, the truth is if I got offered some crazy deal right now I'd have to decide what to do—college or contract—and . . . pointless! What a pointless argument to have in my head with my own self. Focus. I need to focus on what's really happening, part of which is my ever-growing pile of work, part of which is my gnawing need to see Asher.

I am overwhelmed with that romantic itch that makes it impossible to sit still. So much so that I actually get off the bus a stop early and walk the rest of the way just to try to give my racing pulse a real reason to quicken. Just the mere thought of him leads me to a question. *The* question. Will I? Would I?

Would I—given the right scenario—sleep with Asher Piece? Could I get ahead of myself more?

Before I can further investigate my trepidations and expectations, my feet bring me to the flat and by flat I mean face-to-face with Arabella.

"Bloody idiot!" Her voice is loud and exasperated.

"Sorry," I say for no reason save for the guilt in my head and the lust in my loins. A gross image. Loins still makes me think of beef or pork, and while they're tasty with a dried-fruit reduction sauce like Mable makes, it's not something I associate with sex.

"Not you—it's Tobias. He's just crap. You saw him the other night. Passed out, useless. I didn't even come meet you and Chris, and Tobias just couldn't be bothered to so much as lift a finger to help clear up, much less deign to speak to me . . ."

I shift my big bag higher up on my shoulder. Maybe now's not the best time for me to move in. I want to be supportive, but Tobias is hardly living up to the fairy-tale image Arabella projected back at Hadley last term. "Is he worth it? Wait, before you get defensive—and I'm the queen of defensive—just think about something Mable told me once. Guys don't change." I put my bag on the front stoop and hug Arabella. "They say they do, but once the magic of the first weeks or months . . ."

"Try years . . ."

"Fine. Years—and that's like a decade for us. I'm just saying that you're this incredible person." We stop hugging and Arabella flips back her thick brown hair. Even sad, she's gorgeous. "You have everything—and he's a bloody idiot to take you for granted." She pouts and then puts her hand in front of her face to do an old drama trick, flipping her frown into a big grin while keeping her eyes steady. It's harder than it seems, and it shows how much of a smile is in the eyes, not the lips.

"What did I do without you?" she wonders and trots down the steps. "Rehearsal's all of act two tonight. Don't wait up."

"Oh, I'm not sure I'm staying—I just came over to . . ."

"To move in with me, right? Feena and Kizzy beat you to it." She likes to interchange their names, since they're rarely apart.

"And you're sure you don't mind?" I have my keys out, ready to unlock the door.

"Mind? I'm beyond bloody thrilled. It's the only good thing to happen recently. We'll have loads of fun—just wait. Girly time, and a real bath or shower, and real food." She's halfway down the small lane that leads to the main street but shouts back, "And Nick Cooper! He's phoned already looking for you. You should go for it. He's very sweet and . . ." I can't hear the last part of what she says, but I'm willing to bet it has nothing to do with her amazing brother being better for me than a certain Cooper.

Dad—

Again, I can't thank you enough for sending Chris. I'll call you tom. about Mable. Am trying hard not to freak out about it. Am writing semi-grammarless b/c I have five min. before class with PMT—big project needs approval and I'm hoping she'll say yes. First Choir practice (I went from wait-listed to in by way of someone else's misfortune—need serious ethical help with that one) was great. Sang scales, grouped into high-ranging alto position, worked on a capella version of "Only You" (it's a Yaz song, you know "looking from the window above, it's like a story of love . . ."—ask Mable if you don't know it). Speaking of only you, I miss you. Maybe I miss Hadley—no wait—miss elements of Hadley: you, Mable, Harriet Walters and her astute observations in class, the salad bar, Mr. Chaucer, running (I do it here but only to catch trains and buses), the paper. Will you send over a couple of recent issues? Did I tell you I kind of know Clementine Highstreet—didn't you have a thing for her way back when? "Like the London Rain" qualifies as a classic (and has the distressing ability to get wedged in my brain for days on end).

Oh—and PS (not really ps, because it's not a postscript, but a now script . . . can you tell my English is really improving?), at the Choir practice, the leader of the pack told me the way

I say "Love" sounds like I'm enunciating too much. Result = too American. I now have to correct/ change the way I say my own name! Upside of all this is that we have our first "proper" concert in front of royalty at the start of next term (post Easter). I'm working on my curtsy. My name to you (but with a soft L to make it sound Britty),

L.

CHAPTER TEN

♡

In Poppy Massa-Tonclair's office (note to self: Though she is aware of her moniker, one should not refer to her as such during face-to-face contact), I watch her as she reads my essay. By now I'm fairly used to our tutorials, the one-on-one sessions where she reads my papers right in front of me, often articulating my words back so I can hear the finer points I've made (or the drivel).

"You have a knack for tying things up very neatly," Poppy says without taking her eyes off my paper. She likes you to go back and make written comments, thoughts, points to add, prior to handing over the paper, and I can see where she is by what I've noted.

"Is that a bad thing?" It's one of those questions I ask semirhetorically, probably in the hopes she'll respond with something like "No, it's a great thing," and my academigods smile down on me.

Instead, she furrows her brow, which makes her face look just like Keena's, only with some crinkles by the eyes and strands of gray woven into the dark mass of hair piled loosely on the very top of her head (not so much a bun as a donut). "You're at the stage in life where neatness has its own special appeal. If everything's tidy, nothing bad can happen. Order equals control."

I open my mouth to protest but find myself taking notes. Order = control. "Perceived control," I say. She's totally right. "But in academics it seems like part of the point is to tie it all up, make connections, merge themes of migration to evolution or marginalization of women to workforce ideologies . . ."

"Listen to yourself!" PMT laughs. "You've spent far too long in classes and you're only—what? seventeen?" I nod. "I'm not saying you need to go out on the street and forget everything you've learned. I just don't want to see you turn into a looking glass."

"You mean like the second part of *Alice in Wonderland*?"

"No. Not like that. A looking glass reflects only the object in front of it, and it would destroy such a wonderful part of you if all you did was spew back someone else's theories and words."

"I didn't think I was guilty of that," I say. I'm starting to feel like crap, so I take a breath and ask, "Am I just completely unoriginal?"

PMT puts my paper on her desk and opens one of the wooden drawers. Pulling out a folder, she shows me a couple of earlier papers I wrote, plus something else. "Recognize this?"

"Where'd you get that?" I ask and reach for the note. It's a sort of letter slash commentary I wrote to Keena during a particularly boring lecture on the history of British parliament. I wanted to find it interesting, but I didn't—partly because I couldn't hear the speaker very well and partly because, well, just because I want to be super well rounded and interested in everything, doesn't mean I am.

PMT lets me have the paper. "It's funny. Keena gave it to me to read only because she knew I'd have a real laugh. This is the real you, the observer, the one who isn't so much part of the action as dissecting it. You notice so much, Love. All the details that filter in . . . There's poignancy in your writing that is very rare."

"But I can't be like that in academic writing," I say. "At Hadley, they'd—"

"You're not at Hadley. I can't speak for the brilliant minds back in the States, but I can tell you that writing is like a muscle—if you don't exercise it and build it up, it will atrophy. . . . God, that was a terrible sentence. Ignore the words but keep the sentiment, okay?" She takes her hair down from its coil and suddenly looks fifteen years younger. Running her fingers through her hair, she flips her whole head downward and then raises it, mumbling, "Oh, I have one of those hair headaches. How is it possible that keeping it clasped leads to such scalp ache?"

I'm not feeling qualified to comment on anything, follicular or otherwise, so I say nothing. PMT has a way of criticizing and commending at the same time—I feel bolstered and beaten down. "I'm not sure what to do with the information you just gave me. Are you saying I should write really casual papers for you or just keep doing what I'm doing but be funny?"

PMT starts to stack up piles on the desk. I notice her literary awards are tucked discreetly behind the billowy (and dusty) curtain, hardly noticeable on the windowsill. She must be so confident in her work, so nonchalant about the plaques, that if they fell out and were lost, she wouldn't mind. "You have a rather large task ahead."

"The research project?"

"Yes. I'm making a suggestion—it's not a requirement, mind you—that you think of a unique way of presenting it. Or of doing it. Or writing it. Have you ever thought about creative writing?"

"They have classes at Hadley—poetry, prose, memoir."

"And have you signed up for them?"

"No—they're junior electives."

"Aren't you a junior?" she asks. The nearby cathedral bells ring, signaling the end of another London afternoon, bringing me one step closer to calling Mable.

"I am, but I'm here." PMT looks at me for clarification. "It just means that I sort of missed the chance to take certain electives because I'm using up a lot of those slots by taking classes here, like Body—my ridiculous dance but not dance class."

"Hmmm." PMT scribbles something down on her calendar and then says, "I've written a note to myself about being your sponsor. Perhaps, if you show me you're committed to the idea of trying something creative, rather than purely academic, we can figure out a way to beat the Hadley system."

It's a good offer. One I would never refuse, but it sounds too good to be true. "What's the catch?"

"The catch is, use your big project coming up to show me something I haven't seen before, something revealing rather than staid. Enlightening instead of everyday."

There's hardly a moment to process anything PMT said before it's time to race to the antiquated pay phones and call Mable's room at Massachusetts General Hospital. I get to the row of phones and find (a) that they're all in use and (b) the hallway is crowded with teatime takers. In a lovely, though somewhat dated gesture, LADAM puts out tea in the late afternoons. Tables set with real cups and saucers, triangular cucumber and watercress sandwiches, smoked salmon–wrapped endive, all await the singers ("I need extra honey for my throat"), dancers ("I'm not hungry just now"), and painters (they don't talk much but leave charcoal or oil thumbprints in the white, crustless bread).

Saying I'm anxious to call the hospital would be an enormous understatement, but when I think of the worst-case scenario, it's made even worse with the possibility of either having to ask Mable to repeat her bad prognosis or bursting into hysterics (not because I care about crying in front of people but because they'd think I didn't get a part in a play or got chucked—that is, broken up with—rather than something life or death).

So I leave the premises and traipse back into town, now eighteen minutes late in phoning. By the time I catch a bus, run, drop my bag, collect the contents of the spillage, and arrive at the flat, it's nearly an hour past when I said I'd call.

The phone rings. It rings again. Dialing directly was faster than going through the international operator, but when there's no answer, I get worried. So I hang up and check the number to make sure I haven't added a six or deleted a five. It rings again. Four times. Seven times. Two more times and I'll hang up. Wait—that would make nine and Mable said once that nine is an unlucky number. So twelve. Twelve rings is good. Someone better pick up before the *everyone's got a little bit of OCD* really gets cranked up to heavy psychopharm levels.

Finally, a pick up. "Hello?"

"Mable?" I say it almost as a whisper.

"Love . . ." She's breathy. "I'm only a little coherent. The Anastasia." She means anesthesia, I think, but I don't bother to query her. "I'm good. I love you. Loads and loads."

A click. Sweat beads on my upper lip, even in the cold living room. My hands are shaking. "Hello? MABLE?" I yell at the top of my range.

"Jesus Christ, Love," Dad says into the phone as I'm still yelling. "It's me. It's me—everything's fine."

"Daddy." Um, hi, I'm five and need a teddy bear. "Dad, tell me what happened. She sounds loopy."

"She is loopy. Even beforehand . . . No, really, the operation was smooth. The surgeon said she was very pleased with the results. You know how surgeons are . . ."

"Not really," I say. I should have flown home for this—being here feels wrong.

"They have a tendency to be a bit brusque . . . but you can breathe easy now. Mable's groggy, which isn't cancer related, just the anesthesia, as she said."

"And . . ." I clear my throat. "And what's next?"

"Ah, let's see . . ." Dad covers the phone and I can hear Charlie Brown–style mumbling. When he moves his hand I hear "Should I tell her," which again makes me nauseated and wish I were there to get a better sense of what's really happening.

"Dad, you promised you'd keep me informed. You promised you'd tell me the truth!"

"Fine." Dad sighs. "It was going to be a surprise, but maybe you've had enough surprises for now."

"I've never liked surprises—not even good ones."

"Well, maybe you won't mind this one so much. How would you like us to visit?"

I hear a key in the door and check my watch. Arabella's due home from history lectures and yet another *Damn* practice. "Here? With Mable?"

Dad's grin is audible, if that's even possible. "Dr. Cutler said Mable should be fine to travel."

"When? That's so awesome!"

"As soon as a couple of weeks, assuming she has no secondary infections and no fluid in the operation site."

"Infections, fluid—just get here! I miss you both so much. And it'd be so much easier to see you and be sure she's okay. Plus, I want you to see everything."

"I haven't been to London in a long time," he says. This is *the tone*. The tone he reserves only when—even if he doesn't admit it—something has to do with my (missing) mother.

"Were you here with her?" I ask. I'm so beyond being timid about his reticence. "My mother." I add that in not so much as a dog, because it's not the time for one, but so he knows I mean my mother the ever-hidden Galadriel, not Mable.

Dad swallows. "Yes. Years ago." I expect the typical sigh with a grunt to signify case closed, but he goes on. "We had a fun time, actually. It was—she was . . ." And then nothing. But I can hardly press him for specifics now. I'm not so desperate for maternal matters that I'd insist he deliver something from Mable's hospital room.

"So you're coming here!" I say, ignoring the desire to ask more about my mother and father's history in London. As she walks into the room, Arabella gives a mimed *How is she?* Then she drops her bag on the floor and sits next to me. She gives me a thumbs-up and says out loud, "Fab—if they're coming here they've got to stay at Bracker's!"

"Arabella's saying you can stay with her parents at their house. We're all going out there in a couple of weeks for the Bank Holiday Weekend." As I say it, I feel two things: one—kind of English. Not like Hadley Hall's Cordelia, who littered her speech with Frenchisms after a vacation in Marseilles, but like I've made the transition from total foreigner to passable resident. Two—the weekend has the potential to be a comedy of errors. When I picture my tiny family and the Pieces out at Bracker's, with Clementine Highstreet, PM (plus-minus) Jerry or Mick or Rod Stewart and Tobias, of course and his royal clan, not to mention Asher (okay, I did mention him already, but he's worth doing—er, mentioning—twice), it's all a little too much like a Molière farce with slamming doors and mistaken identities. But I digress.

"We'll see. I'd love to check it out, meet the Pieces—Angus's plays are an important part of the new cannon . . . But let's just allow Mable some time to heal up and figure it out."

"Tell her again that I love her, okay?" I say, and it's only then that

I hear someone making noise in the kitchen, thanks to my total phone zone. I finally put the receiver down. (It looks retro, but when I mentioned this to Arabella, she tilted her head to the side like she was confused. I realized it's the same phenom as the Martha's Vineyard/boarding-school old-money world where ratty rugs and outdated kitchens in your Maine coast mansion just show that you have *so* much wealth and class that you don't need to reoutfit with stainless-steel appliances or Brunschwig & Fils fabrics. I'm pondering this again as I stare at the telephone—it's receiver is L shaped and beige.

"Are you expecting it to talk to you?" Asher asks me as I commune with the cord. Before I can deny all charges, he offers me tea. "It's oolong," Asher says as if that explains his presence.

Arabella, ever her huffy self around her brother, takes the tea from him and scolds, "She doesn't like oolong—only Darjeeling. And anyway, I thought you were just coming in for a second."

"How do you know I don't like oolong?" I ask and ignore my fifth-grade impulse to make a joke like *I do like it long,* especially since I really wouldn't know. "I'm so relieved, you guys."

Arabella pats my back and puts the mug of tea on a stack of old art books that we use as a side table. "Seriously good news, Love. And we'll have such a great time when they're here."

Asher shifts back and forth like he wants to offer his well wishes but fears Arabella's wrath. "Yeah, it seems like good news all round."

"Do you want to sit down?" I ask Asher. It's a normal thing to say to someone who is standing, even though I'm scared of seeming too into him or too not into him, either of which might prove my amorous affections.

"No, I can't stay," he says, and then, smoothly, "I was actually just dropping by to give you this." He holds out a rectangle of thick paper with engraved script on it. "It's a calling card . . . not the phone kind.

The social kind." He's halfway to the door, but still explaining. "Why don't you drop by there on Thursday and we can get started on the head shots."

I have no idea if this is a cover of some kind or a real offer, but I go along with it as Arabella watches. "Sure—sounds good. Do I need to wear anything particular?"

"Black—or white—solid color is best. But maybe bring a couple of changes just so we can get it done."

Get it done—or get *it* done. Or, get it *done*. "I have Body in the morning. How's two o'clock?"

Asher unlocks the door and waves. "Two's fine. The models never take a long lunch anyway, so it should be easy peasy." Only very hot English boys can get away with saying things like *easy peasy*. If I picture even the trophiest Hadley guy attempting to use expressions like that it's just sad. But Asher somehow pulls it off.

"Other models?" Maybe we're meeting at a hotel and Asher is just playing up the head shot thing to distract Arabella from the scent of our growing romance.

"See you then!"

The door closes with a click and a bang and then Arabella stands up, waving at no one. "Ta-ta," she says sourly. "God, get a life, boy." Then she sheds her long, sage-green coat (wool, cut like a Russian guard's, lined with paisley fabric—it belonged to Debbie Harry or Madonna or someone) and opens her bag. "Look what I've got!"

"What?" I come over to inspect. "Tickets? You're going away again?"

Huge smile, hand clutching. "Nevis."

"The island?"

"No, the actress—"

"She's Neve."

"Whatever—yes, the place. We're going."

"We?" I ask and lean on an arm of the sofa. It's plush, covered in a deep rose and burgundy pattern that might once have been floral but now is faded. "The royal we?"

"Yes, as a matter of fact. Quite royal. You, me, Tobes, Prince—"

I cut her off. "Me?"

"Please? You'll love it. We're all comped at the Sugar Bay—It's this amazing old refinery. Ten days of pure bliss."

Outside, everything is shades of gray (rather like my brain just now), and I have to admit that some tropical sunshine would be great. "Well, I guess if I were on *The Real World* it'd be just about time for the *oh my God getaway* to somewhere cool."

"So you'll come?" Arabella flicks my chin with her tickets.

"Maybe," I say. Maybe. Depending on Asher (not that I'd miss out on a travel experience because of a new guy, but still . . .), depending on money, and depending on work. "My priority is getting this project for PMT in order." Arabella nods, but I can tell she just wants a firm answer. "Put me down for a yes, but with the right to change my mind, okay?"

A couple of days later, I am in the middle of Choir practice, waiting for the high-alto part. Just saying this in my head sounds weird as it brings to mind images of O-mouthed cherubic German boys in robes singing in Latin. At St. Paul's, however, our practice room resembles a casting call for the latest WB show. The SPGs (St. Paul's Girls) are all Bartons. Keena told me about an English expression called *pulling a Burton,* but when Chris was here we coined pulling a Barton, as in Mischa, as in the lanky, loose-limbed tall girls who never seem to exercise but are all limbs and doe-eyed wonder. The Mischas are a nice enough pack, always willing to lend a pen or make room on the couch, but they all speak as though they have marbles in their mouths.

Our practice takes place in Little Room—which is neither little nor a room but rather a semicircle with a place for an orchestra (the quartet and jazz groups also use the space) and eight arched windows with leather couches, chairs, and a fireplace large enough to actually be the gates to hell.

"Bee-yoo-kowsky," Jemma Yorlsman calls me up to the front. I take my place next to her and two other girls I don't know.

"Breathe in and . . ." Our faculty advisor Madame La Perla (perhaps connected to the fashionable lingerie line, possibly not) uses her fingers to conduct us in scales, ascending and descending, individuals, and then we go over, for the third time, our group part in the Bach piece we're working on for the next show. With the mix of voices around me, I feel trasported, as though this scene with me in it, could take place in another century (granted, young women weren't allowed to sing like this hundreds of years ago, but my point is that there's a timeless quality to the rooms, the sounds, the ruddy cheeks of the Mischas, to the way I feel completely connected through the sound).

When rehearsal ends, Jemma leaves her group for a minute and I feel sure she's about to further admonish my Americana existence and accent. Instead, she says, "You sounded really good tonight, Love. We're glad you're on."

Nothing huge, not wild excitement, but beyond passable acceptance. I'll take it.

Underneath the stone archway, I pause for a brief moment of reflection. The night is perfectly clear, cold, with a bluish black color sky that I've seen only here, nowhere else. The city lights make it impossible to see stars, but I know they're up there.

"Looking for Pegasus?"

I know before I turn around that it's Asher. His voice has the effect on my body that makes me aware of every pore. Every nerve and follicle go on high alert, gut lurching, heart pounding. It's unlike anything else—this instantaneous reaction that puts to shame any trace of Jacob or Robinson, any guy. Even the Vineyard boys—Henry, who when I reread what I've written about him in my journal seems more sweet, safer. And Charlie—well, maybe I had a semi-similar reaction to him, but he bailed before I could know for sure.

"I repeat—are you looking for a particular constellation up there or just waiting to be beamed up?"

"Neither," I say and turn to see Asher directly under the center of the stone archway. Half his face is in shadow, the other half bathed in the dark blue light from the clear sky. "I was just zoning, I guess."

"Listen," he says. "I think it's time for us to have a talk." The way Asher speaks, *talk* comes out as a long word, one with great bearing.

"Oh," I say and make an uh-oh face. Mainly I do this so he'll brush away my niggling Note to self: Add this to words that are useful yet annoying. fears that the *talk* is "the talk."

"What's wrong?" he asks and puts his hand on my back just for a nanosecond before retracting it and guiding me to a bench to sit down.

"It's just that usually when people say *we have to talk*, it's not for anything positive." But I try not to let the already-sinking feeling take hold of me.

"Do you want to sit?"

In truth, I hadn't noticed I was still standing. I sit with a deliberate space between my legs and Asher's and he gives the GGP (guy grace period) before starting with, "The thing, Love, um . . . I don't think this is quite right."

Shit. Other expletives come to mind. "Sorry," I say and deduct myself points for apologizing—too girly, totally unwarranted, again a British habit I've picked up on. "I'm not sure exactly what to say or exactly what you mean."

"I think you do know, even if it's hard to say. Look . . ." He turns on the bench so his right leg is still facing out but his left leg is pulled into a V, and his torso faces me. "I've had fun—really. From the topiary to the closet and . . ."

I nod. "I get it. You don't have to say anything else." Arabella was only half right. Asher and I didn't even need a "successful night in the lake house" for him to dump me on my American ass. He ended it before it really started. But I feel like the wind has been sucked out of me and stare at my lap as if the tops of my thighs will have brilliant insight into this matter. "I should go, anyway."

Asher furrows his brow as I stand up and clasps my hand to stop me from leaving. "Wait—what's the hurry? I didn't even finish my carefully prepared speech."

"You have a speech? You mean there's more letdown to follow?" I admit to the letdown because I'm in a foreign country and just don't see the point of showing bravado with my best friend's brother whom I will have to encounter on many an occasion. "Please, don't let me interrupt, then."

Asher shakes his head and stands up. We start walking toward the back gates as he continues. "It's just that while I am—what's the right word here? Damn, I practiced this in my head and everything . . . While I'm thrilled—is that too much? While I'm happy to have those moments with you . . ." He looks at me to make sure I'm keeping up.

"The closet, the topiary, the gallery—I gotcha." Then, just so I don't kick myself later, I spew out a few choice words of my own. "I'm not into the FWB thing, either." Asher looks confused, so I explain. "Friend. With. Benefits. Not for me. I'm not against the hookup per se, but now that you mention it, it's probably more hassle than it's worth."

"Hold up—about those, uh, hookups. It's not . . ." Major pause. I play fill in the blank SAT style. It's not (a) working for me because

I've never liked redheads (b) enough—where's the actual sex, or (c) worth the aggro of Arabella, the sneaking around, and so on. "It's not enough. If I'm going to date you, then I want to do it properly. I don't want to molest you in a closet. Well, strictly speaking I do, in fact, want to do that—but then I'd also like to take you out to dinner."

What's the opposite of having the wind sucked out of you? Being filled with helium? My brain rushes to keep pace with what he's saying. "So you're saying you want to date me?"

"No." Oh my God—confusion!

"Asher—what're you saying? Just tell me what you mean."

This is the moment—the break up or make out moment, and I wait to see which it is. We pause by the large bear statues that flank the wrought-iron gates. Each bear is mounted on a slab of cement, and I stand on that so as to be more on eye level with Asher. He stands right in front of me, close enough so that I can feel the edge of his suede jacket touching me. His cuff grazes my wrist.

"We're not allowed to date." His eyes lock with mine.

"Then I guess this is good-bye," I say matter-of-factly.

"Bye, then," Asher says and at the same moment, leans in and puts his open mouth on mine. My hands pull him closer to me and he pushes back, so I'm pressed up against the cold metal of the statue. Probably not what Lord So and So had in mind when he donated the bears to the grounds, but a worthy snapshot all the same.

"I feel a Clash song coming on," I say.

"Mmmm—'Should I Stay or Should I Go,' I assume."

"That's the one."

"Listen, before we get kicked off the grounds, what I wanted to ask you all along is . . ." I pull back so I can see his face, and he moves onto the pavement from the cement slab step. "Would you like to go out?"

"I thought you just said we couldn't go out—even though that directly conflicts with what you said in the closet, which is that we should ignore what anyone else thinks."

"Right. I know. We're sort of stuck."

"Which leaves us—yet again—at good-bye."

I start off just so he can take me by the shoulder and not let me go. "Love Bukowski," he says, the only Brit to pronounce my surname correctly. "Would you like to go on a non-date with me? Or many non-dates?" He waits for me to speak as we walk across the street to wait for a night bus.

"Maybe." How I manage not to bounce up and down like a game show contestant with shouts of "Yippee" and "Yes" is beyond me. I can see the bus approaching. "Are you asking me to be your not girl-friend?"

Asher smiles and puts his arms around me. And in the middle of the wide London night, he nods and pulls me onto the bus. We sit at the back, hand in hand, and I lean my head on my non-boyfriend's shoulder.

While pretending to find my inner focus, light on my abbreviated energies, and stretching myself into a linear form (all this from the high-pitched instructive voice of Body teacher). Rather than see Body as a big old waste of my time, I've tried to implement the time-honored Hadley technique of multifunctional reasoning and practice (MFRP, not to be confused with car ads that use the same letters for something entirely different). Basically, there's so much work at Hadley and so many other restrictions on you at any given time, that time-management skills are one of the most valued skills acquired there.

So, rather than simply point my toes toward the mirrored wall, I do it while trying to figure out the angle I want to choose for my PMT project. Instead of singularly allowing myself to "become one with my breath" (not breasts, as I'd originally thought), I toy with the idea of not going to Nevis. It's not that I'm opposed to fun in the sun. On the contrary, going to a tiny island and being pampered by beach boys bringing me beverages sounds pretty damn good. But when Googie Binsworth, an old schoolmate of Arabella's came over, out came the old photo albums. They showed me photos of similar outings, pointed out a couple of old friends, then a sarong and a straw hat, then a stack of beach books—and then casually informed me that these were all items that neither of them had any longer, that the smiling tanned faces were people they'd once called best friends but now no longer knew.

Part of me thinks that this is how money works: You want it if you don't have it. If you do have it you're scared of losing it. And if you have too much of it, everything becomes disposable. And that's what I don't want to be—the Bic razor equivalent. And while I'm pretty confident that my friendship with Arabella is here to stay, the farther into her world of Brit class and calamity I get sucked, the more chance I have of being part of the past—some old photo of a once-familiar girl.

"And arch, using your core to stabilize . . ."

I do a quick check of the class in the mirror, making sure I'm keeping up with everyone while my head is somewhere else. I could allow myself the fantasy of thinking about performing with the Choir in front of Prince Charles and his royal clan, but instead, I'm drawn back to the PMT thing. What I'd like to do is figure out a way of exploring the nature of dialogue, of communicating. I've realized that that's the part of music I like best, how you can deliver a feeling just by performing. You can change the mood in a room, make someone swoon or cry or cheer just by having the right notes and the right words. So somehow I want to have a story and a song overlap and . . . okay, the reality is I don't know how to translate the ideas in my head onto the page. Kind of like when you're this brilliant artist in your mind and then when you get out the pencil or crayons everything looks like it was done by a group of second graders. At least that's what happens to me.

"Hey!" Keena bumps into me after class. "Where'd Piece go?"

"I don't know," I say and zip up my sweatshirt. The plus side of Body is that it ends on the earlier side of the classes (some run as long at two and a half hours), so there's sometimes a couple of minutes to talk or trade stories. "She wasn't in class. I figured she was doing one of the final rehearsals or something."

Keena grins and rubs under her eye where the liner had smudged. She pulls away a charcoaled fingertip. "Am I raccooning?" I shake my head. "Want to grab a coffee?"

The student café is packed so we end up ducking into the shabby pub at the end of Haverston Street, where I've never been before.

"Slumming, are we?" I ask as we wait at the bar.

Keena slides money over to the bartender and nudges me to a back table with a half pint of beer in each hand.

"Isn't drinking during the day bad?" I ask and smile.

"I thought it was drinking alone," she says and sips.

"Either way, I'm sure this would be frowned upon by my State-side counterparts."

"Probably." Keena takes another drink and looks at me over the rim of her glass. Her dark eyes are bright, staring.

"What?"

"You tell me yours, I'll tell you mine," she says. She opens a packet of salt-and-vinegar crisps (aka potato chips but more flavorful) and we each take a couple, chewing on the food and Keena's offer.

"I'm sure I don't know what you mean," I say like a Southern belle. Keena lived for two years in the States when she was younger, so the reference might not be entirely lost on her.

"Don't play coy, Bukowski—it doesn't suit you."

I lick one of the chips and eat it, swig my drink, and then pull my knees up so they touch my chest and I'm tucked in behind the bar table for safety. "What do you think I have to tell you?"

Keena considers for a minute. "Could be a couple of things—though I think I know. But in a million years you'll never figure out my inner doings unless I choose to spill."

"So spill."

"You first," she says. "And I think we both know it goes without saying that this travels nowhere—these secrets live and die in this shitty pub." I nod. "Fizzy and Arabella included—right?"

"Right." I don't know if Keena knows what I know or if she only thinks she knows what I know—mainly that I am now officially dating, or, um, non-dating, Asher. And I know once you tell one person the thing you're supposed to keep hidden, it only opens up the greater possibility of letting the secret out for the world to know. But I am at this point, about to burst. So in a fit of whimsy, I decide to tell her.

"I've been . . ." I start and then retract. No. It's best that no one knows.

But Keena beats me to it. "So how long have you been shagging Asher?"

My palms fly to my face like that will curtail the blushing that seeps from neck to forehead. My redhead skin can take only the smallest shame or worry or nerves before blossoming into a rose garden of reds and pinks. "We're not shagging."

"No?" Keena's skeptical. "What then?"

"We're . . ." How do I explain it? "We're . . ."

"God, for someone who's so brilliant with words, you have a crap way of talking about your feelings."

"Why, thank you Dr. Massa-Tonclair. You should think about

being a shrink—you have real knack for putting people at ease." I laugh and try to wangle the last chip, but she beats me to it.

"Sorry—do go on. You were saying so eloquently . . . ?"

"Asher and I are . . . well, we would be dating or having a relationship—going out, a couple—however you want to phrase it. But since he's off limits to me . . ."

"And you're off limits to him . . ."

I wipe my hands on my sweatpants for lack of a napkin. "By way of default, right?"

"No." Keena tilts her half pint up to get the last drop out. "Arabella made a whole thing about it with Asher. She called from Hadley—no, wait, from the airport in Boston when you all were heading over here—and told him to keep his dirty hands off you. Dirty and dismissive were the exact words she used, I believe."

"Nice. Clichéd, but chilling anyway." I think for a second. "I guess she called when she ditched me at the snack place and went to the bathroom. Why do you know this, anyway?"

Keena examines the lock of hair at the front of her head that's slightly lighter, more mahogany colored than the rest of the strands. "Asher and I took a drawing class together this autumn. He's a good bloke—even if he's misunderstood or in that breaking away from the parents stage that makes him a bit of a prat sometimes."

"Glad to have your approval," I joke. "I just wish it weren't such a big deal."

We're quiet for a bit, watching the sports on the small television above the bar, the people walking by outside, the paunchy guy reading his paper in the corner. "So you really like him, then?" Keena asks.

"Yeah," I say softly. "I really do."

Keena takes out a Labello lip balm, with a hint of pink and offers it to me. I slide some on my lower lip and give it back. "Hey, I almost forgot to ask you about your deep dark secret . . ."

Keena puts her chin in her hand and looks at the table, suddenly very interested in the cardboard coasters that advertise some lager. "This is a big one," she says. "I can't tell you here. Come on."

We stand up and make our way to the very revolting bathroom. Keena slides the brass lock closed and leans on the door. I stand with my hands in my pockets, trying not to step in the dubious puddles on the floor.

"You sure know how to treat a girl right," I say.

Keena grins. She looks so nervous, which I've never seen before. She's the calm collected girl who responds slowly to things, never appears flustered, has a witty comeback but not so fast she seems overprepared. "You know the rumors about student-faculty relations?" I nod and wait for her to continue. "Well, let's just say there's merit to them."

"Is this about Fizzy? She has a different person in that room every day—and I don't want to judge her but . . ."

"No, this isn't Fizzy. This is me. Me and—"

She's cut off by Arabella's singsong voice. "Lo-ove . . . Keens? Are you in here?"

I poke my head out from the top of the stall and wave. "Hiya," I say.

"Are you having a tampon situation or something?" Arabella asks. It does look odd probably, the two of us huddled in here, but since I'm already lying enough to her I say, "No—just having a conference."

"I won't ask," Arabella says and fixes her jeans in the mirror. Keena and I exit the stall and then the three of us leave the pub and disperse, me without knowing what—or whom—Keena was about to tell me.

CHAPTER ELEVEN

"That's me as a little boy," Asher says, pointing to a dark-haired black-and-white image of himself.

"So cute. Where was it taken?"

"Here, actually, which is why I wanted to bring you out this way." Asher jumps down from the riverbank onto one of the houseboats that rock and sway in the Thames. Cloistered away from the rest of the bustle and noise of the city, this little enclave of boats is peaceful and soothing.

"What is this place, exactly?" I get my bearings and begin a tour, which takes all of three minutes—an open area at the stern with empty flowerpots and a layer of frost on the tarpaulin-lined bench, then a long galley kitchen with a two-burner stove, and a cozy main room with built-in couches and throw pillows, all of which center around a wood-burning stove.

"This was Dad's bachelor pad, you know back in his swingin' single days."

"So let me guess," I say and continue to nose around, opening cabinets, finding half-filled spice jars, a hunk of moldy cheese in the top-loading fridge. "Now it's your bachelor pad—your den of delights, your . . ."

"Yeah, that's it. This is where I keep my harem, and I'm bringing you here to join my other wives." Even in the plural and the ridiculous, I can't help but catch my breath. Wives. Wife. Whoa.

"We say harem," I tell him. "Not ha-reeeem."

"Potato, tomato—whatever. No, I stay mainly at the gallery. I only come here every once in a while. More in the spring and summer. It's good for parties." I can envision a floral, wine-soaked afternoon here, sunlight streaming in as the upscale artistic set (read: girls with choppy short hair and Velma glasses, willowy beauties with halter dresses and ballet flats)—I cut the images short before they lead to wondering who else Asher has brought here.

"Maybe we'll have a dinner party here in April," he says while I try to open a latched cabinet. *We.* Nice. Asher comes up behind me, his chest pressing into my back—I think he's about to slide his hands up my shirt or kiss me, but all he does is unlatch the cabinet so it swings open, revealing nothing.

"What're you looking for, anyway?" he asks.

"In general or in this cupboard?" I ask, but Asher only rolls his eyes. "Nothing. I don't know. Just curious, I guess."

We walk over to the couch and both sit with our backs against the arms so our feet just touch if I stretch myself out. I kick off my boots and notice Asher's already taken off his shoes. His socks are warm against mine, his toes rub the bottoms of my feet. It's cold enough in the room that my breath comes out in white bursts.

"I always liked to explore people's houses or their old stuff, letters . . . It's like I somehow think I'll find the core, or some big secret—"

"That just happens to be on display in the overhead cabinet?" Asher folds his arms across his chest, not in the defensive way, in the chilly way. I get on my knees and crawl over to his side of the couch and lie back on him, so his arms are around me, my legs in between his.

"Fine. Maybe I'm just nosey. But I sometimes wonder if someone found my room and went through my music, smelled all the smells of my lotions and shampoo and gross running shoes, if they read my journal, even, if they'd know who I am."

"Without meeting you, you mean?" I nod, then rest my head back on Asher's chest so I can feel his breath on my hair. "I don't think so. I suppose part of you—a large part, even—would filter through. But I think there's this intangible quality, something you can't define or translate by objects that someone has or owns, that you can only get by being *with* them."

"And do you think that part is essential? Like you can't ever know anyone without first getting close to that part?"

"Maybe," Asher says. "One of the reasons I like photography is for that . . . You get a whole other sense of someone by how they photograph."

"Poorly, in my case," I say. I want to be one of those girls who looks incredible, natural, and lovely in each picture snapped of her, but the reality is that most of the time something's off—every once in a while there's a good one, but as a rule, I am not, as they say, making love to the camera.

"No, this is beyond good or bad or photogenic. What I'm saying is that I like the way the lens captures what words can't, or what might escape your notice."

"I can see that. Let me see that picture of you again?" He digs through his layers of jacket, sweater (he calls it a jumper), shirt, to his wallet and hands it back to me. "Is there something missing? I didn't realize before, but what's the deal with this?"

Asher sighs. "Yeah, this is actually a reprint. Arabella took the original, which had the two of us together—like bookends on the whispering wall—and ripped it. I found the negative and pieced it together. Mum looks so young in it. Dad looks the same, probably due to the beard."

"Why'd she rip it?"

"Some adolescent fit of rage, I don't know. She had some argument with Monti about wanting to go to the hunt ball, which of course was far too establishment in Monti's eyes, so Arabella tore up a bunch of family photos."

"Which your dad probably thought was a healthy way of expressing her familial dissent," I joke.

Asher laughs. "You've got us all pegged." He tilts my head back up to his, which no doubt gives him a lovely view of my nostrils, but also affords the opportunity to kiss me very softly on the lips. "What's the story with your clan, then?"

"Oh, dear. The question . . . well, you know my dad is—as the parenting mags call it—the primary caregiver."

"And Mable's, what, the secondary?"

"She's incredible. And my dad is . . . Well, I've never really felt like my situation is weird, even though it is to some degree. I mean, aren't all our definitions of what constitutes a family changing?"

"Yes, newscaster slash journalist Love." I laugh and then switch positions so now we're facing each other despite the fact that I am precariously close to toppling off the narrow couch onto the floor, especially since the wind seems to have picked up, causing the boat to rock more. "Don't you have anything to say about Mater? That's mother, in Latin, for the grim uneducated among us."

"My mother's . . . Well, no I don't have that much to say. I mean, her name is Galadriel, that I know. What else? . . . She . . . You know how I was searching through the shelves in here? It's like instinct— my whole life I've always devoted bits of my week or month or day to digging for clues."

"You have heard of the Internet, right?"

I shake off the thought. "It's not like that. I trust my dad—and there's probably a good reason why he's chosen to raise me like this, without knowing the whole story."

"It just seems odd somehow, for someone who's so into knowing the details, that you'd just accept being kept in the dark. I know if I were in your position, I'd just look and track down all the information I could. So how come you don't?"

"I do—kind of. I found all this clothing of hers last term and I wore it, which pissed my dad off. These boots—those on the floor—are actually hers. My mom's. Or they were."

Asher leans over and grabs a boot, examining it. "London made—good choice." He nods his approval.

"When I was coming here my dad said they were the last thing he ever got her—Galadriel."

"Well, they're from Bella James," Asher says and drops the boot. "So he probably got them here, since they're not sold anywhere else. Monti's friends with Bella, which is why I know such fascinating shoe trivia, just so you don't think I've got some bizarre foot fetish."

I try to let this sink in for a second and then talk. "You know what, though? Maybe he did buy her the boots here. Maybe she took off or something and he couldn't give them to her, and he shoved them into the basement because he couldn't deal with getting rid of them. But . . . you asked why I'm not furiously trying to find her or find out what happened."

"Right. I mean, she's not my mum and I'm dying to know . . ."

Asher holds my right wrist and circles it with his thumb and pointer. Then he takes both my hands and sandwiches them between his. It's comforting and exciting at the same time. "Here's the real thing," I say and stare at our hands. "I've been curious. Of course. I mean, I do ask about her . . . But I've never *needed* to know. There's a difference. My life, with my dad and Mable, it's enough. And maybe if it weren't, if I were just a big fuck up or felt like such a huge part of me were missing, maybe I'd feel more compelled to go on some megasearch." I stand up and stretch, then jog in place to get the blood flowing to my legs again. "But I don't have that gaping hole. Just some mild curiosity that gets inflamed once in a while."

"Fair enough," Asher says. "But when you do find out—someday—even if I don't know you anymore, or we're like eighty-nine years old and living right here together, will you tell me?"

I nod. "If I ever know, yes." Before I get hung up on the prospect of not knowing him someday or of living with him on this house-boat, I find my boots.

Asher does the same, slipping into his shoes without untying them and then, gallant boy that he is, kneels down to help me with my boots.

"I feel like Cinderella," I say.

"I was brought up to be honest, not charming," Asher says, beating me to my princely comment.

"Oh, I think you're charming enough," I say, trying not to gush, and semisucceeding. Asher puts his hand on my cheek and just looks at me. Then we head off the boat and back to dry land, where everything's stable.

We kiss good-bye, and he undoes my hair from its ponytail. "You should wear it down in your head shots. It looks so . . . just unbelievable."

"It's not . . ."

"Just take the compliment." He grins. "And sorry I had to reschedule the shoot . . ." He sounds almost embarrassed, but maybe he is—from what he said, he got in trouble for assuming I could just show up and steal the limelight (or whatever special lights they have) from the gazellelike models. "But we will find a time. I promise."

"I know," I say. "And it's not like it's an urgent matter, anyway."

Asher thinks for a minute and says, "Maybe the simplest thing is to have you come to the gallery. One night soon?"

We look at each other without speaking, and there may as well be subtitles under us like in *Annie Hall*. It's obvious—at least to me—that going to his gallery (fight off the image of him kissing that ex-girlfriend) is really code not just for head shots . . . but for bed shots . . . one night soon. Soon.

"Soon?" I ask, then try to make it a confirmation, not a question. "Soon. Right. Sounds . . . good."

"Good then." Asher gives me a kiss on each cheek, then comes back for one on the mouth. Yes, I think. Soon.

CHAPTER TWELVE

♡

My mail still arrives at LADAM due to the slightly prickly point that while I have permission from my *in loco parentis* (pointed accent on the loco part), Monti and Angus Piece, they've yet to inform my father that I am a mere seventeen years old, living in a two-million-dollar flat with my best friend without rules or supervision. This is a small issue with which we will all have to contend when—or if—Dad visits. For the time being, I dutifully check with the ancient porter for any packages or letters. The thick overnight envelope contains the following note on Hadley Hall letterhead:

> *Love—here's the latest from Mrs. Dandy-Patinko. I made sure to Express Mail it so that you'd have all the information the same day as everyone else. All the class II's are very busy with college prep—including practice SATs (I'm sure you've been doing yours) and even brainstorming ideas for upcoming essays!*

I decipher as I read: Express Mail shows Dad's clear need to demonstrate the importance of this packet; God forbid it arrive three days later. I might miss out on Harvard if a postal delay occurs . . .

"All the Class II's" (Juniors = Class II, seniors = Class I) is meant to defer the pressure from parental to peer—all the kids are doing it, you should, too. Heh. And Dad's surety about my practice SATs is just a little jab to say that if I haven't been, I should. Ah, I am fluent in Dad-ponese. And unless my college essays have something to do with my current obsession with chips (French fries), how to deal with the Asher-Arabella conundrum, or how to complete my course work here while still having a life, I don't think it's fair to say I've been "brainstorming."

I head over to said chip cart, get a paper cone filled with hot fries, douse them with vinegar, and retreat to the student café for a five-minute perusal of the rest of the college package.

Here is a delicious sampling from TCP (the college process). It's thirty-eight degrees, I'm three thousand miles away from all things Ivy League or (gasp!) safety, and yet the fact that college looms ahead is inescapable after reading this from the counseling office.

1. *To get ahead on your college process over the summer, we suggest the following:*
   - *Do extensive research about the colleges to which you might apply. Use the Internet.* (I love the way they change it to "your college process," so it's just that much more personal.)
   - *Visit colleges, if you can, and have interviews at places that offer them.* (When am I supposed to do this? While I'm trekking to Body? While hoofing it to my Shakespearean heroines elective?)
   - *Begin to work on your applications. Colleges often do not have their applications available until late August, but you might find the updated versions of the applications on Web sites long before they are available by mail.* (Thanks for the added pressure . . . like it's not already looming enough.)
   - *Write essays over the summer; this will keep you from having long*

nights of anguish in September. (But I live for long nights of anguish!) *At the very least, keep a journal of ideas and opening paragraphs. Feel free to email the college office with your essays for feedback during the summer months. We would love to hear from you!* (My journal is not filled with college ideas. I doubt Yale would be interested in my half-completed songs, my lists of weird words and English phrases, the merits of various crushes over other ones. In other words, I fully expect those long nights of anguish this fall.)

2. *Remember to "demonstrate interest" at colleges to which you may apply: Schools will wait-list or deny a perfectly qualified applicant if they feel that you have not demonstrated enough interest in attending their college. Showing ample interest is* your *responsibility . . . this includes not just your "reach" colleges, but your "possible" and "likely" colleges as well! You can "demonstrate interest" in the following ways: have an on-campus or alumni interview, attend an information session and tour campus, connect with college admission reps at our two fall minifairs, and/or contact professors in your areas of interest.* (Um, difficult to show interest from three thousand miles away. Read: I'm screwed.)

3. *Get cracking on those SATs! Register now!* (Yay! Here's one thing I actually got right—seven weeks and counting.)

4. *Email us at Hadley Hall for a form that will help you evaluate colleges. Keep these forms with you during your college tour; they are sure to be of help when the time comes to answer application questions such as "Why Bowdoin?" or "Why, in particular, do you wish to attend Wisconsin at Madison?" or "Why are you attracted to UCLA?"* (answer = because it's hot?)

Blah Blah blah. It's an all-encompassing task that lies ahead of me. Maybe all this leads to my needing a "gap year" like the one Asher is taking before he heads off to Oxford. Being out of Hadley, out of any school, sounds like the key to recharging prior to another solid study period. But maybe this is just laziness talking. Besides, I'd still want to apply, with the option to defer. I eat the last French fry and try to find solace in the fact that I can harass Mrs. Dandy-Patinko by phone, mail, or email all summer long. Hadley even gives you the option of setting up an FTF (face-to-face) meeting if you are in danger of self-imploding.

I plan on memorizing the number for her office, but in the meantime, all of this is so far away from the ringing bells of Big Ben, the smells of London at night (smoke, bus fumes, the sugar-slicked roasted nuts sold from a cart near the tube entrance, vague whiffs of perfume and cologne), classes where everyone's in leotards or practicing stage rage; basically my entire life here. So I make a note to write to Mrs. Dandy-Pantinko (college counselor or shrink, hard to tell) and then shove the manila envelope into my bag until later (later = spring? Can I hold off until summer?).

Aside from actually finding a place where I'd like to live and study for four years (three if I come back here—hey, that's an idea), I don't really want to spend my last high school summer plodding along scripting out those all-important essays. Aunt Mable's offered at least a couple times to have me work at the new Slave to the Grind on the Vineyard, and if Arabella can come, too (read: if she can pry herself away from Tobias), it has the makings for a perfect summer. Especially if Asher—Wait. No. I won't do this. I, Love, the Zen master, will live in the now and not try to push past the present to a future that may or may not include a boy I like so much I've kept it hidden from my best friend. Oh dear.

Arsenio Hall once said that "success is preparation and opportunity meeting." Of course, I'm too young to have seen his late-night talk show, but I happened to catch him on a VH1 eighties binge last year, and the words have stuck. For some reason, while I watch Arabella's millionth rehearsal for *Damn Yankees,* it suddenly hits me that this is what she has. She's totally prepped and has opportunity all around her at LADAM. Then her dad, English playwright extraordinaire, will no doubt hook her up with some choice casting director, and she'll be set for life.

I, on the other hand, will need to either audition for a reality show or happen to sit next to some music executive on the oh-so-many bicoastal flights I take in order to hand over the nonexistent demo tape. But I don't begrudge Arabella. Being critical of the hand-me-down effects of wealth and fame won't help me.

In between reading *King Lear* and rereading *Hamlet,* I allow myself the treat of Chris's latest letter. (It's really an email, but I printed it out so as not to deal with the sneers from the long queue—er, line—in the computer centre—er, center.)

Lovey Dovey

Valentine's Day passed with nary a phone call nor flower from Chicago—guess my boyfriend ain't so much a boyfriend as a boy friend. But did get quickie note from Alistair the American in London— semisordid, semiplatonic. Oh well. What about you and yours? Any hearts, chochie, pressies, anything?

As for non sequiturs, you're so right about Bitch Thompson—I am stuck with her this term for my calculus add-on (yes, I do kiss butt for credit) and she sucks. But it's better than Mr. Chaucer's idea of college prep (your boy Jacob—

oops, not your boy—is one of several people writing novellas on the side of all the usual course
work just to stand out from the college app.
crowd. Um, no thanks.)

And cleverly segueing into Jacobland, let me
tell you his tryst with Linsday Parrish has fallen
on its superficial, sucky face. His newest amore
is Dillon Fuchs—(that's fewques, not fucks).
Fade-in on Jacob, pouty with his acoustic, cut to
Lindsay in a new demure Marc Jacobs ensemble. Like
Mary Janes and pleats can mask how cruel she is.
She's probably plotting Dillon's demise while
you're away. (I mean, the girl doesn't do any actual schoolwork, so what else is she supposed to
do to keep herself busy?) Meanwhile, Cordelia,
our fave fac brat, has managed to acquire herself
a little teeny weeny drinking prob, and is thusly
on probation! Call it karma, baby.

I managed to wrangle a straight boy (the very
cute and way too preppy Haveford Pomroy—perhaps
I'll have-er-ford him . . . heh) to help with the
yearbook candid spread. He's got an eye for details (just call me details). His sister,
Chilton, will be a new sophomore next year—one
to watch, I'm sure. Chili (that's not beans 'n'
slop, but Chilton's nickname, for those in the
know) visited last weekend and we had a blast.
She's slumming on the Vineyard this summer—maybe
you'll see her there? Ah, summer sounds so good
right now.

Alas, college crap awaits, and my straight-for-

now buddy Haverford is due to arrive any sec. You
know the only reason I wanted to be photo editor
of the yearbook is so I can demand all the candid shots be of us or ones that make LP look like
the reigning queen of bitch or blemish. Oops—
maybe I'm competing with her in that category! I
must stop the gossip train.

 Am meeting your lovely Aunt Mable for a burger
the day after tomorrow if she's up for it—don't
you miss Bartley's? I'll order extra onions on
your behalf.

   XXS Always,

   Chris

Valentine's had passed without much aplomb. Arabella got a bou-
quet of day lilies from Sir Toby, and I was stuck in my former dorm
hell, and I can't say I missed the frenzy of flowers or forgotten romantic gestures. Chris's email leaves me with enough gossip that I'm
full for a good couple of days, but I make a note to write back and
demand he tell me more about Chilton Pomroy. Chili. Or Chilly. It'd
be nice to have friend on the Vineyard, even if she's a sophomore. And
I wish I either didn't know about Jacob's novella, or, now that I do,
that I could get a glimpse of what's in there, even if it means doing
some Hadley espionage. Cordelia drinking—looking back, I guess I
could see it coming, but it's sad anyway. Maybe she'll be like Drew
Barrymore and emerge a different person, with her life better for her
past troubles. Or, more likely, she'll brag about rehab and just use it
to gain attention.

 Maybe I should write a novella for extra credit. Or do trig. Or perform a one-girl show with kittens and an emu. Or maybe I should forget all that and just deal with my day-to-day here—which sounds like a better plan. I have next year to revert to the Hadley code of conduct and slumming around for activities in the college application add-on route.

After rehearsal ends (during which I must confess I found myself mouthing along to the songs—Arabella nearly chants the music day and night, shower included), we head out to meet Fizzy and Keena at Pizza Express. Rather than do as the name suggests, however, we settle in for a wine, dough, and salad evening. It's become our customary midweek thing, to meet here and give ourselves the luxury of two hours spent hanging and heckling one another. Of course, now that Keena has the recently gained knowledge that is my boyfriend, she'll have to keep mum (nod to the queen) about it. Plus, she never spilled the beans (baked or otherwise) about her big hush-hush thing, so maybe we're even.

"Well, first thing's first," I say. "I talked to him again today, and Mable's doing fine—no postoperative infections or anything. And—big breath—it seems as though my dad has met someone."

Keena slings her postal bag filled with books and papers down on the ground underneath the table and sits in one of the café chairs. "God, don't you hate that phrase? It's such a pathetic attempt at masking the reality—um, hallo, I'm shagging someone."

I make a face and flick her shoulder. "Gross. Please keep from mentioning my father and the idea of shagging in the same sentence. The same universe, even."

"Could be worse," Fizzy says. "He could be like my dad and have a different woman each time I go home for the holidays. It's got so bad I now just call them all Sheila." Then Fizzy lights a Silk Cut cigarette that clouds the table so much Arabella shoos her outside to finish.

"I'll be right back. I told Tobias I'd give a quick ring," Arabella says.

"You can do it from here. I don't mind," I say.

Arabella shakes her head. "No, that's okay. You two order me a margarita and a side salad and I won't be a sec." Translation: See you when the food gets here.

Before Fizzy flits back, I lean in and say, "All right, Keena, enough's enough."

"What?" she asks but knows exactly what I'm after.

"You can't just leave me hanging."

"Fine. I have some shagging news myself," she says and—despite being Ms. Calm, Cool, and Collected—actually blushes a deep maroon.

"Don't tell me it's that guy who puked in your sink?" Keena rolls her eyes. "Well, it's not totally out of order; I mean he was good-looking. Disgustingly drunk and puking, but cute."

"No," she says, suddenly quiet and serious. "It's more than just a quick thing, anyway. It's . . . real."

I'm still playing up the joke, trying to think whom she might have bedded down with when Keena raises her chin to show me Fizzy's on her way back.

"Come on!" I say.

"Someone French," she says and looks me right in the eyes to check if I'll flinch. I don't. She raises one eyebrow to make her point, but I don't get it. "French. Galen French."

"My vocal coach? But he's a faculty member!" No shit. I try to move on from the obvious. "How long?" I ask and right away wish I'd clarified I meant the duration of the affair.

"Two months," she says and smiles. "More on that subject later, but please—whatever you do—don't tell my mother."

"I'm not—though it might come as a surprise—in the habit of discussing your romantic entanglements with PMT—your mother, I mean."

"Good," she says.

"What romantic entanglements?" Fizzy asks and plops down in the chair. Keena gives me a look that pleads *find something to avert the confidentiality crisis.* "Don't let me fill up on garlic bread." Crisis averted.

When Arabella comes back, looking cheerful and chipper after her TB (touch base) phone call with Toby, I again feel that sinking weight of being dishonest with her. Note to self: Think of how to break the news to her or at least hint at it so it doesn't explode later.

Sometime in between salad and slices (which aren't really slices but personal ovals of thin-crusted pizza), Keena complains about her all-knowing, campus-powerful mother.

"I hear you," I say. "I got busted last year at Hadley and my own father suspended me for two days."

"Christ, that's bad," Keena says. "Mine just checks each grade, each paper, with a fucking monocle. She's determined to see me rise to the top of the Cambridge elite."

"At least your mum cares," Fizzy says. "Mine's too busy dealing with my stepsiblings to even notice if I fail. She's like supermom to them—music classes, baby yoga, everything—and still manages to work at night."

Arabella cuts off a piece of cheesy dough and eats it, then adds, "I don't mind it, really. Monti and Angus are sort of in and out—you know, partially invested because they love me and everything, and part just really into their own lives, you know? Sometimes I think maybe parents don't have enough going on so they have to pick through their kids' crap to feel alive."

"Well, not everyone's parents are busy entertaining Sting and Trudie," I say and smile.

Arabella nods. "True. I just think having something else . . . not just living for your children . . . helps." She sips her glass of water, then wipes her mouth on the waxy napkin. "Kind of like Mable." She explains to Fizzy and Keena, in case they don't know. "Love's aunt is, like, really the perfect mix of involved and not. She's got her café . . ."

"And her cancer," I add, knowing that if Mable were here, she'd appreciate my attempt at humor. "But you're right. She is good about that—she'll always talk and ask me about things, but doesn't have that pressured way of making you feel like there's always a correct response, or that she's waiting for me to mess up so she can redirect me."

"Yeah, she's pretty much the best," Arabella adds. She chews her lip, which she does only when she's about to push a subject. Fizzy takes another garlic breadstick and gnaws on it. "Love . . ."

Keena looks at Arabella, acknowledging some unspoken connection between them. Keena clears her throat. Arabella goes on. "Love? Has it ever . . . have you ever thought that . . . ?"

Oh my God. She knows. Keena told her. Bitch. Hear comes the Asher tirade. "Have you ever thought that Mable could possibly be . . . your mother?"

What? What? "What?" It comes out louder than I expected, but I am blown away. Speechless. I sit there in the bizarre fallout and wait for someone to talk.

Finally, Keena does. "We were talking and it's only that—"

"You guys talk about me?"

"Come on, Love," Fizzy says. "Everyone talks about everyone."

"I know that," I say, defensive as hell. "But not about this—you're supposed to talk about someone's sluttiness"—we all look at Fizzy—"or how they're always convinced they're right"—switch focus to Keena—"or how their lame boyfriends don't appreciate them"—hello, Arabella. "I mean, this is your theory? Not, 'Gee, is Love happy?' or 'Did you notice how her boobs stick out of that shirt?' or 'What a bitch she was the other day' . . . but is my aunt actually my mother?"

As I say it, the possibilities and ramifications make me feel sick.

Then, in the quiet that follows, I realize it's silly. Ridiculous. And I start cracking up. To my relief, so does Arabella, which sets the others off. "You guys have been watching too many Australian soaps," I say and laugh so hard I snort.

"Nice snort," Arabella says. "You didn't have to lose the plot about it—it was only an idea."

"Well, enough of your conspiracy theories and crazies," I say.

"And I'm not that big a slut," Fizzy adds as if that's been the focus.

"Yeah, right," Keena says. "But we love you anyway."

In my voice lesson, my mouth is saying la la la, but my mind is going tsk tsk tsk. I consider myself fairly open-minded, but the idea of getting it on with a faculty member has never appealed. Plus, when I think of the various issues of power and possible expelling, firing and so on, it doesn't seem worth it.

But looking at Galen French, his scruffy, slightly crumpled green-and-white-checked shirt, his dark jeans, and those Brit-boy shoes, he's undoubtedly sexy. Why is it that once someone points out someone's sex appeal, you see it in a new light, as if suddenly those sensors have come and that person is a whole different level of present.

He's only a year or so out of university—and college here is only three years, so . . . So, he's still supposed to be off-limits. "Love? Are you still with me? Can you hit the 'c'?"

"Oh, um, right. I can try. I'm not sure." Galen plays a chord and I try to mimic it with my voice. "I'm making progress, right?"

"Oh, without a doubt."

He scratches the stubble on his chin and runs a hand through his hair. He's probably only mid-twenties, maybe right out of university, but still. I tilt my head and try to imagine meeting him somewhere else, like on a beach holiday, like if I agreed to go to Nevis with Arabella and met Galen and he weren't my teacher, if that would seem so bad. Kind of. Maybe not. I don't know. "It's not my problem." Oops. I said that part out loud. "I mean, is it a problem that . . ." I've got nothing. I can't even fake a point.

"That you'll need to demonstrate a clear desire to progress in order to make it into the finals?"

"Is it?"

"No—it shouldn't be a problem for you. Unless you completely slack off, which you Americans seem unlikely to do."

"Good, then. Great."

I can't shake the image of him with Keena—and it makes sense. He's all about powerful women, likes us to have these strong voices, stand tall, all that. He closes the piano and gets his room keys out. Usually, he's one for after-class chatter, but today he's clearly rushing.

"In a hurry?" I ask and lead the way out the door.

"Ah, I'm, I'm . . . I've got . . ." He stutters, hems, haws, and blushes beneath his tawny cool five-o'clock shadow. I want to fill in the blank with *young little illegal hottie* but I don't. I watch his face to find the right thing to say. "I have an important meeting. A tutorial."

Oh, a tutorial. I can only imagine what kind of lesson that will be. I can't help the smirk, but my voice remains calm. "Well, have a fantastic meeting!"

He starts off one way and I go the other way, out toward the back stairwell, but then he comes back. "Did I mention the good news?" he asks.

"No," I say. Maybe he'll come clean about Keena, risking his job for the sake of his love, setting an example I can cite when I—if I—I come clean to Arabella.

"Sublime Records—ring a bell?"

"No, not really," I say. Then I think about it. "Are they the ones with a sort of swervy loop as their logo?" I demonstrate the swervy part by making my pointer finger dance.

"Yes. Rather like a fleur-de-lis upside down."

"Right—that's a better way of describing it." From all the way down the hall, I can see the bright red toe of Keena's cowboy boots. She pokes her head out from behind a wall, checking on what's taking her loovahhh so long, and our eyes meet. It's all I can do to keep from busting up laughing.

"As you know, we do try to further careers here and through some sort of connection or other, it seems we've got two record execs from Sublime coming to watch the upcoming Choir performance—the one in Covent Garden."

"At the Transport Museum, you mean?"

"That's the one." He nods. "Just thought I'd warn you. Might be a real leg up in the industry. In our faculty notes we were told Sublime might be scouting for NRT."

NRT = new raw talent. New = singers no one has seen or heard before who are hot, Raw = singers untouched by overdone demo reels or too much preparation who are hot, Talent = singers who are naturally gifted enough not to need a shitload of work so they can rise immediately to smash single success, that is, if they are hot.

"Wow. Thanks for telling me—no added pressure or anything."

"There's always someone watching. May as well gain exposure to the industry."

"Point taken," I say. Then I see Keena doing a cancan kick from behind the wall and have to turn on my heel quickly so I don't crack up. "Sublime Records. Sounds . . . potentially sublime."

Galen French gives a wave and then makes his way back down the hall to my friend, to give her a . . . tutorial.

"Which is better, this? Or this?" Arabella pivots to show me her two options.

"I like the blue one," I say. "The straps are sturdier."

"Love," Arabella sighs, "it's sunbathing, not lifeguard training—I don't think sturdiness counts."

"Fine, then opt for the halter thingy."

"This one?" Arabella displays a yellow barely there tankini. I nod. "You're right. It's good with a tan. Which I will so have."

"I never tan," I say. "It's the curse of the fair-skinned. I always loved that sun-kissed look, but it just ain't gonna happen."

"Yeah, you're more the reading-under-the-umbrella-shade girl."

"Yup." I try on one of Arabella's sarongs over my jeans. "Is this cool like I'm so cutting edge or lame like some girl at the back of the magazine demonstrating how not to dress?"

"The first, I think. You're cooler than you think."

I roll my eyes at her and tie the top of her string (and by string I mean floss) bikini and watch her inspect all sides before she commits to bringing it to Nevis. The trip's not for another month, but she's insisting on making sure everything's perfect.

"Do you want to try on some swimming costumes?" she asks and drops the suit in her bag. Then she looks at my face for signs of travel trepidation. "You are still coming, aren't you?"

"Totally," I say. "I just have to convince my dad. Plus, it'll take me all of ten minutes to throw my stuff in a bag."

"Just let my parents cover for you," she says. "You know they will."

"Arabella . . . I'm sure they would. But I can't just leave the country without telling him. I mean, what if—"

"What if something happened with Mable?"

"Well, yeah."

"Whether you go to Nevis or not, something could happen. It's not decided by your actions."

"Thanks, Sartre."

"I'm just telling you to take a breather—forget the cold dreary

London of winter and come away with us." Arabella tries parting her hair on the other side, considering its merits.

"Who is this *us,* anyway? Aside from Toby."

Arabella plops down next to me on the floor, pulling a turtleneck sweater (aka poloneck jumper) over her cold self. "Here, try this one on. I picked it up for you at One oh One." 101 = Arabella and her set's latest love, a sort of fashion emporium meets lounge where you can plan on meeting for coffee and wind up leaving with hundreds of pounds worth of scarves, pants, or, in this case, "resort wear."

I shimmy into the suit—it's a two-piece with cotton-candy-pink surfer-style shorts and a top that's a darker pink, almost raspberry. "Hey, this isn't bad."

Arabella agrees. "You look really good." She picks at the peeling polish on her toes. "So to answer your question—you, me, Toby, Bettina Grimly, Tim Webber, Googie, Flask, Wormy, and Anastasia, though she might beg off due to exams."

"Do you realize how many of those people have whacked-out names?"

Arabella nods. "Seriously. But Wormy, you know, it's not like she wanted that name or anything." Wormy got the moniker after wearing unfortunately too-short short shorts one summer, and the string of her tampon escaped and was spotted dangling, swaying, in the beach breeze. The rest is history. Flask is a no-brainer (both in name and in reality), always swigging from his engraved flask. I've met Bettina in passing, half Italian, beautiful, the usual. Anastasia's a duchess or something, studying at St. Andrew's in Scotland and has that UK mix of glamour meets Welly boots.

"Sounds like fun," I say.

"Oh, and Nick Cooper. Who could forget him? He'll be there."

I change back into my winter clothing: straight-legged jeans, Irish jumper that itches if I don't wear a layer underneath—today's layer is the Brown University T-shirt I got when visiting Lila Lawrence—it's already faded from multiple wearings and washings. "He seems really . . ."

"Nice? He is. We're all going for lunch at his place on Sunday. You should come."

I pull my hair out from the sweater, trying to calm its static. "Don't you have rehearsals? And a paper?"

"Yes, Mummy, I do, but the lunch is for only two hours." Arabella undoes the bathing-suit top and slides it out from under her shirt without disrobing. "I'll RSVP for you, okay?"

I nod. "Why not?"

CHAPTER THIRTEEN

♡

"It's me." Mable's voice on the other end of the phone is a welcome surprise; worth rushing through the door into the flat after a long afternoon of Choir practice.

"Mable, how are you . . ." I'm out of breath, and let her talk so I can put my bag down, kick off my shoes, and stop panting.

"Good. Really good, actually. Your dad is busy looking on Expedia as we speak, trying to hunt down the best fare." She whispers, "He thinks I'm calling your dorm."

"So you're coming?" I stand up and dance around the empty flat, flicking on lights and smiling as I go. "I'm so excited—When? Where will you stay? And for how long? You have to stay long enough to—"

"Wait—slow down, there. I think . . . Let me just check." I can hear her paging through her planner, "It's either the first or the second week of April. It depends on your dad and Louisa."

"Louisa?"

"Uh-oh, did I slip up?"

"No," I say. "I know my dad's been 'seeing someone' . . . I just forgot her name temporarily."

"Ah, Freudian."

"No, memory lapse is more like it. Anyway, is she nice? What's she like?"

Mable exhales deeply. "Louisa's very good for him. Really. She's soft-spoken and sweet, with a wacky sense of humor—the kind of person who could laugh hard enough during a sermon or a play that she'd have to leave—your type of person. And she loves books."

"She's the one with the bookstore?"

"It's on Craigie Street, behind that restaurant we went to once."

Silence. It's weird to think of this whole new person in my dad's life, whom Mable knows, whom I don't—whom probably Lindsay Parrish has met at our house. But Louisa can't be worse than Ms. Thompson, my shitty ex-math teacher slash Dad's old girlfriend—or his evil prepster from last summer.

"I guess I should meet her—Louisa, that is," I say.

"I'm sure you will. She's not coming with us in April or anything—that's just for us, you know, for family."

"April's still so far away . . ." Then I realize how whiny I sound. "But still, that's great, and just tell me as soon as you know. You'll miss *Damn Yankees,* Arabella's play, not like that's why you were coming, but . . . so you're feeling well, for real?"

"Yes, for real. It's amazing how good you can feel when they stop filling your body and bloodstream with poison!" She laughs. "Yup, I'm slowly getting back into the swing of things. I have a compression sleeve on, which I have to wear for a while . . . and Miles has been a huge help, taking care of Slave to the Grind for me, dealing with the distributors. Things are good with us, too. He likes my peach fuzz."

"Oh, I can't wait to see your hair!" I say. "It must be really soft."

"It is . . . but it's so cold here I've been wearing that red cashmere hat you sent me. It'll come in handy on the ferry. Miles and I are heading to the Vineyard this weekend to check on everything there."

I sigh and sink into the cushy couch, tucking a velvet throw pillow behind my back. "The Vineyard . . . say hi to it for me—the island, the café . . ."

"Those cute boys . . . ?"

"Mable!" I pretend to scold her. "I wasn't even thinking about that aspect of island life!"

"Well, I was," she says.

"What do you mean?"

She sips at a drink, probably green tea, as she switched from her beloved coffee during the radiation. "Did Chris tell you we went for a burger?"

I nod like she can see me. "He mentioned it in an email."

"So, the lowdown is—we met at Bartley's, of course—in the middle of my meatfest, I saw this guy sitting in the corner of the room."

"At the small tables?" I prop my feet up on the coffee table and proceed to knock a stack of magazines onto the floor.

"No, it was a four-top, but the place was empty. He was there alone."

"And?" One by one I pick up the magazines, pausing to stare at a *Travel and Leisure* with its full-color shot of a white sandy beach: Nevis.

"And he was reading some book about the mythology of wealth in America. A real laugh riot, no doubt."

"Okay, fine, but why is this relevant?"

"Sorry, right. So Chris and I look at him and I'm positive—totally sure—that I've seen him before. Poor Chris had to spend the entire meal with me going through the ways I could know the guy."

"So what'd you come up with?"

"That guy—the one from Edgartown. Labor Day? The gorgeous boating guy?"

I feel my breath catch in my throat. Lurch. Stomach twist. "Charlie," I say. "His name was Charlie." Charlie who wouldn't take my dad's money after rescuing us when our sailboat got stuck. Charlie who kissed me and made me forget myself. Charlie who talked to me all night by the fireside.

"*Is*—his name still *is* Charlie. And he said to say hi."

"Oh, no, you didn't—you actually spoke to him?"

"Jesus, it's not like he's the president or something. I waved and he came by the table when he was done. He knew who I was."

"What was he doing in Harvard Square, anyway?" I ask.

"Oh, what, first you can't believe I deigned to speak to the guy, and now you're wondering why I didn't give Charlie the third degree?"

"No. No. Never mind. I don't care what he was doing. He deserted me at that dinner, remember?"

"Oh, I remember," Mable says. "I'm glad you're not pining for him still . . . but he is something."

"Yeah," I say. "Something."

"So," Mable says, "this calling card is good for eighteen more minutes. Tell me what else is going on."

"Well," I start. "The record company that's coming to my singing performance or the guy I'm falling for? Which first?"

"You pick," she says and it's all so normal, so easy, I forget she's even been sick, it's like I have her here with me, and nothing else matters.

Six hours and twenty minutes spent in one position, and not the fun kind. I stretch my back and try to uncrink my neck. My twenty pages (that's about nineteen minutes a page—not bad—granted, it includes footnotes) concerning Ophelia, Cordelia, and Helena, and Hermia (aka Shakespeare's girls) is finally completed. I didn't want to do the procrastinatory route with Nick Cooper's lunch party on for tomorrow, my clandestine photo shoot with Asher planned for later, and the Bank Holiday Weekend coming up.

I leave the library feeling like a mole emerging into the sunshine. I shield my eyes, open a can of Coke, and make my way to the flat to shower with clear academic conscience. On my way, I swing by the academic buildings and drop my completed paper in the faculty lounge, lest I lose it or forget it somewhere.

Inside, the door, which is usually locked on the weekends, is half open. (Note my optimism—it's not half closed. I am so centered. Thank you, Body.) I can hear Galen French's voice, animated even though he's attempting to speak quietly. "That's not the point, Paul!"

"Yes, it bloody well is," says the other voice—Paul—which could be (a) a Paul I don't know or (b) Paul Trambly, one of the drama profs, or (c) Paul Isaacs, the head of the entire LADAM–St. Paul's combined program. Any of the three are enough to keep me from doing more than sliding my paper into the collection box and pausing long enough to tie my sneaker (read: eavesdrop just a tad).

"She'll be expected to leave permanently," voice of Paul says.

"And you think that's reasonable, considering," Galen French answers.

"Yes. It's the rules—and whether we agree to the measure of her guilt, she's still broken trust. She's crossed the line."

Oh my God. Sounds like Keena's foray into faculty relations have gone terribly wrong. I walk home, opting to stretch my legs and get my ass to wake up from it's butt nap. Should I tell Keena what I heard? She must know. And what would happen to Poppy Massa-Tonclair if her daughter were expelled for bedding down with a voice teacher? Now that's a novel right there.

With the hot water on full blast, I stand underneath the spray of the shower and pick a song to sing. It's always interesting what song pops into your head, like a book I read once in which a girl deciphers people's emotional states by what songs get stuck. What pops out of my mouth is Stevie Wonder's version of "Signed, Sealed, Delivered." It's a good song, and one he makes better, I think. It's one of the songs I got from the mix that Jacob made for me last year. *Like a fool I went and stayed too long, now I'm wondering if your love's still strong . . .* I sing it and try to disconnect it from Jacob, for whom it would have more meaning now than when he first put it on that mix. It makes me feel sad and wistful to think about Jacob. He's this person I could have had so much with, but the truth is that we've spent more time apart than we have hanging out. And the Jacob I knew as a sophomore probably isn't the same after a summer away, a term in Switzerland, and a brief but torrid affair with superswine Parrish. But I guess I'm not the same, either. But I am, sort of, so who knows. Plus, we haven't had *any* contact since I've been here. After our emails last semester I would have predicted otherwise. But I'm not about to start the hellos, especially not after the dirt Lindsay's no doubt spewed.

I dry off, sitting on the edge of the bathtub while I towel my hair so it's only damp, not dripping. It's fine, as far as red hair goes, less the coarse kind, more like an Irish setter's (yes, I take pride in comparing my hair to that of a canine), and it doesn't take long until I'm ready to go. I'm supposed to meet Arabella by HEL, where she went for coffee with Toby and Clementine. For some reason, I can't picture the upper-crust Tobias with the rise-up-from-nada Clem, but I suppose now that she's been "in society," not to mention famous, he'll buy it—it seems like without those two key items of cache, Toby would have no interest whatsoever.

Tobias drives us in his Astin Martin to Nick Cooper's house. Nick is at Cambridge University and lives there, but from what I gather has frequent weekends at his parent's house at St. George's Hill in Surrey, which is about twenty-five miles from London.

"It's an early Tarrant House," Tobias explains to me as if I know what this means. Note to self: Ask the Google gods. "Apparently, when the Coopers bought it, it was in dire need of refurbishment, but I tell you what—it's lovely now. Just perfect for house parties."

"Sounds nice," I say.

Arabella turns around from the front seat and says, "They've got loads of space, so if you want, you can stay the night—I think we might. If not, we'll drop you back at the train, k?" Her okays always sound like the single letter.

Nick's house is as described: beautiful. Not in the overwhelming *Lifestyles of the Rich and Famous* way, like Bracker's Common, not the posh rebuilds on the Vineyard, just a comfy (albeit very large and stately) country place.

We pull up to a double garage and park. A quick hello to Nick's parents inside results in a self-guided tour (six bedrooms, two staircases, cozy library with photos everywhere) through the very lived-in house. Outside, I meet up with the rest of the "youngsters" as his mother called us, who are all getting liquored and fed in the summerhouse. Of course, it's not summer, so everyone's in layers of jackets and scarves, with rosy cheeks.

I proceed to air kiss and double kiss a bunch of people I vaguely know and then some I don't know at all and then cold-cheeked, humble, gorgeous Nick.

"Love, so glad you could join us," he says. He hands me wine, which I accept despite the fact that I've got more work to do when I get back to London later. "Come sit. Flask—move your arse and let the lady sit."

Flask, with his namesake in hand, begrudgingly removes himself from the wicker chair and I sit down. Nick promptly brings over a woven blanket and drapes it across my lap. I smile at the special treatment but then notice that all the females have blankets either wrapped around their shoulders or on their legs like I do.

"Bukowski," a bloke named Alex says. "Like the writer?"

"Spelled the same, yes, but I'm not related, if that's what you mean."

"Oy—Cooper!" Alex waves Nick over and accosts him as only the drunken will do. "This girl's just like you, Cooper. A literary off-spring. If not by heritage, then by name." Alex then sees a tray of sandwiches and dives for them, leaving me with Nick. Again.

"I don't know any writers named Nick Cooper," I say.

"Oh, no, there aren't—at least not that I'm aware of . . ." Nick offers me a mini quiche, which I accept and eat in one bite. Yum. "But my full name's Nick Adams Cooper."

I note the absence of roman numerals. Maybe he's not part of the Cartier set (Cartiers are the crowd who all have a I, II, III, and so on after their names). Then I think for a second.

"Nick Adams. As in the Hemingway stories?" I smile. Ah, Mr. Chaucer would be proud.

Nick nods. "My mum is a great believer in his books. His writing is so clear, but there's always more happening under the surface than you know at first."

"Like Raymond Carver?" I ask. Nick turns his ring around, a habit I noticed at Arabella's flat. He's got one of the family crest rings that are worn on the pinky by both sexes; the family crests (a deer, a shield, some random Scottish thing or tree with curling branches) are a silent reminder of just how old the money or family name is. One of the guests motions for Nick to come over, and we end up inside around a large oval table in the sunroom. Winter light shines through the plate-glass windows, hitting the polished concrete floor and glinting off the sterling-silver flatware.

Anyone can watch *The Princess Diaries* or *Pretty Woman* and learn which fork to use or how to walk like royalty, but actually assimilating to the upper class is something that you can't just study from film.

At Bracker's, or at the mega-mansions handed down to Hadley's finest, it's obvious there's a set of unwritten rules, ones that wouldn't make it into a movie because they are far too subtle. But at Nick Cooper's, everything's easy—the tone, the chatter, all the edges blurred so nothing's defined. Creamy parsnip soup eaten, we move on to roast chicken with "new potatoes" (the little red kind) and *haricots verte* (green beans but French), then right into the best dessert I've ever had: sticky toffee pudding. Each person has their own little ramekin of the stuff and the caramel scent rises up to me. With the light in the room, the sweet and cinnamony smell, this image will be a photograph in my mind. Just as I'm thinking this, Nick Cooper catches my eye and we stay like that, just for a second longer than normal.

As Nick had mentioned at Arabella's flat the night I met him, each time a name is dropped, his mother flings a spoon onto the ground. With Tobias at the table, this has led to Nick's father having to go get more silverware from the kitchen just for the sake of throwing it onto the concrete, where it lands with a clang, causing all of us to laugh. Nick has been guilty only once, when he mentioned meeting the nephew of Bertram Russell, the philosopher. Not to be outdone, Tobias pipes in with, "Wasn't he at that party given by Lady Piper Fuller?" Arabella keeps smiling as Mrs. Cooper cries, "Yet again, Toby!" and pelts a spoon over her shoulder.

"I can't help it, honestly," Toby says with his wide grin. He is the life of the party in many ways, always picking up conversation if it lags, telling amusing (if name-laden) stories from around the globe. I can see why Arabella likes him. In some ways, he's like the society version of her dad—big, brash, funny. It's ironic that she has to hide her relationship from her parents when they'd probably like Tobias, if he weren't titled and everything.

"Are you ready, then?" Nick asks. He has politely offered to drive me to the train station so I can catch the 4:05 back to Waterloo.

"Yup, thanks. Again, thanks very much for having me." I hold up my little recipe cards from Mrs. Cooper, who wrote them down, along with the names of two books she thought I'd like, and I slide the items into my bag so I can add them to my journal later.

The train station could be a set for a 1930s film, where the hero is going off somewhere, leaving the girl behind. In this case, it's the reverse, and I'm heading out, leaving a pensive Nick Cooper. If things were different, if I'd met him somewhere else, some other time . . . Never mind. I didn't. He looks at me as the train approaches.

"I gather you've got something going with someone," he says.

"Something underneath the surface, you mean?"

"Yes, like that." He bites his bottom lip and runs a hand though his hair, which, true to his English birthright, flops into his eyes just enough to warrant swooning. "But I did want to say—if you hadn't—if I weren't treading on someone else's . . ."

I nod and the train slows down. "I hear what you're saying. I like talking to you, too. And your parents are really cool."

"So maybe I'll see you around?" he asks.

"I should think so," I say and feel terribly British. I want to add *I hope so,* but I don't, even though I mean it only in a friendly way. Probably.

I stand on the train; Nick gives me a kiss on both cheeks and says, "Asher's a lucky guy."

Lurch (my stomach, not the train). "What?" I ask.

"I know him. We were at school together. I saw his face when you and I were doing dishes at Arabella's." My face clearly shows that I'm shocked to have been discovered. "Don't worry—I wouldn't ever say anything. He's a good guy."

"Thanks," I say to Nick as the train starts to move. He waves and I'm not sure if I meant to say thanks for keeping it under wraps, thanks for lunch, or thanks for not trying anything, since I don't know how I would've reacted.

CHAPTER FOURTEEN

At Ed's Easy Diner at midnight that night, Asher tries to feed me one more sweet potato fry.

"I can't." I swat it away. "It's physically impossible."

"Oh, go on, then," he says, but when I shake my head he eats it himself. "So, tell me more about this lunch at Cooper's, then."

"I told you," I say. "It was fun—very, um, English, I think. Relaxed. His mother threw spoons every time Tobias opened his mouth." Asher laughs. "Nick told me you guys are friends?"

Asher drains his Coke. "We went to school together—not really friends so much as lived in the same dorm." Asher looks like he's about to go on but doesn't.

"What's the story there?" I ask and take his hand.

"The story is that he did something for me once, and for that I will always be grateful. And then I, in turn, did something for him. So we have an unwritten, unspoken—until now—code of honor between us."

"Care to elaborate?" I ask. The code of honor—how *Three Musketeers* (not the candy bar, the book), how dashing.

"Not really," Asher says. "We all have our little histories, don't we?"

★   ★   ★

Asher walks me back to the empty flat. "Should I come in?" he asks.

"Sure," I say.

Asher puts his arms around my waist and grins.

We spend the next hour playing DJ, taking turns trying to find the cheesiest lyrics from the albums in Monti's old collection. From Cilla Black to The Pet Shop Boys to Sheena Easton, the records span two and a half decades of pop, funk, and flat-out fabulously bad music. Then Asher says, "Wait. Let me put this on. This one's really good."

"I can name this song in two seconds," I say. The trouble is, it's "Signed, Sealed, Delivered," the Stevie Wonder version that I totally connect to Jacob now, so when Asher tries to dance with me, I stamp on the ground a little too hard, which makes the needle jump.

"Damn, sorry. It must be scratched."

"Here—let me put one on," I say. I go over and out on the fifth track of *Clementine Highstreet's Greatest Hits*. (It's so funny to me that people you've never heard of have the best-of albums when you can't even think of *one* song they've done, let alone enough to warrant an entire greatest hits). "Be Here, Be Now" plays, its crackling only adding to the dim light, the way Asher kisses my neck. We sway and kiss, the words swirling around us: *Stay with me, be here, now, baby—my heart is a pocket, you're searching for lost change, I'm the one you're looking for . . .* Not bad for a song that I will connect to this moment. But then the last line, which I haven't really paid attention to comes on as Asher undoes the buttons on my shirt: *Someday you'll leave, let time pull you away, and I'll be left with only thoughts of yesterday, but for now just stay, be here, be now.*

In the morning, I wake up and just look at him, wondering if I should I have said yes, yes I'll sleep with him—not resting sleep, the other kind. But then I'm glad I didn't. With my luck, I'd lose my virginity and Arabella would bust in and discover us, or the house would catch on fire or Tobias would use his flat key and shout out to the world. Not yet. Not now.

Dear Dad,

In one hour I'm leaving to meet Arabella to shop for Nevis! Thank you a million times for saying yes. Nick Cooper's parents will be great chaperones, really. And I'll send postcards . . . But I still have to get through the SATs before we go. Plus, I need to do an outline for my project with Poppy Massa-Tonclair—she liked the idea of a personal narrative. (You can tell Mr. Chaucer I got the idea from him.)

My name to you, L.

PS. From your latest email, sounds like Louisa's really great—looking forward to meeting her. Ask her if she's read Alain de Botton and what she thinks of his ideas.

Dear Chris,

I just wrote my dad and told him Nick Cooper's parents are chaperoning the Nevis trip, which is essentially true in that they have some villa there, but I think it's chaperoning in the loosest sense of the word (i.e., come and tell us if someone's bleeding or needs to be airlifted, but otherwise, you're on your own). Fun in the sun. But I wish Asher were invited.

I also told Dad I'm psyched to meet his current flame, Louisa, but I'm actually kind of dreading it—by all accounts she's great, which in some ways might be harder to fathom than his other two (lame!) girlfriends . . .

Anyway, I'm about to go meet Arabella for an hour of shopping before we head out to Bracker's Common for the long weekend! Think of me while you deal with midterms (insert pity face here). I'll be trying to contain my excitement (and failing) when I watch the Celebrity Life shoot. (Think me, Mick Jagger, Tom Jones, Paul—I mean, Sir Paul—hanging out, or rather, think of me fetching them tea. Heh.) Actually, I need to study study study this weekend for the dreaded SATs.

I bumped into your crush, Alistair the American today—as per your wishes, I poked and prodded a little. Which of the following info did I glean? Fill in the oval completely to show your answer) (a) Alistair is single (b) he was way into you (c) he was kind of serious about that Cali visit—he asked me about UCLA again as a subtle way of mentioning we should stop by (d) all of the above. Yes, D is the correct answer . . .

And for all this info I want the following: to know what Jacob's like now (however you wish to define this), a jpeg of some of the yearbook, and more scoop on the Lindsay Parrish situation, plus this Chilton Pomroy girl. Chili? Chilly? Will the name insanity never end? And what happened with Haverford, your straight-boy quest? There's stuff happening here, too. One of my friends might be heading for a faculty fracas—still waiting for the details . . . and I wrote another song! Or, the beginning of one—more journal fodder—if those pages could talk. Actually, thank God they can't. Good luck w/ exams & your boys. I'm going to email shiny Lila Lawrence now—have been OOT (out of touch) but she finally wrote, so now it's up to me! LLS—Big xxxs, L.

Dear Lila,

I know, I know, it's been way too long. I'm glad you ended the email strike! I've been busy, too, so I get what you mean. Art History—sounds like a perfect major to declare. I'm sure you're great at it (and even more reason now for you to head to Paris for a semester, oui?).

I nearly peed in my pants (okay, slight exag.) when I read your email. Let me get this straight— Henry my (not my, but you know) little prepster from the Vineyard wrote to me? I totally forgot he thought I went to Brown with you . . . but impressive that (a) he remembers me (and my Ivy League lie) and (b) that the mail reached you.

The fact that a postcard was delivered to me at Brown University where I am not even a student is testament to the wonder of the postal system—good thing you rescued it from the lost letters pile. Should I write him back? Do I have to deal w/ it now or just wait until I inevitably bump into him on Martha's Vineyard? Speaking of which, what are your summer plans? If all goes well, I'll be working w/ Mable in Edgartown—

maybe w/ my English boyfriend along for the ride . . . not kidding. He's amazing—but will fill you in on details later. Tell me more about your love life. I'd never have pegged you for such a single girl . . . Write back soon—and have a fun spring break. You said you're heading some-place warm—which tropical place are you jetting off to? Miss you—L.

All my emails out of the way, I tube to Knightsbridge to meet Ara-bella at Harvey Nichols. We fondle ouishies, the new Japanese shawls made of some space-age material; then she tries on the newest shade of NARS lipstick and I head to the shoe department to ogle the bal-let flats. I can't shake the image of me in London in spring, record-ing contract (after the Sublime Records people sign me, of course), hottie boyfriend, perfectly simple skirt and top, hair clean, work done, with these shoes to complete the picture. When I turn the shoes over, however, they make the whole vision even less of a real-ity; they cost a very reasonable three hundred fifty pounds (nearly double in dollars).

I'm still fondling the flats when Arabella sidles over and picks up a pointy-toed version of the same shoe, considering an icy blue color.

"I know," she says flatly. No shoe pun intended.

"Sorry?" I ask.

"God, you sound so English."

"I'm not trying to," I say and examine a cream-tipped loafer with a heel—not my scene.

"Well, you do." She sounds so bitchy I have no idea why. "These shoes are revolting."

"What's your problem?" I ask and try to balance the shoe back on its little pedestal only to have it topple off.

"The problem is . . . I know. I know about you and Asher, and before you even think of opening your mouth to defend or deny, just
know that he knows I know and now you know that I know."

"That's a lot of know-ledge," I say. Heart speed beyond cardiovas-
cular conditioning mode. More like shit hitting fan mode. Then I try
a different way of averting confrontation. "Why didn't you say something sooner?"

"I was going to—I had it set, but then, that day when I got back
to the flat was the day you were on the line with Mable and then . . ."
Insert drama voice . . . "Coincidentally . . . Asher was there at the front
door, which only confirmed my suspicions. Then I heard a message
he left for you."

"Maybe it was for you?" Pathetic, Love.

Arabella's cheeks flush, her tone rises, and she pushes her hair out
of her eyes, launching a cascade of hair onto the other side of her
face. (Note to Vidal: Why do we all look *so* different with hair parted
on the not-usual side? Note to self: Do I make such superficial observations in times of turmoil to protect myself from feeling too
much—survey says, ding ding ding. "Love, the one fucking thing I
asked of you when you got here—the one person I told you to steer
clear of—and you just couldn't do it."

My eyes study the patterns on the floor. Sunlight and shadow create a hexagonal prism with bits of rainbow, all of which hold me cap-
tive until I find the right words. "Okay. I would never go against what
you said—you know that."

"But you—"

"Can I finish?" Arabella nods and I go on, "The first day I got to
Bracker's, back before Christmas, when you weren't there—and no,
I'm not blaming you for not being there and that's why all this happened—but it is part of it. You were off with Tobias and I was in this
new place, feeling . . ."

"Like a slag?"

Major eye rolling from me and then, "No. I don't know. I felt bewildered and tired and like I was ready for anything. You have no idea how different it is being here." I breathe in, watch her face for signs she's ready to bolt, but she keeps listening. "So I went for a walk . . ."

"The teacup thing? Is this what you're about to describe? Asher told me, and for once, I don't want to sit through one of your start-to-finish stories."

Ouch. And ouch again. "Hey, don't turn this into a whole pickfest, because I can do the same to you—I just thought we were well beyond that . . . My point is—skipping the details—Asher and I connected well before the warning." News flash—I am not a whore! I am not a bad friend! "Obviously, if I'd known it was such a big deal I would have prevented it."

"So by prevention you mean it's inevitable."

"You're getting semantic now?" I shake my head. "Fine. Yeah, I guess I do mean that. Because we like each other and I guess it feels unstoppable. Like aging or decreased lung capacity from smoking or"—I stare at her with my mouth twisted in annoyance—"dating someone who treats you like crap and finding out that they won't change. Ever. Even though they're the life of the party and fun guy."

"Just don't . . ." Arabella raises her palm in a traffic warden attempt to avert further dumpage. "But that's what I'm saying. If it is *so* powerful between you and my brother, then how can you say that if you'd heard from me earlier it would've changed everything?"

"Because." I drop my hands at my sides, giving up. "Because you're my best friend—and I respect you and don't want to piss you off."

"And yet . . ."

"I know. I know I did the reverse of that . . . But I still feel that if you'd told me sooner I would have been able to (a) at least know who the guy was and (b) decide not to get involved—even though staying away from him would have been hard."

An uneasy five minutes of silence go by. I examine various tops and skirts, sliding the hangers, so I appear at least to be doing something other than waiting for her to speak.

"Right then."

"What?"

Arabella shrugs and gets her hair into place, securing it with a blue elastic. We bought a pack of multicolored ones from the kid section at Peter Jones, the posh department store near the flat. The bottom of my bag is now littered with red, fuchsia, orange, and azure circles for those spur-of-the-moment hair-care needs. "There's not much else to say."

"ButwhatamIsupposedtodo?" I ask and it comes out all smushed like one word.

"Well, for one thing, you can talk so I can understand you." She grins but only from the side of her mouth—not really happy, but not on the verge of chucking a heeled boot at me, either. "I *think* that I'm a big enough person to get past this, if that's what you mean."

I open my mouth to tell her how glad I am when she uses a single finger (not the middle one) to shut me up. Arabella puts on her stage American voice, very OTT (over the top) 1950s perky. "Before you get all *Oh, let's go out on a double date and drink milk shakes together . . .*" I roll my eyes. It's just as annoying when she does the faux accent as when I do it with Brit-speak. "I'm neither here nor there."

"So basically I'm not supposed to talk about my life with you."

"It's not like Asher's your entire existence."

"No, but I mean, it's either okay or it's not. And if it *is,* then I have to be able to at least mention that *part* of my existence." I flip over the price tag on the T-shirt I'm considering getting and instantly regret it. Somehow, I don't foresee ever spending a hundred dollars on one white tee—it seems morally vile.

"First, it doesn't have to be okay or not—it could in fact be in the middle, which is where I stand. And second, I just don't want to be held responsible."

"Oh, is that what all this is about?" I ask. "Just that you don't want me to blame you if he acts like a dick or winds up breaking my heart?" I say it casually, at a normal pitch, but then one of those floor polisher machines comes by, making all sorts of noise, and I have to shout to be heard, so the break my heart part comes out echoing— too loud, too focused, too unpleasant for both of us.

"Spot on." Arabella wipes the corners of her mouth with the points of her thumb and first finger, then leaves them on her lower lip.

"I won't—how could I blame you?" I shake my head and put a consolatory arm around her. "I promise, okay?" Of course, now I'm filled with paranoia about whether this is a pattern that she knows well. Maybe Asher is all about hooking up with his sister's friends and she's had enough of it after watching him break hearts and buck confidences.

"It doesn't matter—as long as you know what you're in for . . ." she says.

After we leave Harvey Nics, we walk to the tube station. We're going in the same direction, but different stops. The train door opens and we step up, being careful to mind the gap between track and train.

"What do you mean about as long as I know what I'm getting into?" I ask. There are no seats, so I find a sweaty pole on which to steady myself. Arabella opts for the hands-free approach, her feet on either side of her shopping bag. When the train lurches forward, so does she, and I pull her back.

Over her shoulder, she clarifies. "Asher's always the same. Tobias might not be the best boyfriend in the world, but he's a prize compared to Asher. He leads girls on, using and wooing them—even smart gorgeous girls like you—and then drops them."

"So that's what you predict will happen?" My voice is calm, but inside I'm worried. I have to either trust her (and she's known him her whole life) or my instincts (which, though often muted by my brain, tell me this is real—it's something, something important).

"One successful night in the lake house at Bracker's and you, too, can phone endlessly in tears wondering where he's gone, what happened—and cry every time you hear your song." She looks at me. "You do have a song by now, right?"

I think of Clementine Highstreet's vocals and nod. "Well, that's your opinion."

"I know, but I'm putting it out there. Oh—here's my stop." She stands in front of the doors, waiting for them to part. "We can just be normal now, as long as you're aware of the situation."

"Fine," I say even though it's not fine—or wouldn't be if what Arabella says is true.

"Fine," she says back to me even though she's kind of stuck, too. If she's right, I'll get really hurt, and if she's wrong—well, who knows. All I can do is hope that she is.

"Have a good weekend," she says. "I'll be here."

I know she means it, that she'll be at the flat (albeit with Tobias), and be there for me—no matter what happens. I just hope I don't have to take her up on her offer.

CHAPTER FIFTEEN

On the train to Bracker's I read my journal, flipping through entries from when I first got to Hadley Hall, then to unfinished songs, then the one I wrote about Jacob, the one I started when I found out Mable was sick, the cringe-worthy poem I attempted when I met Charlie, liked him, then was left hanging on the Vineyard. I've been adding to my list of British slang, so I tack on *rare as hens' teeth* (very uncommon, nonexistent) and *rare as rocking horse shit* (same thing, but funnier). Then I jot down *milkers,* Toby's oh so lovely way of talking about breasts.

I take a taxi from the train station to Bracker's Common. The house is just the same as it was: huge, heavenly, and homey. The only difference is that on the main lawn, an Oriental carpet the size of Massachusetts is spread out, topped with big metal lights, people holding those light-deflector thingies they use in model shoots, and the familiar faces I see belong to the Rock and Roll Hall of Famers who sip tea, crack jokes, talk about their recent travels and kids.

"It's so totally otherworldy to be here," I say to Asher, who is in full PA mode, dashing between one camera and another, setting up shots and then breezing by to give a hand squeeze. He nods but can't talk to me. I stand off the carpet, near the heat lamps, which are warm enough that all the stars are wearing summer clothes; this is for the August cover of the magazine.

Clementine waltzes over to me, bringing with her kisses, accolades, and Martin Gregory Eisenstein, the indie film guy who produced all those Sundance winners: *If This Is Life, Between Hours, Grapefruit Moon,* etc.

"You've just got to meet him," Clem says and shoves me forward so I'm shaking hands with Martin.

"Hi," I say to him.

"Oh, hi! Finally we meet," he responds, like I'm someone—someone famous, that is.

"Isn't she lovely?" Clem asks, hopefully rhetorically. "Oh, bastard. I've got to go—that's my signal. They're trying to frame us in the best possible light . . . It's getting harder and harder!"

"Are you a musician, too?" I ask Martin Eisenstein.

"No, God no. My wife's the one over there, in red." I'm about to say "Lady in Red," like that infamous slow-dance song, but the singer, Chris de Burgh, is actually here, so it'd be really lame.

"She looks familiar," I say. I can't place her though.

"Teeny, née Christina Fuller. She modeled in the seventies, then sang that song—"

" 'All the Queen's Wishes'—yeah, now I remember," I say.

"That's way before your time," Martin says. Then he puts his hands on his hips and says, "Wait—go back. Say that same thing." I do, even though I feel ridiculous. "Yes. Now, I know you've done voice work. Clem mentioned that."

"Just local stuff, back in Boston."

"I'm doing a film just now—we're in post-production at Ealing Studios—but one of the girls couldn't nail down the American accent. She either sounds Southern or like an import from Britain . . . Any chance you'd like to dub?"

In my head: Um, yes, jump up and down, scream and shout! In reality: "That sounds really interesting!"

"It's not a huge part, but maybe a day or two?"

"Where do I sign?" I joke, but Martin actually responds with, "We'll get the contracts to your people on Monday—you can come on Tuesday."

My people. That's funny. I am my people. Tuesday. Tuesday. Why is that day registering as—registering . . . SATs. Crap. "Ah, Martin? I just remembered that I have the . . . a prior commitment on Tuesday. Could we postpone it?"

I mean, sure I want to be in this movie—who wouldn't? But I can't miss the SATs. That one would be impossible to explain to my dad, would never fly with Dandy-Patinko, let alone the college admissions offices, or with my own sense of academic obligation.

"I suppose. But we'll have to do it by the following weekend or we'll run into scheduling conflicts."

"Fine. Great." I jot down my number on a piece of paper and feel totally unprofessional. Note to self: Should I get business cards or will that only ensure that something like this never happens again?

Without Arabella around, and with Monti and Angus swamped with old friends and crooners, Asher and I steal away to my room. I'm on my back with his head on my stomach.

"Nefarious," he says.

"Ugh, that's on my list of words I despise—meaning: despicable, vile."

"You have a list of words? Let me guess, in this infamous journal?" I nod. "Any chance a bloke could take a look at that thing?"

"You're in it, if that's what you're after . . . but no. It's not for public consumption. Ask me another one."

"Apoplectic."

"Enraged."

"Good. Attenuation."

"Decrease, a reduction in," I say and play with his hair. He makes little appreciative noises.

"I think you're good to go—are you secretly a wonk?"

"Not so secretly, actually. I just want to do well. These tests basically determine what you do with the next four years of your life."

Asher sits up so he's looking down at me, spreads my hair in a fan around my face, and snaps a pretend photo. "You could come here for uni," he suggests.

Lurch. Future. Mild palpitations. "Right—me at Oxford . . ." But as I say it, it doesn't sound bad. "It's something to think about, anyway. For the future." Insert girlish laughter to cover instant thoughts of investigating application procedure for said school. Asher kisses me and then pauses a half inch away from my mouth. It's a warm, perfect moment. He's wonderful—I'm lucky—and Arabella is just plain wrong about him.

"And speaking about the future—the near future—I've been thinking. Want to meet me later tonight?"

"A midnight rendezvous?" I say with a bad French accent.

"Oui, Chéri."

He gives me that look, that guy look, that says it all: It's time. At least, he thinks it's time—for *it*. I spend the rest of the day and evening wishing Arabella or Chris were here so I could discuss the pros and cons of sleeping him. The idea of sex is definitely appealing. Asher's pretty much all I've wanted, and I'm leaning toward the *yes* I know he wants to hear. That I for the most part want to say. But the smallest part of me—maybe just a couple of cells—isn't sure. It's not any moral thing. It's just the idea that you can't go back. You can't change the how or when—the circumstances are just there forever.

And I don't know if I want to commit to the forever part. But I might.

The lights from the photo shoot are packed up, but down through the topiary gardens, the lanterns are illuminated, each one a different color, swinging in the night air. I follow Asher's instructions and go to the teacup, where, on top, there's a torch (a flashlight) switched to on and a note that reads *keep going*. Trying not to overinterpret his words, I follow the pathway through the high hedges to the lake house. Asher has set up the heat lamps from the photo shoot, so as soon as I'm inside the arched and pillared entrance, it's warm. Waist-high candles, petals scattered on the ground, and Clementine Highstreet's "Be Still, Be Now" comes from the PAL speaker off to the side.

"Wow," I say and stare at him. He's set up a floor bed, with fluffy duvet, king-sized pillows, white sheets, all with a view of the moon on the lake's surface. It's all perfect. He comes over and starts to lead me to the bed, kissing me, and then I suddenly get chills, despite the heat lamps. Candles. Kissing. Lake house. It's too perfect. It's just like Arabella said. Her prediction is coming true.

I stop in my tracks and drop Asher's hand. "What?" he says in a Johnny Depp whisper, all drama and dark-haired ambience, "Is something wrong?"

"Is this a stage?" I ask calmly, slowly.

"I don't know what you mean. Come dance with me." He holds out a glass of champagne and says, "Here's to a successful night."

"Successful?" I shake my head, my voice getting louder. "This—this place. The music, the lighting. I can't believe it." I fight off tears because I'm more angry than sad—sad comes later. "Arabella . . . she knew—she actually prepared me for this. But it didn't even occur to me she'd be right. Not for one second. I don't want to be one of your many girls."

"Love—wait. Let me explain," Asher says. He's ardent, but the whole scene, the mood, is broken.

"You don't need to explain," I say. "I get it. You just added me to your list, figured you'd get me with all your usual charms. I'm not like that. You're a cliché, Asher. Just a regular, lame-ass guy who's after one thing. It's my fault for allowing myself to get wrapped up in the mirage." I start to walk away. "And I'm not what you're look-ing for, trust me."

I walk in a determined fashion, but slowly enough that he could easily catch up. But he doesn't. So I do the only thing I can think of when I see Clementine in the hallway, heading to the loo. I ask her for a ride back to London.

"Oh, no, dear." She shakes her head. "I'm here for the night." She sees my face, my sad mouth, my eyes. "But go wake Lundgren Shrum, the driver. Tell him I sent you. He owes me one."

The car ride is silent, and I get to the flat feeling guilty I've pulled Lundgren into the mess, woken him, but glad to be back somewhere safe and guy free. Correction, about-to-be guy free.

"And fuck off for good this time," Arabella chucks a shoe at To-bias, who's half clad and backing out the front door with a sheepish expression.

"Come on, Bels—don't throw a fit," he says, but it's no use. Ara-bella pulls me inside, gives a wave to Lundgren, who leaves, and closes the door with Tobias still struggling to keep his pants up.

"Don't ask," she says.

"I won't," I tell her. "I've had enough truth and consequences tonight."

"Bed or tea and talk?" she asks, ever the rock of friendship.

"Bed, thanks," I say. She already knows what happened, most likely, knows that it would have to be pretty bad for me to come back in the middle of the night, proving her right all along.

* * *

It's the morning after the night before, as the English saying goes, and Arabella and I are slightly the worse for wear. She and Toby have apparently split for good, and I am single by choice, so we do the only sensible thing there is to do: meet Keena and Fizzy for a horseback ride through Hyde Park.

Trotting along in a surreal and yet fun turn of events, I yell up to Arabella, who's a natural rider. "You look regal!"

Arabella smiles back at me and kicks the horse into a faster gait, whatever is after trot but slower than gallop—there is a third speed in there, right? Keena, who has been riding only once before, clings to her giant steed for dear life.

"Don't run anywhere, horse," she commands. Then to me, she adds, "Got a second?"

"Well," I say, holding the reins, glad to control at least one creature, "does it look like I'm about to bolt?"

"Nice mood, Love. Bad night?" Keena stops her horse, and I try to reverse mine so we're next to each other while Fizzy and Arabella veer off to the left.

"Crappy night. But what did you want to say?"

Keena lowers her voice and I have to lean over in my saddle to hear her. "The shit's about to hit the fan."

Right—the conversation I overheard in the faculty lounge. "Are you going to come clean about it?"

"Me?" Keena makes a face. "I didn't do anything—oh, well, true I did do *that*. But I'm not the one getting kicked out."

Just as she's explaining, Fizzy approaches with Arabella. It's obvious we've been speaking about something in a hushed way and Fizzy, always straightforward says, "Have you told them I'm being sent away?"

Arabella's mouth falls open. "What? Why? What've you done?"

"I so love that you don't even ask if I've been put in the wrong. But you happen to be correct in this instance. I got caught—no, not with someone in my bed—I . . ." Her strong exterior wavers and she starts to cry. Her horse takes a dump, and she laughs while shaking her head. "Shit, guys. I just . . . I broke the honor code. I used my texts during my history take-home."

"How'd they even know?" Arabella asks.

"I scored too high—it was too perfect or something. Not really believable that I would either retain that much information or phrase it that way. My essay was structured the same way as the introduction in the textbook. I'm leaving tonight, no later than seven, as per the orders."

"Where are you going?" I ask.

"Well, I'm not welcome at home—my mother's got her hands full with the kids, and since I'm skint . . ."

"You could stay with us," Arabella says and I nod.

"No—thanks just the same." Fizzy makes her horse turn in circles. Then she tries to ride sidesaddle, nearly winding up on the ground. "After I got caught I went to HEL—God, that sounds so repentant! But I went there and Clementine, that woman who owns it, said I could work there for a while. Just until I get my head straight."

"You can still audition," Keena offers. "The stage companies won't care if you got—"

"Right, that's true," I say.

"But it doesn't change the fact that I've permanently messed up my record. I'm screwed." Then she pulls a Fizzy and fluffs out her frizz, chuckles, and wipes her tears away. "Fuck pity and self-loathing. Let's ride!"

She takes off and we follow, all of us letting the wind, the new spring air, the faintest hint of warm weather, tempt us into forgetting our troubles. I admire Fizzy's ability to push aside the damage she's done, the mix of guilt and fear she must have. Somehow, when I picture big things like that happening (not that I picture myself cheating or breaking major Hadley rules), my world falls apart, cracking and splintering until there's nothing left but shards. Maybe that's the point, that life does splinter—the guy you thought was perfect isn't, people get sick, friends disappoint, but there's the upside of everything, a continual cycle of up, slide down, and the self-correcting that can happen only over the course of time.

"I can't believe you're backing out!" Arabella pouts.

"I can't believe you're going," I say. I watch her zip closed, then re-open, her suitcase every time she remembers another article of clothing or book she wants to bring.

"You said you'd come."

"That was before all this—do you really want me to miss out on this experience? When will I ever get the chance to dub some ingenue's part in a Martin Eisenstein film?"

"Big sigh," Arabella says. "Look, I'm not saying I don't agree with you. I'm just saying it—as the Americans say—sucks."

"Why are you still going if things are off with Tobias?"

"Because he'll see me there in my suit, flirting with Flask or some island boy, regret being a shithead, and want me back." She looks at me. "And before you even hit me with the psychobabble, no, I'm not planning on taking him back if he asks me. I just want him to want to ask."

I'm standing with my SAT prep book in my hand, weighing down my arm, my wrist, my life until tomorrow afternoon, when they are officially over. "I'm hardly one to tell you how to live your romantic life when mine's in shambles," I say.

Arabella swallows and bites her top lip. "No, sure, I . . . you should go study, anyway."

"And you know what? If the dubbing thing gets rescheduled yet again, I'll come. Seriously."

Martin Eisenstein is my new best friend, phoning every couple of hours to tell me my time has been changed. Note to self: Do not tell him where the SATs are being held as he will probably come and yell to me through the window—"three forty-five on Friday." "No, next Monday at 2 p.m." And so on. As a result of the rescheduling, I have negged the Nevis trip and been reimbursed by Jess Montgomery, a new friend of Arabella, who was gagging for a chance to hang out and drink daiquiris while writing a freelance article for some magazine. She came round to the flat yesterday to get the ticket, which had to be totally cancelled and reissued for security reasons, and gave me a wad of cash and a smile. She's one of those Lila Lawrence–like blondes, really pretty in a freshly scrubbed way with very believable highlights (could be real, I'm not an expert) and a sweet demeanor.

Arabella sweetly makes me dinner while I do another practice test, and we retire. She's up before I am, leaves a note saying she'll see me in ten days, and wishes me luck. Since she didn't have to wait for me to finish, she went early with Fizzy to Nick Cooper's house, where everyone's gathering before the airport trek on Friday. It does sound fun, and, if Mable's right with her advice, which she usually is, I will probably regret not going. Mable says that it's the things you don't do that you regret the most when you're older, not the things you did do—even if they don't turn out right. But it feels like a fair trade, fun 'n' sun for a cool experience dubbing a role. After all, Glenn Close did the same thing for that model girl in *Greystoke,* and look where she is now.

CHAPTER SIXTEEN

♡

Song of the moment: "Buffalo Stance" by Neneh Cherry, even though it has nothing to do with my current environs. But her attitude is strong and so is the beat, carrying me away from the Masonry (read: old cold stone building where the hour upon hour of multiple choice hellaciousness known as the SATs took place) and off to LADAM for Choir practice, then home (home! I do think of it that way now) to the flat for a solitary evening of cooking and catch-up Brecht and Churchill (Carol not Winston) reading for British Playwrights. Plus, I could use a moment to decompress, write in my journal, and unload the mix of feelings I'm tugging along regarding the lake house incident and all that it encompasses.

On my way back, I pass by Wild at Heart, a flower store in this funky little area of West London. They make bouquets that burst with colors; all the spring ones have either hyacinths or tulips cut very short, adding to the robust feel of each arrangement. I stand surrounded by all the smells and bright blues, hot pinks, soft ivies, until one of the assistants asks if I need anything. I shake my head, no, but I feel otherwise. I want to roll around in the soft petals, have one of those movie endings where the right person at the right time says the right thing and it's all—yes, say it with me—right. But I stand there in the mildish air and then move on.

Another phone message at the flat leads to the further rescheduling of the voice-over project. By now I've begun to doubt it will actually ever happen. Martin Eisenstein has informed me that the ending didn't "test well" with audiences (who knew they even did that stuff with independent films?) so they've gone back for reshoots, thus changing the part, thus changing the time I'd need to be there, and so on. So basically, I could have gone to Nevis.

Three days slide by and I am past the mental rescripting of Asher's "successful night" scene in my head. I've made progress; I no longer feel teary about it, no longer feel like kicking myself or Asher where it counts (in the heart), but just feel let down. I call Keena from the flat and ask her to meet me at the cinema, but she's busy doing whatever illicit things she does with Galen French. I get my coat on and am locking the door when a taxi squeals to a stop and Arabella bounds out. She looks normal (normal = stunning), but staggers.

"Are you drunk?" I ask.

"I need to go inside," she says. "And yes, I am. Not drunk. Tipsy. Wine on the plane. The flight attendants took pity on me."

Inside, Arabella gets a cup of water, changes into her pj's, and sits on the kitchen counter, waiting for me to do the same. It's where we've had some of our best talks, my feet dangling off the edges, her feet nearly resting in the small stainless-steel sink.

"It's finished," she says and I don't have to ask for clarification. "For good this time. He chucked me. I guess he's tired of lurking around, not being out to my parents."

"Really?" I ask, surprised. "That seems like an"—how to phrase it without sounding like Tobias is kind of a schmuck—"honorable reason."

"Well, that plus he got off with—" She stops short. "You won't believe it. Seriously."

"Fizzy?" I ask. I wouldn't have said she's unethical, just a bit easy, but after the honor code thing, maybe she's in a moral quandary.

"God, no. She'd never . . . Lila. Lila Lawrence. Your good old buddy."

My mouth hangs open and I literally have to grope for words. "Okay. Wait. What was she doing there? No—lame question. On vacation. She just told me she was going somewhere warm. I didn't think to ask where. But now that I think of it, she's been there before. I just assumed she'd be in Anguilla."

"Enough of the geography, Love. She's a bitch."

"She's not, though. I mean, not that you want me to defend her. Nor should I. But she's a good person."

"Not in this case." Arabella plays with the taps with her toes, trying to stop the constant *pling pling* from the leaky faucet. "It's Tobias's fault more than hers. She didn't even know that he was my boyfriend until the moment of truth when I walked in on them. Really pleasant."

"I'm so sorry, Bels. Really." I reach out and squeeze her hand, and we stare at each other. She's still a little off-kilter, her words slightly uneven from the wine or tropical drinks she's consumed, and she looks sad. Suddenly, she starts to cry. "Oh, sweetie, no. Don't. He's not worth it."

"No." She shakes her head and wipes the trickling snot onto her T-shirt. "It's . . . you were right. I was just really jealous and scared and . . ."

"I'm confused. Slow down."

Arabella leaps down from the counter and I follow her into the bathroom, where she reaches for some migraine medication (American: my-grain, British: me-grain). "You and Asher. You should be together."

I have no idea where all this is coming from. "Can you please try to make sense? I really don't know what you're saying here."

"What I'm saying"—she gulps down the pills and sits on the toilet, knees tucked to her chin—"is that I lied. Asher never wanted a successful night in the lake house, all the candles and everything. I made that up."

I shake my head emphatically. "No—no, you were totally right. Just as you predicted, it was all there." I fight off the image of the scattered petals, the lanterns, the bed, his face.

"But it was real. I knew what to describe only because Asher, in one of our rare close moments a few years ago, admitted to me that the lake house is his favorite place. That when he found the right person, he'd take her there, set the mood with candles and flowers . . ."

"Oh my God." I can't take it. Chills run down my arms, my legs. I hug myself, trying to both protect and preserve my emotions. "So he's never been out there with anyone else? I'm not one of the *many girls* you talked about?"

Arabella stands up and massages her head, looking truly sorry, her lips curled down. "I'm not saying he's an angel—he's had his fair share of flings and girlfriends, but not like this. Even Monti noticed it. He's in love with you."

The words hang like cartoon bubbles in the air, and I want to collect them, put them in my pockets for later, as proof. But instead, I walk out, leaving Arabella to tuck herself in and nurse what will be some mixture of hangover and headache and try to collect myself so I can sort this out once and for all.

If you want your movie setting, sometimes you can plan it, sometimes it just happens. Nervous as hell, I manage to put one foot in front of the other and head to the Westminster area, near a big Ferris wheel, where he's part of a day for night shoot (day for night = shot during the day to look like night, with cool dark lights and reflectors, resulting in that purplish mottled finish). Off to the side, models are smoking and strutting in next winter's gear, cape-style coats and military-cut jackets, while the reality is that the sun's out and the buds are on the trees. Dad told me that back at Hadley it's still Farch, muddy, the ground in a half thaw. Here, spring has sprung suddenly, and my fingers tingle as they always do before I'm about to do something important.

Asher, holding a reflecting circle so it casts a glow on one of the models, spots me and turns so I am hit in the face with the light. Then he turns back to the set and I wait for him to finish. He walks over, hands in his pockets, face steady—no smile—no emotion, really.

"Hi," I say, maybe too friendly for someone who dissed him rather recently.

"Hey," he says. "I've got only a couple of seconds. Can I help you?"

Big breath. Stop fidgeting with buttons on coat. Gulp. "I'm really . . ."

Asher tries to save me from my muddling apology. "It's cool. No worries. I misconstrued . . ." He edits himself, looks at me one more time (and I swear I see him stare at my mouth, which I read in *Teen Vogue* is one of the signs someone wants to kiss you), and then checks over his shoulder at the shoot. I dare myself to step closer to him, and accept, moving so I'm either inappropriately near to him, or the perfect distance for kissing. I turn his head so he's facing me again and wrap my arms around him. First, his arms stay at his sides and I panic, not about having made an ass of myself, but that he's severed all ties with me.

Then he whispers in my ear, "Want to ride the Eye?"

This sounds like prep school drug lingo or some deviant sexual thing I know nothing about, but my blank look inspires Asher to point to the very large and very obvious Ferris wheel towering nearby.

"That'd be great," I say. I'm not much for scary rides; to know me is to understand I do most activities with a degree of caution not meant for upside-down roller coasters or gravity drops, but I think I can handle this. We get into the mini pod, seated close together, and in one gentle motion, we're off the ground, with a view of London that I haven't had since arriving (and I was a tad too tired then to appreciate it).

"It's amazing," I say. It has been like falling down the rabbit hole in many ways, the people I've met. Clementine—with her wide smile (minus the hookah)—could be the caterpillar, Arabella the bunny that led me here in the first place. "I have to tell you," I say and Asher looks at me. "I'm analyzing my life in terms of *Alice in Wonderland* at the moment."

"How intellectual of you," he says. "Have you considered who I might be in this Lewis Carroll scenario?"

To our right, bridges and water, to the left the gracious historic buildings, and everywhere, a creeping spring green. Everything feels on the verge right now, about to explode into blossom, about to break open. Asher takes my face into his hands, his fingers in my hair, and right before he kisses me asks, "Would it be okay if I fell in love with you?"

Before I can answer, before I can formulate an answer even—or even know what I think—I nod and he kisses me, the sunlight seeping in the domed top of our capsule.

"You see, rather than just being suspended under gravity, these things"—he tries to shake the pod to demonstrate—"each one turns . . . They've got circular mounting rings fixed to the main rim"—he smiles as I watch his Joe Science explanation—"thereby allowing a spectacular three-hundred-and-sixty-degree panorama at the top."

We swing and tilt, his arm draped over my shoulder, and circle a few more times while discussing plans, his goals, mine, then ours.

"And if I were to get a placement with Annie Lebowitz or something, then I'd postpone Oxford for another year. But maybe I should just forget the photo stuff, keeping the gallery of course, but go back to my first love . . ." He checks my face. "No, not a girl. You might laugh—but the first subject I was ever really good at was maths."

"I love how you guys say maths, plural. We just say math. So you're this brilliant mathematician?" Ah, the allure of brains.

"Not now, but it's what I'll read at Oxford." Asher puts his hand on the capsule window, where it sticks out from the blue of the sky. "And you? Think you'll stay on here?"

This, along with the jolt we get at the bottom of the wheel, produces a silence. Finally, when I'm back on the ground, I try to answer. "It's not really an option, I don't think. I mean, I was lucky to even get over here in the first place. Hadley Hall requires that something like four-fifths of your credits be taken there, like you can take a summer science class or—in my case—a term away, barely. But to get a diploma from there, you have to . . ."

"Be there." He looks disappointed. I wonder if he really thought I'd just be the London version of myself, eschewing my life back in Boston. I have to admit, it's an appealing thought. If I could just import my dad and Mable, and maybe sign Chris up for a frequent-flier program. "When exactly is your return ticket?"

"Late spring," I say. "The end of May there's the Avon Breast Cancer Walk, and I need to be back for that. My friend, Chris, has already been coaxing contributions from everyone within a fifty-mile radius of Hadley, and Mable's going to walk with us, so . . ."

"So until then." Asher waves to his photo shoot people, giving them the two minutes sign.

"Until then, what?" I ask. But it's clear what he means. We have until then to be us, the new open, nonhidden us. We hug good-bye.

In my ear he asks, "Love? Will you come to Bracker's again?" I start to pull back, but he keeps me in hug position. "You don't have to answer now—and it wouldn't be a lake house thing. Even though that was sincere, maybe it's not right to try and re-create that. But will you come out there for a long weekend? Maybe Mothering Sunday?"

Mothering Sunday. How ironic to have that be when I go out, motherless, as per usual. Though Mable will be here then, and Dad, which counts for something. My experiences with Mother's Days of yore have been watching families parade to brunch together, or watching those ads on TV about getting flowers. I always divert my attention to Father's Day, finding safety and practicality in the day of ties and tools.

My words get semismushed into his chest. "My dad and aunt are coming then. We'll all be there."

"Good," he says. "I want to make it up to you."

"I'd like that," I say.

On Easter, Asher invites me to his gallery for a day of egg dying prior to meeting Angus, Arabella, and Monti (Clive's gone romping around Spain for a holiday—*bueno*) for a 'family' supper on the houseboat. Now that it's springish, the boat is the perfect place for a dinner.

"If you use the wax like this, you can make a pattern," I say, showing off my egg-dying skills with Paas pride.

"You never informed me of your tremendous skills," Asher says, lowering his egg into a puddle of red dye.

"One of my hidden talents." I let my finished blue and purple egg rest on the kitchen roll (kitchen roll = paper towel. Loo roll = toilet paper. Apparently, *toilet* is only for the lower class. How incredible that even words connote class here.)

"So," Asher starts, keeping his fingers steady on the spoon so the egg doesn't drop. "How was Stratford?"

I check Asher's face for signs of anything other than casual interest. Chance of jealousy, several percent. "It was good," I say. "Seeing

Shakespeare in the round, the way he intended, is a really different experience. Very cool." I don't say anything about how during our field trip there, PMT (one of the chaperones) led us to a pub in which Nick Adams Cooper happened to be seated with his intellectual, groovy parents.

"Anything else happen up there?" he asks.

He clearly heard something, even though there's nothing to tell. "Hmm . . . not really. Bumped into Nick Cooper, but that's about all."

Asher wipes his hands on his trousers, leaving red fingerprints. "How is old Nicky these days, anyway?"

"Fine," I say and start another egg. "He's . . ." I don't complete my sentence because the egg I'm holding breaks, causing big-time drippage. Asher laughs and gets the mop. While he wipes the floor (read: sexiest male Cinderella ever), I think about what I might have said. That Nick is sweet, smart, that I'd like to know him, but there's not much point, and he's sort of on the outskirts of my life here. Would I mention that Nick could have liked me? No. It all leads back to possibilities and potentials and the choices we make to skip one road and take the next. Asher grins up at me and starts to wipe the spilled yolk from my hands—his is the face on the path in front of me.

CHAPTER SEVENTEEN

♡

On my way to school, I count the weeks until Dad and Mable get here. Almost three. Then I count back and tally up the time Asher and I have been together. What if things progress enough between now and then that I want to say yes to Asher's overnight invite? To the whole thing? That would make almost four months of seeing him. In my mind I try to equate time with emotion, to see if I feel like that's enough, if that makes it okay to have sex with him. Then I berate myself for thinking in such mathematical terms. Should it matter how long you've been together? But I come back to yes, for me it does. Like the time spent together adds up to the realness of the relationship. But maybe that's just a cover-up based on fear. Maybe it's all about passion and love and lust and it could feel right after only being together for a couple days. I begin to drive myself crazy dissecting all this, so I try to focus on what's ahead.

While waiting for my turn at the computer terminal, I take out my journal and jot down some scrambled lists (like scrambled eggs, only not runny).

Hey—this journal is almost complete! Not too many pages left. Then it'll be done. How weird to put closure on some chapter in my life—and where will I be when I'm on the last page? Here? With Asher? At the Choir finale? Finally finally finally (I wrote that so many times it now looks wrong. Thank God the SATs are done) doing the voice-dubbing thing? Or will I be home already, with summer in full swing? I will have turned in my PMT novella project by then, and so many of my daily questions now will be answered. I'm using the pen Chris gave me to write this—wonder how long the ink will last.

"I'll be just a second," the girl using the computer says. "Just one more min, okay?" I give the okay, if you must sigh and keep writing. Sometimes it's better to look agitated to hurry people up, but Galen French isn't expecting me until half four (that's four thirty—yeesh, I'm going to sound affected when I get back), and the curtain for *Damn Yankees* doesn't rise until eight. Which should give me plenty of time to email, meet Asher for dinner and, um, dessert at the flat. Then we'll go meet Monti and Angus for opening night.

List of Questions/Comments
- To sex or not to sex?
- Long-distance vs. home court—get the sense A. would <u>not</u> be into commuting relationship.
- Explore poss. of coming here for another term? University? No. Dumb to plan around a boy. But I like it here for my own sake.
- What will my transcript say from here? Oh—note to self: Ask PMT for college rec. Can't hurt to have one of greatest living British authors talk me up.

- When Dad said he's "serious" about Louisa, did he mean like moving in w/ her serious? Hey, maybe Louisa can move in with me and Lindsay Parrish. Now that's good times right there.
- Note to self: Talk to Lila Lawrence ASAP about Tobias/Arabella conundrum before it gets weirder than it is—esp. w/ Arabella coming to Vineyard this summer. Need to find friends there (possibilities include: Henry, Charlie, that girl Chris met—what is her name? Cold? Chilly . . .)
- How much can I reasonably expect to make this summer? Enough to buy a ticket back in August for a vacation? Look at STA's deals.
- Ask Mable about job at Slave to the Grind II—and about renaming it. Contest for this? Also, what are my hrs.?
- Deal with college essays/make appt. for summer meeting w/ Dandy-P. to go over TCOMC (don't even know what my choice place is, though).
- To sex or not to sex—yes, it's on my brain
- Beg Mable for big batch of music from her collection—am bored w/ mine (note to self: copy—or take—Clementine's record?)
- What is Mable thinking these days?

"All yours." The girl pushes the chair out and leaves, and I sink into that weird warmth created by someone else's ass on the seat. The answer to my last question is waiting for me in my in-box.

Love! It's me, Mable! Taking your advice, I got one of those handheld PDAs and am writing to you while waiting for my checkup with Dr. Cutler (yes, I know, Cutler sounds like Cut her, which she did and for the better—Gosh, can you tell we share some of the same genes? Who else would dissect names like that?). BIG NEWS! Now that Miles re-proposed and I said yes, we've been hunting for a place. We've settled on Labor Day at the Whaling Church in Edgartown. And you can wear whatever you want; we're beyond the wedding-attire BS. It's not the outfits or food that matters this time around. Just the emotion. I know it's fast, but he's been a star during the past few months. I guess sometimes it doesn't matter how long you've been together—you just know! Did I ever tell you that story about your dad? Remind me—I will. (Just say 'the one with the sushi' and I'll know what you mean.) Official Vineyard plans are all set. I'm sure you've thought about this, but would you like Arabella to come for the summer? We could use another barista. Your preppy friend Henry said his dad can arrange a work-stay visa. (I guess that's what being the Island's answer to Trump can do—though he does have an interest in the café, so . . .) Oh—they just called my name to the Dr.'s office. Let's hope for another good appt. Love you more than air, M.

I print out the email to add to the other Mable paraphernalia. Since her diagnosis, I've been slightly OCD about keeping any and everything—a napkin from our dinner on Martha's Vineyard, notes she'd left for me around Slave to the Grind, even phone messages I can't bare to erase from my cell phone back home. I just keep saving and resaving them. Just in case. It's dumb and superstitious, but I can't help it.

Then I look at the rest of the junk in my account—some nonfiltered spam, a couple of library overdue notices from St. Paul's, and a name I haven't seen for ages.

```
Hi, Love—

It's been a while. Wanted to check in and see
how London's treating you. Have you been singing?
Hadley's pretty much the same, with the odd vari-
ant. I'm performing at the May Festival—a high-
light in an otherwise college-centric early
spring. I'd like to hear from you, if you want.

—Jacob
```

Points for pleasantry. Simple, not too revealing, but not bland (what exactly are the "variants" of which he writes?). No mention of Lindsay (not that he would) and no mention of which colleges or what he's performing at the May Festival. Part of me wants to write back, but most of me just wouldn't know what to say right now. Nothing here has anything to do with life there, it seems, and Jacob is a reminder of a long time ago—days that feel far away, younger. Before Mable's diagnosis, before my internship in NYC, before TCP even started, way before London.

LOCALE: CHARLTON THEATRE.
TIME: TEN FORTY P.M.
MOOD: EFFERVESCENT.

"Bravo!" Angus bellows in his brogue. His voice stands out in the packed audience. *Damn Yankees* rocked. Arabella was incredible, not so much stealing the show, because everyone was good, but bringing it up to another level. She's no amateur.

"I fully expect to see your name in lights," I say to her when she's emerged from backstage, still in her stage makeup and costume.

"Fabulous!" Monti glows with pride, hugging her daughter. I instantly miss my dad. It's the longest I've ever been away from him, and I suddenly feel this intense need to hug him, to hear his voice— just to show him my world here.

"Well done, Bels," Asher says and gives Arabella a quick kiss on the cheek. It's the first time he's bothered to come see her in anything, so it's a big deal. She, in turn, went to his gallery today, which she'd blown off since he bought it and put his work on display. So maybe their sibling rivalry or disinterest is fading, if not perfect.

"Let's have a drink to celebrate!" Monti says and leads the way to Brasserie Fontaine, where platters of oysters, caviar, escargot, and calamari await (if there's one thing the wealthy have, it's an affinity for slimy seafood). I bypass all but the caviar and gladly toast to Arabella—and Angus, who has completed his new play.

"It's called *Beast Within the Burden*," he says. "Title subject to change, of course."

"It's very Rolling Stones," I say.

"Shit," Angus exclaims. "I knew it sounded familiar. Ah, well, we'll see."

"Thanks for coming everyone," Arabella says and tosses back her flute of bubbly. She hasn't wiped off the makeup completely, so her face is a deep tan, her eyes rimmed with dark liner; she looks older. She looks happy. To me she adds, "You guys okay now?"

"Yeah. Better than okay." I squeeze Asher's hand under the table and tell Arabella again how awesome she is on stage.

After an hour of boozing and bragging about Bels's talents, we all call it a night. As Monti leans in to double kiss my cheeks she says, "And Love, before I forget, we made a pledge for the Avon Breast Cancer Walk."

"Oh, great!" I say. "Did you get forced into it by Chris? He's a friend of mine who tends to be quite pushy at times . . ."

"Not to worry," she says. "It was actually your dad who rang up—not about that, but he mentioned it and . . ."

"Well, thanks a lot—for everything, really," I say. Monti has her hands on my shoulders and looks right into my eyes, so deeply, so kindly, so probing, that I'm left wondering what, exactly, the rest of her conversation with my dad was about. But if there's more to it, she doesn't let on, or doesn't say more than, "Good night. Sleep well, Love."

And I do. I sleep soundly, cuddled up next to Asher, whose chest rises and sags into my back as he holds me.

"I wish I could photograph you like this," he says, his voice hushed and sleepy.

"In bed?" I ask.

"Hmm," he says. "Not sleezy, just comfy. Natural." Then he pulls me closer and says, "That's what you get for having a boyfriend who thinks with a lens."

"Actually, you're not the first," I say, and then try to clarify that I don't mean first as in first sex first, but photo-boy first. "It's weird, actually. My first boyfriend at Hadley was into photography. But not like you—more like a hobby."

"Funny coincidence. Were you together long?" Asher doesn't change his calm breathing, his tight hold on me.

"No—not at all. He was pretty much a giant liar, a disappointment, and a cheat. The trifecta of crap."

"Poor you," he says, then rises on his hands so he's looking down at me. "Rather, poor him. He completely missed out." He kisses me then resumes spoon position.

Outside, a soft rain hits the rooftops, pinging onto the window boxes Arabella and I filled with flowers from Wild at Heart. It's the first time I've spent the entire night next to him—next to any boyfriend—and it's a solid A, a perfect score.

CHAPTER EIGHTEEN

The Easter holiday weekend is late this year, and by the time Arabella and I have decided which train to catch for the long weekend out at Bracker's, the city is in full bloom. Trees have unfurled their leaves creating an umbrella of green as I walk back home after my final meeting with PMT before the holiday. Praise be to the college gods that she agreed to write a recommendation letter for me. She also decided to give us all a break from the usual twenty-page handwritten tomes she assigns. I am free of work for the vacation. We have twelve days, and Dad and Mable will arrive on Monday—only six more days! We spoke yesterday and went over our loosely planned itinerary (Tate Modern, Thames riverboat trip—not on *the* houseboat, though—curry at Malabar in Notting Hill, tour of LADAM and St. Paul's, and so on, but first a couple of nights chez Piece).

When I get back, Arabella and Asher (together!) are waiting for me.

"It's time to celebrate," Asher says. "And not in the Kool and the Gang way." He knew exactly where my mind would go upon hearing the word *celebrate*.

"What're you guys doing?" I ask. They have a bag between them and I can see a baguette sticking up from it, a bottle of wine, a blanket. "Care to inform me where you're off to?"

"Our plan, Bukowski," Arabella says and stands up, "is to have the lovely Lundgren Shrum drive us for an outing."

"An outing . . ."

"We're going punting," Asher says. "In Oxford. You know, the English gondola."

"I have always wanted to do that," I say. I saw *Oxford Blues* on late-night USA and totally fell for the whole scene—picnic on a boat, hot guy pushing the boat along through the scenic town. "Do I have time to change and drop my things? I have to get my camera."

"Ah, I believe I have that covered," Asher says. He holds up a digital and a long lens, displaying his wares. "You just need to bring yourself. Oh, and maybe a jumper in case it gets chilly."

I head inside and immediately scour my room for clothing. The whole space is a tip. The Choir finale concert is right after break and we are all supposed to look the same, with white trousers, white shirts, hair back. I'm the only red-hued person, and I think I stick out, but what can you do? I think we'll end up looking like a row of waiters, but it's not my call. In light of the required uniform, I went digging through my clothes and unearthed a couple of passable tops, but no white pants (pants here = underwear and Asher will often say it rather than swear—example: Oh, pants! I've forgotten my keys—again!). So I fling clothes around, searching for a clean pair of jeans underneath the various white articles.

As I'm half dressed (the bottom half), the phone rings so I go to the living room to pick up.

"Love, so glad to have caught you." The voice belongs to my frequent phoner Martin Eisenstein. "Can you hear me? I'm in the car on the 101."

"The 101?" I ask.

"In L.A.," Martin says as if everyone in the world should know the California roadways.

"But that means—" I start but don't get to finish before he interrupts.

"Sadly, yes. So look, darling, just please don't take this personally, but we've had to recast the part you were set to dub . . ."

Not that I thought it would come to fruition, but I'm immediately bummed anyway. "Oh . . . that's too bad."

"But we'd like to use you for something—just not quite sure what." He beeps at someone and then comes back. "Any chance you'll be in L.A. anytime soon?"

I'm about to say no, which would be the honest response, but then I think about Chris and what he told Alistair the American. "It's possible," I say and sound aloof when really it's just that I have no idea. Or, I do have an idea (that'd be a *no*), but I want to see what he offers.

"That's my other line. I have to take it—but I asked Clementine Highstreet to pass along my details Stateside. Seems I'll be here for bit dealing with this complete cock-up, so do phone when you get here."

As if I'm due to take up residence as the Chateaux Marmont next week I say, "Sounds good—will do."

Then I take my half-clad self back to the bedroom to get ready for punting. I can totally see it: Arabella happy (even though Tobias has left many a groveling message for her—and one threatening one when she didn't respond. He threatened to go to the paparazzi with an old photo of them together just to force the issue of their relationship. Rock-steady Bels didn't budge), Asher in love (with me! I haven't said it to him, but I will. I think. I know. I'm getting close to positive about doing more than just sleeping *next* to him . . . maybe tonight? Ah, freaking out now that I've thought that), me feeling totally and completely—

Can't complete that thought as the phone rings again and Arabella, probably impatient as hell to get going, comes inside to answer it. Asher wanders in, too, ogling me from the doorway as I pull on a cream-colored snug-fitting henley top.

Asher comes over and is about to kiss me, and I'm about to tell him what I *think* is going to happen tonight when Arabella bursts in.

"You've got to go," she says, her brow crinkled, her face worried.

"I'm almost ready. Hang on," I say.

"No." She scrambles around my room, throwing items into a bag. "We're taking you—"

"How much stuff could I possibly need to bring punting?" I ask. "I lent my heavy sweater to Keena, anyway, so . . ."

"Fuck the sweaters." Arabella hands the bag to Asher, who, through some unspoken sibling lingo gets what she's doing and continues to pile things in. "Love." Arabella stands before me. "You know that emergency ticket your dad gave you?"

"Yeah?" My voice cracks when I suddenly click in.

"You're gonna need to use it," she says.

CHAPTER NINETEEN

♡

The next hours are a blur of travel, talking, tears. Mable went into the hospital again, fever spiking, trouble breathing, possible sepsis, and while there, found that the cancer has spread to her other breast, some axillary lymph nodes.

"Just pray that it's not in the blood," Dad said when I called him from Arabella's phone on the way to Heathrow. "You wanted me to be forthright with you, so I am. I love you. I'm glad you're coming back." That he's glad I'm coming back had two sides—one, he misses me and two, Mable is critical.

We left the flat in a complete hurricane of academic papers, clothing, souvenirs, my journal. Asher rounded up Fizzy and Keena, who came to say good-bye, Keena looking really off—probably just concerned—Fizzy scared for me, for Mable, but really liking her job at HEL. She brought over an envelope from Clementine, which she said contains Martin Eisenstein's info, among other things.

Arabella walks me to the passport check-in and hugs me good-bye, at which point I burst into tears. I stand there, sobbing.

"I hate that I'm leaving so quickly," I say.

"I know," she says and wipes the tears that are streaming down her own cheeks. "But you'll be back, right? This can't be it. No. We'll just figure out a way to get you back here, k?"

"K."

"I'll call you every day," she says. "And I'll explain to all your teachers, or get your work for you, or whatever."

"Thanks," I say. Asher has been standing off to the side, waiting for us to finish. Once Arabella kisses my cheeks again, she backs away and Asher steps forward.

I look at his face, the color creeping up into his cheeks the way it did on the London Eye. His eyes are sad, taking all of me in.

"I'm just so sorry," he says.

"Me, too." I nod. There's so much feeling here, I can't even hug him, can't bring myself to touch him. But finally he does, he kisses me, and I taste my own tears in the kiss. "I don't want to go."

"And I don't want you to," he says. "But you know you have to."

I start to cry again. My passport digs into my thigh from the front pocket of my jeans, and my henley top is spotted with tears. "I know it's a long way off, but, just in case I don't get back here right away . . ."

"Let's just plan that you will," he says.

"But I might not," I say. I can feel the defensive demon kicking in. "I might not, so I was just trying to suggest . . ."

"Just take it one day at . . ." He hugs me again. "I'm here for you."

I can't take it anymore, so I hug him, put my carry-on bag on my shoulder, and walk through passport control. He's *here* for me, I think, but what about anywhere else?

As I shuffle through the lines that lead to the plane that will bring me home, I take out my reliable journal. Eight pages left. Without extra commentary, I make a list of all the random words and thoughts in my mind: Mable, blood, Dad, Vineyard, college, back here, what would have been tonight, voice-over, Asher, ask-her. I pass by Boots Pharmacy, WH Smith, and then, as I'm meandering in a haze to my gate, I see a pile of newspapers. Always looking for onboard distractions, I pick up a couple of the castoff papers. Then I see it: me, Arabella, Tobias, and enough of the prince boy that he's identifiable. Our club photo (which Asher said he had gotten away from the guy) is smack dab in the middle of the front page of *Top Star,* the celebrity rag. I keep it with me, but don't even know how to react.

On board Virgin (irony duly noted) Atlantic's flight to Boston, the welcome music is familiar—strumming, musak version, but familiar. The notes get stuck in my brain as my carry-on gets stuck under the seat in front of me. All my emotional baggage weighs too much to fit in the overhead compartments. I open the music and video channel guide to find out the song before it drives me crazy.

Then I see it: "Like the London Rain" by Clementine Highstreet. Of course. Thankfully, it doesn't lead into "Be Here, Be Now," but I go through those lyrics in my head as we take off for whatever waits for me across the large expanse of ocean. Then, as I'm quoting the song in my head, I look at the finer print, the other credits—"Like the London Rain" 1990 rerelease (no wonder it didn't register right away) on Gala Records. Gala. My mother = Galadriel. Could it be the same? I slip the idea away into the safety of my journal and look out the window at London. The "Be Here, Be Now" lyrics echo in my head: *Someday you'll leave, let time pull you away, and I'll be left with only thoughts of yesterday, but for now just stay. Be here, be now.* I wish I could. The ground recedes, the buildings smaller, the people hidden, my England world growing farther away as the plane rises—pulling me from my rabbit hole of wonder and back to reality.

And then . . .

To: Poppy Massa-Tonclair
From: Love Bukowski

Enclosed please find my novella. I know it's not exactly what we spoke about, but please allow me to explain. I had to leave suddenly, as Keena told you, and things are hanging in the balance here—barely. But this novella, my journal, isn't a cop out. On the contrary, this journal is the truest part of me, the realest story of my life so far. I've edited nothing, except for a couple of names for privacy's sake (theirs, not mine), and if you just give it a chance, you'll find everything you asked me to write about is all there. That I'm all in there. Please consider it my final paper, my big project. You asked for the truth, and this is it. I'm sending it registered mail; it's hard to part with it—but it's yours for the reading. Thanks, Love.

And then . . .

Journal Entry # Who Knows What

Can't believe I had to leave so suddenly—what will happen with Asher? And what about my London coursework? Not to mention that movie voice-over gig. With London cut short, I guess I have to get used being stateside again (not easy), dealing with Aunt Mable's illness (worse), Dad's somewhat hidden agenda (suspicion brews), college catalogues (read: pressure wrapped up in a glossy mag), my upcoming summer on the island of Martha's Vineyard (read: beaches, boys, and basic fun), and of course—those boys I keep trying to forget (not to mention names . . .). Why is it that the path to love is never a shortcut? And why is it so difficult to figure out what—and whom—I want? Maybe all I need is some time to think. Maybe all I need is some perspective. Or maybe all those songs on the radio got it right and

All You Need Is Love

The next book in *The Principles of Love* series

— Coming in Fall 2006 —

Want to send an e-mail to the author? Want to have LOVE visit your school, book group or camp?
Check out www.emilyfranklin.com.